THE NE

CREDITS

Firstly I must thank my editor, Jenny Hewitt, for her work in polishing the text and spotting my worst punctuation and grammatical howlers, and Simon who proof read the final draft. The original was written pre-computer days so I would like to thank Tracie who spent many hours redrafting it in proper form, and Jo Smith who typeset the final version. Any errors of fact or spelling are down to me.

I must also thank: Chris and Tom from Frensham Pond SC, and Justin and Sarah from Datchet SC, who read parts of the text and advised me on sailing matters. Also many friends from Chichester Harbour.

And of course: Eve, Charles, Amanda and Pamela, who encouraged me at those times when I wondered if I would ever make it into print.

Needless to say, no character in this book bears any relation or resemblance to anyone in the real world.

AUTHOR

Jim Morley has sailed and raced small boats all his life. He spent forty years in agriculture and forestry before changing to a career in freelance writing. He lives near Petersfield in Hampshire and sails a small family yacht on Chichester Harbour.

COVER: Itchenor, near Chichester, West Sussex

THE NEMESIS FILE

James Morley

DEDICATION

To all sailors and helpers at Frensham Pond Sailability.

The Nemesis File
First published 2004
Second edition 2005

Published by Benhams Books, 1 Fir Cottage, Greatham, Liss,
Hampshire GU33 6BB

Typeset by John Owen Smith

ISBN 0-9548880-0-6

Printed and bound by Antony Rowe, Eastbourne

PROLOGUE

COPENHAGEN MAY 3rd 1945

The soldier could easily have killed the three men guarding the bridge, but tomorrow his war would be over and he'd exhausted his hate. He stood in shadow, looking once again at the Sydhavnen Bridge. Five years ago, as a young student, he had fled this place and found his way to England. Now he had come home, a hardened fighting man, physically and mentally scarred, who by extraordinary fate was to be the first liberator of his native city.

The German soldiers backed away from him and from the barrel of his levelled Sten gun. He'd taken off his steel helmet and in its place wore a simple fawn beret and a badge with a winged dagger. Every man in the defeated German army had heard of these people. They came in darkness, killed, and vanished into the night.

'Who commands here?' He spoke in German

'I do, sir.' The corporal of the guard was a thin undernourished boy.

The Germans were staring at him. He guessed that like everyone in this restless unsleeping city they had only one thought. Would the end come with a Russian army or one of the Western Allies. At least they had the reassurance of his British uniform.

'The war is over for you,' his voice was commanding but not unkind. 'You'd best return to your barracks and await orders.'

'Will they be Russians?' The young corporal had a tremor in his voice.

'Field Marshal Montgomery's forces – British. Do as you're told and no harm will come to you. Just be glad – soon we'll all be going home – no more killing.'

The Germans let him pass and the soldier walked on over the bridge. He strode briskly into the old dockside and seaman's quarter of Copenhagen. An almost unbearable nostalgia embraced him with every step. Each street name, each road, every alleyway, returned to fond memory. Twenty minutes from the bridge and once again he walked among the historic buildings of the Nyhavnen.

At no time did he relax his guard. His senses, refined by a year of fighting, were watching, feeling, hearing. He halted beside a narrow alleyway, before melting into the shadow of a door; voices echoed in a hubbub of angry sound. A flicker of light came from the far end of the passage and with it the silhouettes of shadowy figures. He looked around warily and then moved silently towards the light. The passage between the two ageing warehouses was barely a metre wide. He reached the end and again froze into a convenient doorway. Before him lay a cobbled square surrounded by high buildings. He couldn't recall this place from the old days, although it was typical of that part of the city. On the far side blazed a bonfire of derelict timber, its light creating a lurid backdrop to the scene in front.

In the centre of the courtyard was a group of people, young noisy and drunk. Boys and men alike, they were shabbily dressed, and from such speech he could hear Danish. He estimated there were some thirty of them, tightly clustered around an object that seemed to have aroused their anger. Even as he watched, the crowd let fly a derisive jeer. Stepping into the light, the soldier walked the few paces to the edge of the throng. In the middle of the ring stood a small child.

It was a boy, perhaps six or seven years old, tidily dressed with polished shoes and a little brown overcoat. His fair hair was clogged with dirt that ran down to smudge a tear-stained face. The boy stood in frozen bewilderment and terror as a youth in the crowd hurled another horse turd, striking the child full on the forehead.

The soldier reacted instantly. He forced his way to the front of the crowd, swinging his fists and elbows viciously as angry drunks tried to obstruct him. He stood beside the child who, sensing security, clung to the soldier's leg, burying his face in the rough battledress trousers.

'What's going on here – who is this child?'

He had no need to raise his voice; his tone of command reduced the mob to a sullen whispering. Perhaps it was his words; for he spoke to them in the manner of an educated Dane.

'What's it to you?' called a surly voice. 'This brat's a Nazi lover, like all his family.'

'That's right,' shouted another voice. 'Yeah, his sister sleeps with a German, get outa' the way while we kill him … none o' your business.'

The soldier's face was expressionless, but inwardly he was sickened. Memories from twelve weeks ago were screaming in his head. He could see the flames, hear again the terrified cries of the burning children; their parents shot down as they fought to reach them.

'You scum, have I fought the length of Europe to come home to this?'

They were listening now, by God. The callow youths shrank back, mesmerised by the man's personality.

'Tomorrow, justice and law will be returning to this city. Any of you who harm this boy will pay a penalty – I personally will see that it is so.' His eyes swept around the gathering. The crowd shuffled uneasily, not one of them prepared to meet his gaze.

Gently the soldier bent down and lifting the boy, placed him astride his shoulders. Ignoring the crowd, he turned on his heel and walked into the darkness beyond.

LEIGH PARK, HAMPSHIRE, FEBRUARY 10th 1989

Even encased in her motorcycle leathers, Mandy was cold. An icy, cutting wind blew down the cul-de-sac and with it a flurry of snowflakes. The road had been salted some hours before but the pavement was slippery and covered with piles of broken ice and dirty snow.

Mandy loved Leigh Park. It was her hunting ground, the place where she'd cut her teeth as a journalist. Not many people loved the Park. This infamous post-war planning disaster: a featureless, almost Soviet-style, housing scheme set down in the country to the north of Portsmouth. For Mandy the life was good; she'd always wanted to be a journalist. Now, at twenty-three, she was a senior reporter with a major provincial paper. It would be conceited to say so openly, but she knew she was good. People liked her and they trusted her. It was this gift that had delivered the Dane into her hands two days before. She took a firm grip of her emotions. She could still hardly believe that this was happening. She was on the edge of delivering two linked stories. The first was the criminal conspiracy of the decade. The second story, one of the most harrowing and poignant human-interest tales of the century.

She'd gambled five hundred pounds of her wedding fund to make the trip to Copenhagen. She'd get it back of course, when the story broke, but she could hardly expect her editor to sanction this escapade on expenses. On the second day she'd found the boy in a gay bar. He was a pitiful sight, more underfed waif than the gifted chemist she'd been led to expect. He hadn't talked that time but he'd wanted to; her experience told her that much. She'd learned one thing; he was

7

travelling to Gatwick the next morning. She had no trouble booking on the same flight; the aircraft had been part empty.

It had taken less than thirty minutes for the boy to break down. Tears had flooded almost as fast as the secrets he'd spilled. Incredible as it seemed, her instinct told her every word was true. She put her arm around him and soothed him with comforting words; Mandy was very good at that. On arrival she'd given him a lift on the back of the Harley as far as Petersfield and left him with her contact number scrawled on a piece of paper.

At last she could see movement. They were dragging open the double doors of the loading bay. This was what she'd been waiting for these three hours. Ten days ago she'd found this place. A London reporter, following a related story, had tipped her off. They had shared ideas to her advantage. The other man, for all his experience, had no inkling of the sensational news she was about to reveal to the world.

Good, here was the same white transit van she'd seen earlier; driving slowly out of the loading bay. Now she could see it parked on the concrete in the full glare of the security lights. Mandy had no view of the driver; the man shutting the doors was a stranger. Heart pounding, she concentrated on the other one standing by the passenger side of the cab; yes, it was Larsen. She felt a wave of exaltation and almost at once, cold fright. For the first time she wondered if she could handle this. Too late to wonder now. All three men were in the van and moving into the street. Mandy swung herself onto the saddle of the Harley Davidson and crammed on her crash helmet. The van passed her and before its taillights had turned the corner, she'd pressed the starter button.

If she was right, the van would head for Chichester. Once they'd reached the house she would phone Frank. The police would have their great prize; she would have the story that would blazon her reputation around the globe. The van did not turn right onto the Emsworth road but continued straight through the village of Rowlands Castle. She suppressed an expletive; where the hell were they going? She dare not ride too close but already her target had turned into a maze of twisting side lanes. She had no choice but to speed up. She'd better watch out. No one had salted these roads and the surface gleamed white ice in the moonlight.

'Oh shit!' This time she screamed the words as she slammed on her brakes. A huge boxy vehicle had driven from a field gate straight into her path. The Harley spun sideways and parted company with

Mandy. For ten yards she slid across the icy surface to bump into a hard grass verge. She swore again in a fury. She wasn't hurt but she'd lost some dignity and worst of all, she'd lost her quarry. So near and yet so bloody far … She climbed to her knees. People were on the road. Someone had grabbed her by the shoulders. She tried to strike out as the crash helmet was wrenched off her head. The man who had hold of her hair had an animal quality. He was twisting her head. Out of the night came a searing pain. She'd never known such pain and the spontaneous scream emerged from her throat as an awful gurgling rattle. The pain had gone now. How bright the colours – was she dreaming? She was floating in this strange inky black tunnel. The pretty colours had gone now. Only this black hole and that blinding white light at the end. She wished she could shade her eyes.

CHAPTER 1

CHICHESTER, SUSSEX, AUGUST 1990

In Steve's surreal dream world, he had become a teenager again. He stood in the boxing ring at Woolston Boys Club. Facing him was the gaunt figure of Mickey Peacock and Mickey was closing in for the kill. Suddenly Steve's hands dropped and his legs became leaden. Mickey's punches thudded into his chest and arms. Steve could do nothing; his limbs lifeless and his ears ringing.

'Wake up, Dad – wake up!'

He opened one eye. Sarah was kneeling on the bed beside him. As he awoke fully she pounded his chest with a further punch.

'God, who taught you that right hook?' He rolled away from her and shut his eyes again.

'It's twenty to nine,' shouted his daughter. 'You can't stay there – you've got to get up.'

'Don't want to get up – never again.'

'Please, Dad – you must – it's not fair.'

'Why?' he mumbled blearily,

'It's not fair on me, that's why.'

She stood at the foot of the bed, her fists clenched, eyes tearful.

'All right, love. I'll get up.'

'Good, that's better. I'll cook you some breakfast.'

'Don't want anything.'

'No, you will have breakfast. I'll be late for work but I'm staying to see you eat it.'

'I don't want all this fuss.'

'Well, that's tough.' Sarah turned abruptly and stomped from the room.

Steve glanced at the clock and swore silently. It was eight forty and the old neck pains had surfaced again. He shuffled down the passage to the bathroom. From the kitchen he could hear Sarah petulantly banging and crashing. He shut the door and turned on the shower. He glared at the vision in the mirror. The macho blond hairstyle, once his sporting trademark, was nearly all grey now. Here he was: Stephen Simpson, professional yachtsman and one-time Olympic gold medallist, degenerating into a forty-five-year-old arthritic cabbage.

Returning to the bedroom, feeling slightly more mobile, he pulled on his working clothes: cotton denim trousers, a freshly pressed shirt and a white cricket sweater. The pressed shirt had been his daughter Sarah's handiwork and, feeling a pang of guilt, he made his way to the kitchen. This week had marked the second anniversary of her mother's death and Sarah had borne the brunt of Steve's moodiness. On the kitchen table was a boiled egg, a rack of toast and a pot of coffee. Sarah watched silently as he sat down.

He smiled wanly at her 'Thanks, love.' The two words were enough to dissolve the tension; they were friends again.

'Dad, Doctor Anderson's insisting you see him; what about tomorrow?'

'I can't finish that mainsail of his for another ten days. He's been told already.'

'Of course it's not that. You know perfectly well what I mean. He's worried. For God's sake, I'm worried. You're not getting any better and people are beginning to notice.'

'Notice what?' he snapped and instantly felt guilty.

Sarah was unfazed. 'Ever since Mum died. You've changed, withdrawn, and it's not getting better. It's almost like we've lost you.'

She stared defiantly at him. How very like her mother she looked: same face, same soft blue eyes and lovely straight blonde hair.

'Yes, all right, love, I'll see him whenever you like.' He sighed; he was not in the mood to argue.

'Five o'clock tomorrow afternoon,' she said cheerfully. 'I'll put it in the book when I get to work.'

When Miriam died, Sarah had left the hospital where she worked and taken a job with Doctor Anderson, the family's friend and GP. It had been a move to the advantage of both. Sarah was able to keep house for her father and the practice had gained a conscientious and well-liked nurse.

'I'll be OK if you want to go now,' he said.

'Yeah, better move it, I'm late. Tell you what, it's a nice day, let's go sailing later.'

'What about work?'

'I'll get off early. The doc won't mind – not if I tell him why.'

Steve stood up and looked at the tide tables pinned on the sideboard. 'High water's not until seven-thirty tonight. Tide's against us so we won't get far.'

'Doesn't matter,' she said, planting a kiss on his cheek. 'I'll come to your office – say four o'clock?'

Sarah departed and Steve poured a second cup of coffee. This was the moment of truth, another day to be faced. He had to grit his teeth, walk out through that front door and go to work.

Five minutes later, he reversed the Volvo out of the garage and sat looking at the bungalow. The front lawn needed mowing and Miriam's beloved garden was returning to jungle. He often wondered if a move of house would help lay these ghosts but as always, dismissed the idea. The memories were there forever but the ghosts were inside himself; welded in place that night in the terminal ward of the hospital. The night he had sat with Miriam holding her hand while the cancer sucked away the last flicker of life.

A ten-minute journey and he was parking the car in the manager's slot at Easterbroke Sails. The title 'Sail loft' was a misnomer. Easterbroke's Chichester premises formed a modern steel-span building, housing cutting floors, offices, and a chandler's shop. The whole place was part of their American parent company's massive investment in the European yachting scene. Similar units had been built in five other major centres. Steve remembered the decrepit clapboard loft at Hamble where he'd served his apprenticeship. Sailmaking then had been a craft, little changed since Nelson's day. It was amazing to think that the new cloths, the new masts and all the computer technology had been developed in his working lifetime.

Steve had sprung from modest roots and he had never known his father. A merchant navy officer, he had died in the war, drowned when his ship was torpedoed on an Arctic convoy. Steve's mother had somehow raised her three children while working in a variety of menial jobs. Steve was her youngest and from an early age he had shown a natural ability for sport – all sport. He had dropped out of grammar school at fifteen to take his chance as a professional football apprentice. One day a former teacher had taken him for a day's sailing. It was the most formative moment of his young life. Steve had discovered his vocation; he was hooked.

Sailing at any level is expensive; he needed a job that would take him into the world of boats and give him the entries he needed. The sail loft had a vacancy for an apprentice, so Steve had parked himself on the doorstep at six o'clock in the morning. He could offer no previous experience but his enthusiasm impressed the loft manager. He was taken on for a month's trial. Steve would have accepted almost any job on offer. Sailmaking was only one option, but he soon found he loved the work and he was good at it. One day a customer of the loft approached Steve. His son, Anthony, had a Cadet dinghy but lacked the confidence to race. Would Steve like to helm the boat with Anthony as crew? It was another moment of destiny. Within eighteen months the pair had won almost every trophy available. When Steve became too old for the Cadet, his mentor bought him a National Twelve dinghy, and in one last trick of fate, Anthony's elder sister, Miriam, offered to be his crew. It was to be a partnership that was to take them to more glory and then to marriage. However, there was a price to pay. Ill health and two miscarriages had dogged Miriam. She had given up sailing and Steve had switched to single-handed Finn class dinghies. By now he was manager of the sail loft, but a generous proprietor had encouraged him to take the time off to compete internationally. He'd won British and European honours culminating in the prized Gold Cup in Copenhagen.

Two years later he had sailed that incredible last race of the greatest competition in the world. He had to win it to clinch the title. He recalled the wind and the waves; the euphoria when he knew that he could conquer the conditions while all about him were failing the test. Hours later, in a heady daze, he had stood on the rostrum whilst the Olympic gold medal for his class was placed around his neck. The band had played the national anthem, while in the crowd Miriam had stood, full of pride, holding baby Sarah in her arms. It all seemed so long ago, that wonderful pinnacle of success. Then came the car crash, injury, hospital, and recovery. There followed the long years building his business and reputation. Then Miriam's last illness and the bleak world that he faced today.

Steve went into the office and flopped down behind his desk.

'What's on this morning, Carol?'

Carol Fox, Steve's PA, was a thirty-two-year-old business school graduate married to a Sussex policeman. Recruiting her to the company had been Steve's most inspired management decision. Before Miriam had died, Steve had taught navigation at evening school, where Carol and her husband Norman had been amongst his students. That had been four years ago and a firm friendship had grown between the two families. Steve's technical skills had been complemented by Carol's business know-how and the company's order book had filled rapidly. Now, it was not so easy. In a recession-hit economy, new yacht sails were nobody's first priority.

'Do you want the good news or the bad news?' Carol stood over him shuffling a handful of faxes.

'Oh, God! Let's have the bad then,' he sighed wearily.

14

'This is from Boston. Winterbirch Holdings have made a bid for the whole of Easterbroke's European operation. Sam wants your reaction.'

'Winterbirch!' Steve stared in disbelief. 'What the hell does Kenny Lindgrune want a sailmaker for?'

'For the same reason he wants to get his hands on every yachting marina on the South Coast.' Carol sat down opposite. 'Come on, Steve, wake up; yachting, sailing, boating, whatever you call it, is big money. But it's a fragmented industry and right now it's in trouble. There's a recession, so you've got dozens of yards, yacht builders and companies like ours all going cheap. Rich pickings for a chancer like Lindgrune.'

Steve sat silently waiting for more. In these matters he trusted Carol's judgement. Kenneth Lindgrune had burst on the local scene five years ago. He was a Scottish property developer, with big interests in Scotland and the north of England. His Winterbirch company covered the south coast and had latterly taken over two yacht marinas and associated businesses. Lindgrune himself lived in Millbury House, a brash executive mansion a mile away from the yacht basin. Steve had met the man only once and found him rude and abrupt.

'So,' he said at last. 'What do we tell Sam?'

Sam was Samuel Easterbroke the second; legendary American yacht helmsman and seventy-five-year-old president of the company that bore his name.

'You can tell Sam, that if he really wants to sell his lofts, there's money around that's a lot cleaner than our Ken's.'

Carol spoke the words almost in a whisper but in a tone that commanded its own silence. In the background, the workshop machines whirred and some children shouted and laughed on the pontoon outside.

'Norman knows something, doesn't he?' Steve moved his chair closer to the desk. 'He was dropping hints about Lindgrune the other day. Carol, are you seriously telling me that the law thinks Ken Lindgrune's a crook?'

'In a nutshell, yes.'

'Does Sam realise?'

'I shouldn't think so, but he's shrewd enough to ask our views.'

Steve frowned. 'Lindgrune must be dangling one hell of a lot of cash for Sam to even consider it. Christ! What's the man playing at? We've all worked our guts out to build this business. For God's sake we've landed that Whitbread Race syndicate. That's practically a licence to print money.'

'Yes,' said Carol, 'and if we don't nip this in the bud now, it's all going to Lindgrune. Then he'll strip this firms assets and we'll all be out of a job.'

'Like hell we will!' Steve was wide-awake now. 'Do the other branches realise what's going on? I shouldn't think they know Ken Lindgrune from Santa Claus.' He reached for a note pad. 'We'd better start ringing around now. I want to confront Sam with a unanimous vote by tonight.'

'Actually, I rang Kiel this morning before you came in. Early risers these Germans,' Carol stated disconcertingly. 'Do you know what Wolfgang said? Well surprisingly, he knows quite a lot about our Ken. He told me that Lindgrune's father was Danish. He's the one who made the millions and he was a nice guy by all accounts.'

Wolfgang Bartels, the veteran German helmsman, and fellow Olympic medallist, had been something of a father figure to Steve. Now he was the manager of Easterbroke's German branch. Steve had a deep respect for Wolfgang and valued his opinion.

'Does Wolfie know our police say Lindgrune's bent?'

'I don't think so, but he says the man spends a lot of time in Copenhagen these days and the Danes don't exactly love him. Wolfgang says he'll give you the details at the Olympic reunion.'

'Oh sod that, I told you I'm not going.'

Carol pursed her lips into what Steve called her collision-course expression.

He stared back defiantly. 'I don't see the point in going all that way to spend four days swilling lager with a couple of hundred other has-beens.'

'Well, we'll see.'

'Winning that medal was twenty years ago. I don't want to become some silly old fart boring on about the past. My problems are here today.'

Carol's eyes were glinting dangerously. 'God, you make me bloody angry sometimes.'

'Oh, what now?' he snapped

'Well, somebody's got to tell you what a conceited self-pitying prig you are.'

'What! No bloody woman talks to me like that …'

'Yes they do, I just have.'

'You've no right. I go through hell most days and what support do

I get. Both you and Sarah – it's all, "pull yourself together, Steve", and, "get yourself a life, Dad". All day long – yackety-yack – bloody women!'

'Now you're turning into a small-minded misogynist. What would Miriam have said about that?'

'Don't you dare drag Miriam into this! You've no idea what I go through and you don't care – either of you.'

Steve was still angry but in an odd way he was relieved. He guessed that Carol had planned this confrontation with Sarah's blessing.

Carol stared coldly at him. 'When Miriam died, everyone here rallied round and we ran this place on our own for six weeks because you were fit for nothing. Some of our people did overtime and I had to force them to take the money. Why do you think that was?'

Steve said nothing.

'Odd though it may sound,' Carol continued, 'we like you. The younger ones look up to you. They respect you and they're proud of you. You're Steve Simpson. You were Cadet World Champion. Then you and Miriam won the Burton Trophy. On your own you won, the Finn Gold Cup, The Olympic gold. You were on the Seventy-Nine Fastnet – you're a role model.'

'I've told you, that's all dead ...'

'Shut up and listen!'

Carol was in complete command as she silenced his bluster.

'Then there's Sarah – she's put her whole career on hold for you. That girl's as pretty as her mother. She's intelligent and full of life. Sooner than you think she's going to find some young chap – where will you be then?'

Steve said nothing but his face must have shown that the thought had struck home.

'That's better,' Carol smiled sweetly. 'I say you should go to Copenhagen for that reunion.'

'All right, I'll think about it.'

Sarah appeared at ten-to-four, dressed for sailing. She sat impatiently in the office while Steve and Carol fended off a barrage of calls from sailmakers boatyards and an electronics company who were also facing a Lindgrune take-over. Further calls came from the yachting press and from anxious customers. Leaving Carol to hold the fort, Steve grabbed Sarah and fled. Ten minutes later they were parking the car at Itchenor.

When Miriam died, Steve had sold the family cruising boat, a much loved and travelled Contessa 32. The same week he bought a little Sonata-class sloop and gave her to Sarah as a gift. *Glorfindel* was now the family boat. Sarah raced her at weekends with an all girl crew, while Steve made solitary trips in her, often at night.

Long ago Itchenor had been a fishing village; a long street of cottages ending in the hard, a gravel landing where the crab-boat men still unload their catches. Steve had never bothered with the plush surroundings of the yacht basin. The family boat had lived for years on a mooring, a quarter of a mile upstream from the landing place. Here the channel wound its way through the mudflats fringed by fields and trees interspersed with the houses of the seriously wealthy. It was a peaceful spot and never failed to raise Steve's spirits even on one of his bad days. This evening, it had lost some of its charm. As they rigged their boat, a helicopter swept down the centre of the channel, a little above the mast height and disappeared behind a belt of trees. Sarah turned to her father and made a face. They both recognised the machine as Lindgrune's, heading for the landing square at Millbury House.

A knot of tide was against them as *Glorfindel* sailed down the harbour. The wind had shifted to the northeast, giving them a fair breeze for the entrance. Sarah steered the ship towards the bar beacon, a wooden structure rising from the sea, marking the treacherous shingle bar below. Even on as tranquil a day as this wind and tide in opposition added an uneasy menace to the swell. Steve stood in the cabin hatchway watching the set of the big Genoa jib. Satisfied, he turned his gaze to the sea ahead. He stared intently, reached for his binoculars, and then scrambling onto the cabin top, he stood with one hand on the mast. He focused the glasses.

'Sarah, quick – over there!'

'What's up?'

Steve saw her jump at the rasp in his voice.

'There's something in the water. It looks like a body– if so it's a dead'un. Keep going as fast as you can – I'll point you there.'

Before Steve married he had spent two years with a lifeboat crew and now he felt a familiar chill of unease. He knew exactly what he was looking at: floating face down was a dead body. He was relieved that it was Sarah who was with him. For all her tender years, her nursing background had accustomed her to grim sights.

Two minutes later the boat was level with the body – a man, with fair hair, of slim build and fully clothed. If they were to recover him it would take all of Steve's strength with only a slender girl to help.

Sarah turned the ship into the wind while her father lowered the mainsail.

'Sail back, just off the wind,' he called. 'Try and stop her by the casualty, starboard side on.'

Sarah nodded, her lips pressed tightly together, her face pale beneath her suntan.

Steve made a noose with a bowline in a mooring line; then he picked up the boathook. He watched Sarah, pleased with the way she was handling the boat. They were rolling horribly but she kept steering, carefully judging the distance between ship and body with just enough power to make a perfect stop alongside. Six feet ... four feet ... two; Steve leant over and dug the boathook into the studded leather belt around the man's waist. Sarah had already let fly the jib and was climbing forward to help.

'I wonder how this poor sod got out here.' Steve grunted. 'He's not a fisherman or a yachtie, that's for sure.'

'Dad,' Sarah's voice was quivering, almost squeaky. 'I don't think he died out here either. It's the neck – look – it's broken clean in half.'

CHAPTER 2

The boat was rolling heavily and Steve knew they were drifting towards the shallows. They would have to move quickly.

'Come on, let's get this line round him.'

Steve opened the loop and leant outboard under the guard-wires. The body was still alongside with Sarah now steadying it with the boathook.

'I've got him,' he called. 'Hold my ankles and don't let go whatever.'

Sarah gripped his legs. The body in the water was a horrible sight as it surged towards him and away again as the yacht rolled. The corpse was contorted into a grotesque foetal position with the dislocated neck bent forward across the chest.

'This one's as stiff as a board,' he called. 'If I can get this loop under his arms it should be easy.'

'He's been dead several hours if he's in rigor,' said Sarah. 'Oh do be careful!'

Steve gave what he hoped was a reassuring grunt and concentrated on pushing the loop under the corpse; not easy with a floating line. At the third attempt he succeeded, pulled the noose tight, and made the line fast to a mooring cleat.

'I don't fancy having him aboard,' he said, 'we'll call the lifeboat.'

They were starting to drift towards the East Pole, the large expanse of hard sand that lined the approach to the harbour. Although they were in no immediate danger it was time to be moving. Steve started the little outboard motor that was their reserve power and they motored towards the beacon. It was an uncomfortable ride, the motor racing and gasping, as the pitching yacht lifted the propeller from the water every few seconds. The body surged and bumped alongside adding a sinister dimension; neither of them cared to look at it. They were relieved when they were back in the safety of the channel and able to make sail again.

Steve picked up the hand-bearing compass. 'Sarah – get on the radio and make a pan-call. Ask them for the inshore lifeboat.'

Sarah nodded and dropped down into the cabin.

'Our position,' he read the bearing, 'Our position is ... one hundred and five degrees true from the Chichester Beacon, about a

20

quarter of a mile.'

A 'pan-call' was an emergency plea of a lesser status than a 'mayday', but it would nonetheless set the wheels in motion. Sarah came back on deck to report that the inshore rescue were on the way and please could he have a flare ready to show *Glorfindel's* position.

Twenty minutes later they sighted the rescue boat, a blob of colour against the darkening Hampshire shore. The lifeboat was a rigid-inflatable, a RIB, with a crew of three. Expertly handled she dropped alongside, recovered the corpse and sped away. It was neatly done as even Steve had to admit. The fact that the coxswain seemed a mere boy, he supposed was a sign of his own advancing age.

In sombre mood they hoisted sail and turned northward into the harbour. The radio crackled once more calling their name; instructions from the coastguard to the crew of, *Glorfindel* – they should report to the nearest police station upon arrival in port.

For a quarter of an hour neither of them spoke. Steve stole a glance at Sarah. She was sitting hunched in a corner of the cockpit, her hands clasped around her knees, as she stared at the horizon in deep reverie. It was the posture she had always adopted as a little girl when someone upset her. She turned suddenly and met his eyes.

'Sorry, Dad.'

'Why? It's not your fault, it's just one of those things.'

'No, I mean I'm sorry I brought you out here tonight. It was meant to cheer you up.'

'Never mind, love, it's certainly not a sail I'll forget in a hurry.' He paused for a moment while he trimmed the mainsheet. 'I still can't make out how that boy came to be in the sea – there's something that's all wrong.'

'How come?'

'Well, you saw him, he was hardly dressed for the water, he looked like he was about to play a game of snooker.'

'It was the neck that got me.' Sarah was staring at the horizon again. 'It was a clean break. It must have taken a hell of a shock to do that.'

'Maybe.'

'No, I'm sure I'm right. We had one like that in Casualty – but that was a road accident. Nothing we could do, the patient had been dead an hour.'

Their eyes met and he could see that there were tear marks on her cheeks. 'There's another thing; it was his face. I'm sure I know him,

21

or at least I've seen him before and quite recently, but where? I just don't know.'

It was nearly dark with a dying breeze when they motored the last half mile and picked up the mooring. Before going home, Steve drove into town and stopped at the police station. Making their statements was something of an anticlimax. The desk constable had heard nothing of the incident but took the details. If the stiff, as he referred to their casualty, had been collected by the Hayling Boat, it would be taken to Cosham, the other side of the county line in Hampshire.

'More paperwork,' he grumbled.

Sarah, who had been only half listening, was suddenly alert. 'I've got it, I know where I saw him: it was at Francine's party. He was staying at the house. I don't know his name but I expect Francine does,' she ended somewhat breathless.

The PC pulled out another statement form.

'Do I understand, miss, that you'd like to add something to what you've already said?' he asked indifferently.

Sarah explained. A week ago she'd been invited to her friend Francine Luterbacher's birthday party, held in the house of Francine's stepfather, Kenneth Lindgrune, no less. She was certain that the dead man had been at the party and was a guest in the house.

The mention of Lindgrune had a startling effect on the young policeman. With a hurried apology he sped across the room and began a rapid conversation on an intercom. A minute later into the room came Steve's sailing friend and Carol's husband, Sergeant Norman Fox. Norman whisked them into a small interview room and called loudly for coffee.

'Take a seat,' he said. 'This place is a bit Spartan but it's where we talk to our villains.'

'I hope that doesn't include us?' said Sarah.

'Not today, I think.' Norman grinned.

They were more relaxed now. The Foxes and the Simpsons were such close friends that it seemed strange to remember that they had only met four years ago.

Norman sat down. 'Carol broke it to me that you've become a target for Ken Lindgrune. I hope it's OK – for me to know, that is?'

'Just about the whole world seems to have heard,' said Steve, 'so I don't see why not.'

'I gather Carol told you the name Lindgrune arouses some emotions around here?'

'She said you thought he was a crook.'

'We don't use that word normally, it's too dramatic, but in this case it fits – yes.' Norman switched his gaze to Sarah. 'That body you recovered, you say you know him, and you say his neck is broken.'

Sarah nodded nervously. She'd never seen Norman in this sort of mood before. A knock at the door relieved the tension. In came a young woman PC carrying a tray of coffee cups. She was a pretty auburn-haired girl and shapely beneath her uniform. Steve caught her eye as she handed him a cup and she smiled. Sarah looked at her father speculatively; for the first time in two years he'd noticed a girl. Maybe the shock of this evening was better therapy than she'd realised.

'Look,' said Norman. 'I think it's just possible that you may be able to help us and because I know you both I'm going to tell you something about Lindgrune. It's unofficial though – strictly off the record.'

'We'll help you all we can,' said Steve. 'But I doubt it'll amount to much, I hardly know the man.'

'No, but you soon will if he takes you over.'

Norman sat still for a moment; he seemed to be weighing his words.

'Ever been to *HMS Hudson*?' he asked.

'Not since the Navy pulled out,' said Steve.

HMS Hudson was a one-time Navy shore establishment, a so-called 'stone frigate.' It had mushroomed during the two world wars to cover some fifteen acres on the waterfront between Gosport and Fareham. Defence cuts and changing times had seen its closure and its personnel re-deployed. Then a year ago there had been plans and scale models. A new marina was proposed with shops, restaurants, fancy waterside flats and boutiques; the whole project to be called, Port Paradise! Steve grimaced at the memory.

Norman was grinning again. 'I know, bloody Port Paradise; I'd charge our Kenny for that name alone.'

'So Lindgrune's behind that scheme as well, is he?' Steve was not particularly surprised.

'You bet he is and that's how we first became interested. Not us, you understand, it was the Hampshire force, but they told us what was going on, or at least Frank did while he was around.' Norman seemed to be weighing his words again. 'Yes, Frank, or should I say, Superintendent Frank Matheson, Portsmouth CID. Ever hear of him?'

'No, I don't think so.'

'No reason why you should, but if you were a villain you would and with reason. Frank was special, he had a reputation and he got results'

Steve looked puzzled 'You talk as if he's not around anymore?'

'Frank took early retirement under pressure. It was either that or face disciplinary action and this is where Lindgrune comes in – and Port Paradise for that matter.'

Norman looked at the clock and then back to Sarah and Steve. 'I hope I'm not boring you with all this? You two must be shattered after what's happened today.'

'Please go on, Norman,' Sarah said. 'You were saying you thought we could help.'

'Right, as far as I am concerned, Frank Matheson broke only one rule; he got himself emotionally involved. You see Frank was something of an expert on fraud, and in Hampshire he had plenty of scope, all the devious bastards live there – here in Sussex we're just country boys.'

'Hey!' said Steve. 'I was born in Southampton.'

'And you're a devious bastard – ask anyone who's raced against you.' Norman was grinning again. 'Anyway, I don't know the precise details except that when the *Hudson* site came up for grabs, it seems everything was done to smooth the path for Lindgrune. It was a Government sale and there were a dozen after it, including the Council – there was talk of putting a new hospital there.'

Norman stood up and began to pace around the room. 'Now, at this point there enters another player and about the most unlikely you could think of. A lovely, twenty three-year-old little dolly, called Mandy Wallace. By the way, don't tell Carol I called her that, will you?'

'That depends,' said Sarah, 'on how you re-phrase it.'

'OK, you win. Of course what I meant to say was Ms Amanda Wallace, investigative journalist for the *News,* and she was good – people would talk to her when they wouldn't to us. She dropped us a few good tips, although she was a pain in the arse some of the time.'

'Well, Frank was pretty sure Lindgrune was oiling palms in London, but neither he nor the Met could pin down whose. Then that Mandy found out something and she was going to spill the beans in print. Frank got wind of it and told her, "not until you've spoken to me".' Norman half smiled and shook his head.

'Now Mandy was a sporting little girl, used to drive everywhere on a bloody great Harley-Davidson motor bike; you could hear her a mile off. She'd promised to talk to Frank but she never turned up; a few hours later they found her dead in a back lane near Rowlands Castle. She was lying in the road and the bike was on the other side of the hedge. There was nothing anybody could do – her neck was broken clean.'

Sarah let out a gasp 'Yes, I remember, I was in Casualty that night … Dad, that was the one I saw, the one I told you about – just like the one today.'

'Now you see why I'm so interested.' said Norman. 'Coincidence always interests coppers and these two are not the only ones who've ended in the morgue with links to Kenny.'

Norman sat down again rubbing a finger across the Formica-topped table. 'The effect on Frank was devastating, but although he was pretty shaken, he made a search of Mandy's flat. He was too late; all her notes had been cleaned out. Same thing at the newspaper office; everything gone. The next day there was a Home Office instruction to the Chief Constable; "drop the fraud investigation". Said *HMS Hudson* was covered by the Official Secrets Act – bullshit!'

'Good God – can they do that?'

'Too right they can. Anyway, Frank didn't drop the investigation. He said this was Portsmouth and if Nelson could turn a blind eye … There's something else I should've explained. I told you Frank was emotionally involved. Well, Mandy was his God-daughter and she was engaged to his eldest boy Paul – they thought the world of her. I don't need to say anymore, Steve, I reckon you understand.'

Norman mopped his brow with a discoloured handkerchief. It was pitch dark outside and a sticky humid evening.

'Norman, what do you want me to do about this?'

'Nothing dramatic; but if Lindgrune takes over the sail-loft you'll get an insider's view of what goes on.'

Steve was worried. 'I don't want Lindgrune taking over the loft, but honestly I've no reason to think he's not making a perfectly legitimate deal. I'll fight it tooth and nail of course but I'm not expecting anything to happen that might interest you.'

'In that case you've nothing to worry about. Look, you know that I wouldn't expect you to break faith with Sam Easterbrooke. But if anything happens that you don't like, then tell Frank Matheson. He's not police now. He runs his own agency and he's earning more than his old pay; but he misses the real work and he's still after Lindgrune – and this time there's bugger all the Chief Constable or the Home Secretary can do about it.'

'Why can't I talk direct to you?'

'Of course you can but there's nothing we can do at the moment. We can only act on hard evidence. We can't unleash a full-scale enquiry just on rumour and supposition. Lindgrune would say we were persecuting him.'

'I don't understand this. You say the man's into bribery, fraud, murder even – you can't just do nothing.'

Norman sighed. 'The only policeman ever to come near producing a case against Lindgrune is Frank Matheson and it got him busted. Matheson's unofficial but he's still a good copper. He's got his teeth into Lindgrune and he'll never let go. Frank's one of the best – trust him.'

They left the police station and drove straight home. Steve poured them each a drink. He had been worried that Sarah might react with delayed shock, but on the contrary, she seemed controlled, if inwardly pre-occupied.

'Dad,' she exclaimed, 'It's all beginning to come back – Francine's party, that is.'

'You told me the next day that you didn't enjoy it.'

'That's right. It was too organised, too flash. I can't really say what was wrong. You know, the food was great and the DJ with the disco was a real pro – not the usual local prat. It's just that it was all a bit flat, like an overgrown kid's party. We sort of felt Mr Lindgrune wanted the evening to show how clever and in touch he is, and poor Francine got forgotten.'

'I form the impression Francine doesn't like her stepfather?' Steve commented, sipping his whisky.

Both Sarah and Francine were twenty. They had met at convent school five years ago. They remained a typical schoolgirl duo. Sarah: pretty, athletic but hard up, was the one who pulled all the boys. Francine: plump, rather plain but generously supplied with cash, tagged on, somewhat in awe of her friend.

'She hates him!' Sarah snapped. 'She says he's a pig and what's more, she knows he's a crook – she told me.'

'It's the nature of things for kids not to like step-parents.' Steve mused.

'I wouldn't know,' she said meaningfully. 'That's something I've yet to find out.'

They were on dangerous ground. Sarah had lately joined the tiresome chorus of busybodies telling him he should think of remarrying. He quickly steered the talk onto a new tack.

'What was it you say you remember from the party?'

'If you mean the dead man; I'm not sure I'd have noticed him at all if he hadn't been acting so oddly.'

'In what way?'

'Well, he was supposed to be a guest in the house, but whenever Mr Lindgrune came near, he did a sort of disappearing act. I even saw him hide behind some curtains – quite comical really. Nobody seemed to know who he was, except that he was a foreigner and some of the girls reckoned he was gay.'

'And that's it?'

'I'm afraid so. Maybe we'll find out more tomorrow. I'll get it all from Francine.' Sarah shut her eyes and yawned. 'I'm going to bed. I've an early start and don't forget you're seeing the doctor in the afternoon.'

Steve could not sleep. As he lay awake he saw nothing but the bloated corpse bumping alongside *Glorfindel*. Sometime in the early hours he must have drifted into slumber. He felt as if he was awake but he knew he was entering his recurring dream. It was the same dream that had invaded his sleep at irregular intervals ever since Miriam's death.

He stood at the harbour entrance among the sand dunes of East Head. The colours were vivid so much so that they hurt his eyes. The sky was all blue, the sands a blinding white. The wind was blowing; squalling in mighty gusts out of the north. He looked out to the entrance bar and felt a cold fear. The seas were boiling, tearing, rending each other in awesome combat as the gale fought the incoming tide. Steve was not alone; he felt the presence of another whom he could not see but he had the warm feeling of someone he was deeply attached to. He knew that person was a woman and that they were both in danger and afraid.

This time the dream entered a new dimension. As he shaded his eyes against the glare he saw a figure, a young man, standing on the edge of the pounding surf. He turned to show his face, and Steve knew him: the face was that of today's dead body. The man stared for a few seconds, then beckoned Steve to follow him as he turned and strode, very slowly and deliberately, into the breaking seas.

CHAPTER 3

At nine a.m. Mr Lindgrune had a visit from Sgt Fox and a uniformed PC.

Fox stood for a few seconds admiring the front of Millbury House. 'Real style,' he said approvingly. 'It's got to be a Lutyens.'

'A what?' The PC looked mystified.

'Never mind. Let's dig out our friend and see what he's got to say.'

Fox recognised the girl who opened the front door as Lindgrune's stepdaughter, Francine.

'Hi, you come to arrest Ken? It's about time.' She was a fat jolly youngster, who spoke with a faint trace of some foreign accent.

'We'd like a few words with Mr Lindgrune on a routine matter,' said Fox.

'OK, wait in here and I'll get him.'

Francine showed them into an office and left them amid the expensive furnishings and flickering computer screens.

Two minutes later Lindgrune strode into the room. Fox had met him a few times at public functions; Lindgrune liked to make a show of supporting local charities. Certainly the man had presence. He seemed to fill the room with his personality, as much as his physical size. In every way he was a big man: well over six-foot with heavy features, and hair so dark, that Fox suspected it was dyed.

'How nice it must be for the police – you never have to make appointments.' Lindgrune had an intimidating smile and a deep but not unpleasant voice. 'Now what's all this? You can have three minutes.'

'It's only a routine matter, sir, but we'd like to clear it up quickly. A young man was found dead in the sea yesterday. Unfortunately we can't identify him, but a witness who has viewed the body, believes the man to have been a guest at your daughter's birthday party.'

Lindgrune frowned. 'I don't know what you think I can do. There must have been a hundred of them there. Mostly student types. All no-hopers – I wouldn't employ any of them – sorry can't help.' He turned as if to leave.

Fox was not impressed. 'The dead man is aged eighteen to twenty. He's five foot eight inches tall, slight build, with short fair hair.'

'As are ten thousand other kids in Sussex.'

'I know that, sir, but we have a definite statement that he was here in your house. We'd like to clear this up. The boy will have family – parents. We're thinking of them.'

'But, Daddy?' It was Francine; neither the policemen nor Lindgrune had noticed her standing by the door. 'Couldn't it be Per? He was at my party and we haven't seen him since.'

Lindgrune spun round. Fox caught the spasm of real anger that flickered momentarily on his face. 'Stupid girl – this is a private discussion, I didn'a invite you.'

Lindgrune could not conceal he'd been unsettled and his mild Scots accent had become broader.

'But it could be Per and he was at my party.' She turned to Fox. 'I'll come with you if you want an identification.'

'You'll do no such thing,' snapped Lindgrune.

'I'm sorry you are taking this line, sir,' said Fox. 'It really is only routine. As I said, we're concerned for the boy's family.'

'Well I'm not. I've my own business to attend to. I gave you three minutes of my time, and time, to me, is money. I think I've been very considerate, Fox. Why not try catching the people who scratched my car instead of bothering me with trivialities!'

Francine interrupted him. 'I've told you I'll go. Anyway, Daddy, it might not even be Per. Come on, you two – let's get it over.' Ignoring Lindgrune, she marched out of the room.

Fox watched admiringly. Presumably the girl knew Lindgrune as well as anyone, but all the same the man was an intimidating force and it took some courage to outface him.

Lindgrune was breathing heavily as he mopped his face. 'You're all bloody fools, but I suppose I'll have to come too, or God knows what that silly little bitch'll say.'

The police took Francine with them; Lindgrune followed in his Rolls Royce. At the mortuary, Fox handed over the proceedings to the Hampshire Police. An officer explained that the body had no documents, and that even the clothes labels had been cut out. In the circumstances they must view the body for real.

The mortuary attendant pulled open the drawer, and Francine, pale faced but calm, leaned over the corpse for a few seconds. She turned away with a grimace. 'Yes it's Per.'

'Mr Lindgrune?' said the presiding officer.

Lindgrune stepped forward with obvious bad grace.

'Yes that looks like the boy Elgaad,' he grunted.

'May we have the full name please?'

'He's Per Elgaad. He's Danish and he comes from Copenhagen,' said Francine.

'Thank you, miss. We'll go upstairs and log this officially.'

'I want to know where the body was found and in what circumstances?' It was Lindgrune. He was looking pointedly at his watch; clearly irritated.

'Have you a reason for asking, sir?'

'That's a damn stupid question. This Elgaad is the son of a business associate of mine, so I suppose it'll be me who has to explain things.'

'That's reasonable, sir. The body was found in the sea yesterday between Hayling Island and Wittering. A yachtsman and his daughter recovered it. No ordinary sailor either – it was Steve Simpson.'

'Wow, Sarah and her dad,' said Francine.

'Simpson, from Easterbroke Sails?' Lindgrune snapped. 'I can see where this is coming from now. He's been trying to obstruct my business. He doesn't know that I know, but he soon will. Perhaps those two had a hand in murdering the boy.'

'That's a pretty wild allegation, sir. You told us half an hour ago that you'd never heard of this man, so how d'you know that he was murdered?' It was the young constable, speaking for the first time. Fox nodded in agreement.

'One more funny crack like that and I'll have you busted; I can do that you know.' Lindgrune regarded the man icily, 'I'm going – all this foolery's lost me an hour already.'

At the sail loft, Steve was relieved to find yesterday's furore over the Lindgrune bid had died down. There'd been no response from Sam Easterbroke to Carol's subtly worded fax, only an acknowledgement from Boston saying Sam was in Tokyo. Steve spent a happy morning working on a new asymmetric foresail. A tricky set of problems and it helped him to forget the last twenty-four hours. Then, after lunch, in walked Norman Fox.

'I'm off duty, but I thought I'd have a word.'

Steve whisked Norman into the inner office, where Carol joined them. Norman gave a description of the morning's events, laughing out loud at Lindgrune's discomfiture at the hands of Francine.

'Who exactly was this Danish bloke?' asked Steve.

'We don't know yet,' said Fox. 'In the normal way we wouldn't be interested, but it's a murder investigation now. Hampshire are waiting for the post-mortem report. Secondly, Lindgrune's reaction was odd.' Norman looked at them pensively. 'A warning, be careful – watch your back.'

'Why?'

'Because Lindgrune threw a wobbly. He said you've been obstructing his business, then he said that you and Sarah might've had a hand in that boy being in the sea.'

'But this is ridiculous!' Steve spluttered. 'What's he mean we had a hand in it?'

'Yes I know, that's only Lindgrune, don't take it to heart. I only hope it doesn't hurt you when he takes over the Loft.'

'He's not going to if I have anything to do with it.'

Norman changed the subject. 'Are you going to this do in Copenhagen?'

Steve sighed. 'I honestly don't know.'

'What's it about? Carol said something about a lager brewery. That sounds too good to miss.'

'It's a publicity gimmick. Copenhagen are making a bid for a future Olympic Games. The Brewery's sponsoring a reunion of two hundred former medal winners. One of them's me for some reason.'

'I should bloody well hope so. You really ought to go, you know.'

'To tell you the truth, I've mixed feelings. I don't feel up to socialising, but all the same Copenhagen's a great place. The Danes are sport crazy and they really want the games for their own sake, not just as a commercial rip-off.'

'It's not for me to put pressure on you, Steve, but you could be in a position to mix business with pleasure.'

'How so?'

'I spoke to Frank Matheson after you left last night. You remember, I told you about him?'

'The Pompey copper who ran foul of Lindgrune?'

'That's him. Frank's after Lindgrune but his investigation's hit a brick wall as far as England is concerned. But by coincidence, Mr Lindgrune has a very high profile in Denmark. I took the liberty of mentioning you and, the long and short of it is, we'd like you to listen out for us.'

'No way, Norman!' Steve was emphatic. 'I'm sorry, I don't want to be involved.'

'You'll be moving in exactly the circles where you might learn something, and you've got a legitimate concern about Lindgrune.'

'I've said no.'

'I'm not asking you to play detectives. I'm asking you to have a word with Frank Matheson and ask the questions he wants you to.'

'Why can't he ask his own questions?'

'Because it'll come better from you. You've legitimate reasons for asking questions without arousing suspicion.'

'All right, I know. Just leave it off – you're crowding me!'

Steve suddenly felt intensely weary of the whole business. Sod them; they could solve their own problems. He didn't want to go to Copenhagen, and he was tired of being pushed around.

By mid afternoon the black mood had taken full possession, but he kept his promise and arrived at the doctor's surgery on time.

Sarah grinned as he entered and pointed him to a chair in the waiting room. 'Phil's got a patient in there at the moment – one of our malingering whingers,' she whispered. 'He'll see you as soon as he's free.' She winked and disappeared into the office.

Dr Phil Anderson was an old friend of the family. He'd warmly encouraged Sarah's nursing ambitions and when Steve had begun to have depressive bouts, it was Phil who had offered Sarah her job as a nurse receptionist at the clinic. Steve slumped into the proffered chair and stared bleakly at the magazines on the adjacent table. The window was open and through it wafted a warm breeze, a pleasing scent of roses and the clatter of a lawn mower. These things meant nothing to him and he barely noticed them. He only wanted to complete this charade and escape.

Phil Anderson stared at his patient with a half smile. 'I've given you a thorough examination and, as usual, I can find nothing wrong with you. I could give you a reference for any life insurance company, and that's unusual for sports stars – middle age does for them in swathes.'

'Big deal,' said Steve morosely. 'Quite honestly, I wouldn't mind if my time was up tomorrow.'

'Now that's pure self-indulgence. You've got a lot more to contribute to the world before you're allowed to go, and it's up to me, professionally, to see you do.'

'So, you're the doc. What's wrong with me, what'll really work? And no more of your tranq pills – I won't touch them.'

'Do you really want to know – man to man?' Phil sat watching.

Steve made no reply but for the first time he felt a flicker of interest.

'Good, now you know I'm not a shrink. I know as much of that side of medicine as the next man. I wouldn't attempt to unscramble what's in your mind, but I may be able to point the way for you to do it yourself.'

'All right, but no bullshit. None of this back slapping pull-yourself-together-all-you-need-is-a-bit-of-willpower. That's what I get from Carol at work and I'm about sick of it.'

'No, nothing like that. Here's practical advice. Accept a challenge. Something requiring total focus, and maybe a bit of danger. That's my prescription. Please remember, in my opinion, you've been very near the edge of severe clinical depression, and once you're sucked into that, you're in big trouble.'

'What sort of challenge, Phil?'

'The Whitbread race is coming round again. That's one hell of a challenge. I can tell you for a fact that several of the top boats would be happy to have you.'

'No thanks, that Southern Ocean's a bloody awful place – I don't want to go there.'

'Single-handed or two-handed trans-Atlantic race then. I'll lend you *Andrina* – in her you'd have a fighting chance in the cruiser section.'

Steve was startled. *Andrina* was the Anderson family's pride and joy. A custom-built cruiser-racer, and something of a flyer.

'That's generous of you, Phil. I might just think about that one.'

Outside the waiting room, Sarah was ready to go home. While Steve said goodbye to the doctor, she set off first in her red Mini. Steve followed a few minutes later. He noticed little on his way home. His one thought was for a glass of whiskey and an armchair. He never noticed the large car stopped in the lay-by at the end of the street and which followed him as he passed. He parked his car and walked into the bungalow.

'Dad,' called Sarah. 'There's a Roller coming up the drive.'

'A what?'

'Rolls Royce – shit – it's Lindgrune!'

'Oh bloody hell – that's all I need.'

'Shall I tell him to go away?'

'No, I'll talk to him. It might as well be now.'

The front door, which had been left slightly ajar, was flung open. Standing there, blocking out the evening light, was Ken Lindgrune. Steve knew the man to be much the same age as himself and he felt a little smug at the other's obvious lack of fitness. He tried to dredge his memory for what he knew of Lindgrune. He recalled reading some-where that this man was an exemplar of the nineteen eighties: a role model for the new aggressive capitalism that those years had valued and encouraged.

'You might give us the courtesy of knocking before you crash in here.' Steve eyed the man coldly.

Lindgrune's face looked flabby and chalk white. Beads of sweat ran down his neck into his expensive tailored suit and shirt.

'Simpson, I want to talk to you, and when I want somebody, I'll walk in where the hell I like.'

'The important thing is I don't want to talk to you. I don't have to and I won't until you learn some manners.'

'Oh look, man,' Lindgrune was suddenly conciliatory. 'I've some-thing to say and I'll need five minutes of your time – that's all.'

Steve nodded and waved him forward.

'That's better.' Lindgrune grinned. 'For a moment I thought you were going to stop me. It seems you're making a hobby of getting in my way.'

'I don't get your drift.'

'Then I suggest you listen well.' A touch of Scots crept into the voice, and some menace as well.

'You sent a message about me to Sam Easterbroke, dinna deny it because I've got my ways of knowing.'

Lindgrune was standing in the centre of the room, his back to the open door, legs astride. With the light behind him, he seemed to tower over them. Sarah, a few feet away, looked pale and frightened.

'My advice to my employer is confidential and I'm not discussing it with you.'

'Oh come on, Simpson. I'm buying Easterbroke Sails so just you accept that. I'll give you some credit, man, you're part of my plans too, and if you'd a grain of sense you'd be celebrating.'

'Why should I be celebrating?'

Steve's voice was neutral as he stared back. He'd heard that Lindgrune could be an overwhelming, almost hypnotic personality. The way to handle him was to stand your ground. Certainly the man had compelling eyes. They shone out of the flabby face with a message of power and intelligence.

'Of course you should be celebrating.' Lindgrune pointed around him. 'What sort of a place do you call this?'

'It's our home and we're happy here.'

'For God's sake, man. You're a sporting legend. In any other country you'd be a millionaire for that alone.'

Steve said nothing, but he knew the shot had gone home. Unwittingly he and Sarah exchanged glances. Lindgrune was uncomfortably close to things that were in their thoughts unsaid.

'Hey, that struck a chord, didn't it, Mr Nice Guy.' Lindgrune laughed, though he had no humour in the eyes, or the small narrow mouth.

'Mr Lindgrune. If you've come to make me a proposition, let's hear it.'

'All right, I'm a businessman, I go where there's money to be made. They tell me you're good at your skill: the best maybe. I'm not interested in that side of the thing; you bring in the punters and part them with their money and I'll maybe share some o' it wi' you.' The eyes flickered as the accent became vivid.

'That's a pretty simplistic view, if I may say so,' Steve replied wearily. 'There's not a lot of money around at the moment, and your super-rich yachtsman is a bit of a myth, most of them have to count the pennies...'

'I know all about that.' Lindgrune interrupted brusquely. 'I hear you're soft on losers.'

'Losers?' Steve was baffled.

'Aye, losers. That young fellow from over the way; the one you gave stuff to. Aye, all from the kindness o' your wee heart.' Lindgrune laughed. 'Well you'll not do it from now on.'

Inwardly Steve groaned. He knew what was being alluded to; a young potential Olympic contender, whose business had gone into receivership. The man had been forced to sell his boats, car, and almost everything he owned. He had just managed to save his house from a repossession that would have put his young family on the street. Steve had persuaded Sam to buy him a new boat and provide sails for a year.

'The man had bad luck in his business. Bad debts owed to him, none of it his fault and he's not a loser – he wins races. He's one of the brightest prospects I've seen in ten years...'

'Oh, gi' over the bleeding hearts. A loser's a loser in my books. Man, you've a lot to learn. I can guess how you voted.'

'Mind your own business.'

'Aye, I will. I mind my business and that's why I'm a winner. Just you remember that.'

'Mr Lindgrune, if this is all you've got to say I think you'd better go – now!'

'I'll go when I'm good and ready. Now, what's Easterbroke paying you?' Lindgrune's voice had dropped to a whisper, almost a hiss.

'Mr Lindgrune, I'm trying to be patient with you, but I'm never going to be part of your plans, and Mr Easterbroke pays me what I'm worth, no more, no less.'

'My, you're a stubborn fellow. You're also a blind fool. Well here's my proposition.' Lindgrune leant forward, hands on hips. 'You'll keep your job and whatever you're paid I'll double it. In return, you'll stick to cutting and stitching. You carry out every instruction I give you, however unusual, without question, and,' Lindgrune was openly menacing, 'you'll keep out o' my private affairs – see!'

'I don't give a damn about your private affairs.'

Steve was angry now. His pride was stung. For the first time he faced a man on a completely different wavelength. Steve had never seen himself as other than a professional. He sold his expertise and was rewarded with fair payment and the goodwill of his customers. Lindgrune was saying he would use Steve's reputation to part customers from their money and more money than was due.

Lindgrune took a pace forward. 'You've already meddled in my private affairs. What were you up to yesterday, picking up dead bodies and trying to implicate me?'

'From what I've heard, you've been trying to make out I had something to do with that poor boy ending in the sea.'

'Well this lassie here seemed to know the fellow pretty well.'

Lindgrune's tone held just enough innuendo to leave no doubt what he meant.

'That's not true! You know it's not true,' Sarah was bristling with fury. 'I only saw him once, at Francine's party, and that was in your house!'

Despite everything, Steve almost laughed. The lopsided expression on her face reminded him of the time when she was twelve, and Mrs Blenner-Hasset had falsely accused her of nicking plums.

'That's as maybe,' Lindgrune continued. Not for a moment had his eyes shifted from Steve's. 'But in future when you work for me, you'll keep the lassie's mouth shut, because in my organisation it's loyalty that counts. Loyalty, morning, noon and night. Remember that and you'll get on.'

'I think you've forgotten something,' said Steve. He also had taken a pace forward and was standing not six inches from Lindgrune, still eye to eye. 'My loyalty is to Sam Easterbrooke, to our customers and to the people I work with. I don't need your money, I just want to look in the mirror of a morning and know my dead wife would be proud of me.'

'My, that's some speech,' Lindgrune chortled. 'Hey, man, they should sign you up for yon theatre. Go on, you can't mean all that stuff. What good's a dead woman anyway? I wonder where you get your comfort these days – that copper's wife in your office? Is that what you mean by people you work with?'

'Sarah,' said Steve. 'Mr Lindgrune is leaving. Please show him to his car.'

His ears were ringing, his chest had tightened, and his head drummed with pent-up rage.

'I'm not going anywhere. I'm na' finished wi' you.' The man was openly playing with him.

'Lindgrune, leave – go now!'

'Then ye'll have to throw me out and I wouldna' fancy your chances.'

Steve could see Sarah watching, horrified by the verbal dual. She was quite unprepared for what happened next. Steve swung his right hand viciously, catching Lindgrune by the front of his jacket and thrusting him backwards. Caught off balance, the full sixteen stone of the man toppled to the floor. His head struck a table, dislodging a vase, which shattered beside him. Steve stood over the prostrate figure and dragged him to his knees. Lindgrune, half-winded, gasped and spluttered, fingering a small cut on his head. He staggered uncertainly to his feet as Steve grasped him by the collar and propelled him through the front door, slamming it and dropping the latch. He turned, slightly breathless to face Sarah.

He smiled. 'Trouble is, I rather enjoyed that. My God, that man! He's one for the record book – what a shithouse! Did you hear all that? He tries to buy me. Then he makes a dirty insinuation about you and that boy, and to cap it all he accuses me of knocking off our Carol.'

The tension and anger were draining away. Suddenly he laughed. For the first time in nearly two years, he laughed. Spontaneously, he walked across and kissed Sarah on the forehead.

'Have you got the number of Norman's old police mate in Pompey?'

'Yes, it's on your desk.'

'OK, let's ring him. I've changed my mind about one thing; if

Kenny out there wants a fight he's got himself one.'

CHAPTER 4.

After lunch the next day Steve drove to Gatwick Airport, following a frantic morning of packing and several phone calls. He had confirmed his place on the trip and arranged to stay with the Hansen family; old friends in Copenhagen. He left the Volvo in a garage owned by a customer of the loft and walked the last quarter of a mile to the terminal hotel. The brewery organising the promotion had obviously spared no expense. On arrival, Steve was given his name badge and a lavish brochure with the weekend's programme. The lady tour guide explained that the British and American delegations would leave on a special charter flight the next morning. The organisers would appreciate it, she said, if former Olympians could wear their original team blazers.

Steve retired to his room and rummaged in his suitcase. The blazer was visibly too small, but would just about pass muster, if nobody expected him to button it around the middle. Beside his suitcase was another bulky holdall that Sarah had pushed into the car at the last minute. He unzipped the top and had a peep inside. It was filled with a mixture of sailing gear and casual clothes. He shook his head; as he understood it, the travellers to this bash were there to talk about sport, not to participate.

He went downstairs to the main lounge. Emerging from the lift his ears told him that the place was already full of Americans. As Steve edged into the room looking for a familiar face, a hand clapped him on his shoulder.

'Hello, Steve, I was rather counting on you being here. What are you doing these days? You seem to have dropped out of the frame a bit.'

Steve and Chris Bainbridge had become firm friends fifteen years ago when both had served on a committee to promote youth sport. If Steve was an important figure in his own small world, Chris by contrast, was a national institution. As a distance runner, he had won honours for Britain the world over. The man seemed little changed, although his shock of curly hair was greying now. He still gave the impression of suppressed energy that was infectious. Steve found himself shaking hands and grinning happily.

For just one moment Chris seemed uneasy. 'I was sorry to hear about your wife…'

'I know, it was a bad blow for all of us, but we're trying to put it behind us – that's what Miriam would've wanted. Anyway, what are you doing – still running?'

'Not the serious stuff. I do a bit of fell running and orienteering. Me, plus wife and kids, we're into orienteering in a big way. You should try it – it's all navigation – right up your street.'

'No thanks.' Steve laughed. 'I like my navigation sitting down. How do you earn your living these days?'

'I'm in the security business. Nation wide security firm – been with them twelve years, last four on the board. And you?'

'I'm still in sailmaking, but I don't know for how much longer.'

'How so?'

'Tell you tomorrow. No talking shop, today is for memories.'

It was good to have Chris around. The big ex-runner was not everyone's cup of tea; many found him noisy and conceited. Steve knew the other side of the man. He had a big-hearted generosity and a shrewdness with it. Already Steve had the stirring of an idea. He badly needed an ally in his quest. He was feeling out of his depth, and didn't relish the task of asking pointed questions of total strangers. Chris might be the man to help, if he could be persuaded.

'Where are you staying in Copenhagen?' Steve asked.

'The sponsors have booked me into some flash place near the Tivoli.'

'I'm staying with a family I know. Why don't you come with me? They're lovely people and I guarantee better grub and better company all round.'

'I must say that does sound tempting. I've been booked in with all these Yanks, and it's not that I don't like Americans, but three whole days of them...'

'That's settled then,' said Steve. 'I'll go ring my friends straight away, but there'll be no problems, they've stacks of room and they'll be over the moon to have someone like you staying.'

Steve slipped from the room and phoned the Hansens from the lobby payphone. As he expected, Olga Hansen made no difficulties over an extra guest. Any friend of Steve's was welcome. It was arranged that young Pedar would collect them from the airport and drive them direct to Hellerup.

The aircraft they boarded next morning was a One-eleven of uncertain age specially chartered for the occasion. Steve and Chris found themselves seats towards the rear and settled down as comfortably as possible for the trip. Chris spent half the journey immersed in a crossword puzzle. Eventually he flung down the paper and looked at Steve.

'Something's bothering you. Why did you say you might be out of a job?'

The abrupt question took Steve by surprise, but seeing his chance, he seized it.

'Chris, your firm guards property. Have you ever come across Winterbirch Holdings?'

It was Chris's turn to look startled. 'Yes, I have as a matter of fact, but you've touched a raw nerve there.'

'Can I ask why?'

'Well it's professional pride really. Yes, OK, I'll tell you. Winterbirch own two warehouses about a mile from the docks at Felixstowe. We had a three-year contract to mount security on that property and I know we did a good job at a fair price.' Chris's face had hardened – it was clear the memory still rankled. 'The first eighteen months went as smoothly as anyone could reasonably expect. Then one night there was a very minor break-in. Some idiot shot out a perimeter light with a .22 rifle. When he tried to climb over the fence, all the alarms went off, as they bloody well should, and the joker lit out fast.

'Then Winterbirch turn round and say they're cancelling our contract and bringing in their own security. And that wasn't the half of it. About a month later, I had a tip off that the man they'd hired to take over was an American ex-con: a bogus doctor who'd done time for drug pushing. The only good thing about the whole affair was that when our solicitors protested, Winterbirch paid out the rest of our contract and some more besides. It still makes me bloody angry though.'

'Who did you deal with at Winterbirch. Was it Lindgrune?'

'The boss man, yes – I don't talk with minions in a case like this.'

Steve sat deep in thought. He was not sure whether he should be surprised or not, but this was certainly a fortunate coincidence. It was, as they say, a small world.

'I've a good reason for asking all this. You see, Lindgrune's my problem as well.' Briefly he recalled the events of the last few days.

Chris listened intently. 'I can see your dilemma. Why is your parent company selling you down the river – have they got problems?'

'Not financial problems, but Sam Easterbrooke, our president, is a shrewd old fellow. I would guess Lindgrune is offering the sort of money you just don't refuse.'

'If he is, then the money must come from some other source than the Winterbirch company. When we had that run-in with Lindgrune, our lawyers had a look at their books, and they weren't that flush. They lost a lot of money in the early eighties, though they've recouped some of it in the last few years.' Chris looked thoughtful. 'It's still a mystery though. That place at Felixstowe; Winterbirch paid for this massive security but they didn't run the place – they leased it to an importer. It was a fertiliser store, farm chemicals in one unit, pharmaceuticals in the other, all completely legit – our people on the site were quite definite about that.'

Steve sat and listened to the background whine of the aircraft and the now boisterous sounds of the other passengers.

'Chris, did you know that the police in my part of the world are interested in Lindgrune? But they suspect that he's being protected in high places.'

'I've heard a rumour or two. We have to be careful ourselves, who we work for.'

'I've been asked to put a few tactful questions in Copenhagen; apparently Lindgrune's active there. They say because my job's on the line, nobody will be surprised if I'm a bit nosy.'

'Who's "they"?'

'The police, up to a point, but they've been told to lay off Lindgrune's business activities. There's a private detective in Portsmouth, an ex-superintendent, called Matheson. He has a score to settle with Lindgrune, so the official police are letting him make the running. They want me to ask the questions and then I'm to report back to Matheson. Frankly, I've got severe reservations about the whole business.'

'Well you shouldn't. As you say, your job's affected, and you're a responsible citizen, for God's sake. No, you go ahead, I'll give you moral support; in fact I may ask a few questions myself. How do you intend going about it?'

'I was going to start with the Hansens. They're the family we're staying with. The old man, Karl, is a government lawyer and a pretty influential guy. You see, Denmark's a small country and old Hansen seems to know everybody, and most of what's going on. He doesn't say much normally, but I'm sure he'd help me when I tell him about it.'

'That seems good thinking. Now, our firm does work for both the Copenhagen breweries, and for their British connections, so maybe

I'll ask around as well. You know I'd enjoy that. I didn't like Lindgrune, bombastic sod. It'd be nice to put one over him.' Chris held out his hand with a wide grin. 'Shake, I'm up for it – count me in.'

The flight arrived in Copenhagen to an enthusiastic welcome. Steve was surprised when the whole party was raced through the entry formalities and then into the terminal. A posse of children with flowers, a brass band, sundry politicians, the city mayor, and the PR Director of the brewery greeted them. It was clear that in the matter of their Olympic bid, these Danes meant business.

Following the twenty minutes of welcoming speeches, most of the visitors left for the transport that was to bus them into town. Steve had already spotted Pedar and Else Hansen on the fringe of the crowd and quickly made his way towards them while Chris followed with a luggage trolley. Danes are not emotional, but there was no mistaking the joy in the Hansen's greeting. The years melted away, and amidst the warmth of the handshakes, Steve was seized by a twinge of conscience.

Twenty years earlier, he had boarded with the Hansens on his first visit as a competitor in the Finn Gold Cup. For Steve and Miriam, it had been one of the happiest ten days of their lives, concluding in triumph as Steve won the trophy. They had returned to stay with the Hansens on several occasions. A bond of friendship had developed between the families that had led to several exchange visits. Then, with Miriam's death, Steve had allowed the contact to lapse. It had been Sarah who had sent the Christmas cards and acknowledged the Hansen's births, marriages, and deaths. None of this seemed to bother Pedar and Else. Steve introduced Chris, and saw their surprise and delight, as they realised the identity of this new guest.

Pedar loaded their luggage into his battered family car and they set off on the drive across Amager Island to the bridge over the Sydhavnen, the gateway to the capital. They encountered a traffic hold up on the bridge and they were able to look across the picturesque waterway to the Nyhavnen, the oldest part of the city. Then they were moving again over the bridge and along the wide Hans Christian Andersen Boulevard, past the famous Tivoli Gardens.

All the time Steve felt a mood change, almost a release, as he took in the views of his favourite city. Its green and gold-spired buildings and the streets leading to the Langelinie Park, complete with the Little Mermaid, all a stone's throw from the commercial port.

"The Paris of the north", some Danes call their capital. Certainly one thing Copenhageners have in common with Parisians, is their style of driving. Both Steve and Chris winced as Pedar hurled the car at a crowded roundabout, and then onto the ring road towards the Tuborg brewery. The Hansens lived in the commuter suburb of Hellerup, an area of housing straddling the road to Helsingor. Their house was on Gruntvigs Vej, one of a number of Vej, or leafy side streets, that run down to the coastline. The long Baltic strand between Copenhagen is the city's summer playground. Steve recalled its length being dotted with beaches and yacht harbours.

One such harbour was within walking distance of the house, and it was from its club slipway that Steve had set sail to win the Finn Gold Cup. He was alert and excited as he picked out familiar landmarks and long-remembered street names. As they alighted from the car, he heard the sound of a distant starting gun.

'It is the first day of the regatta,' said Pedar. 'Your race is at the eleventh hour tomorrow morning.'

'What d'you mean, my race?'

'Oh yes, you are to sail in the Laser race, a guest appearance – Morgensen has found you a good boat.'

'The hell he has, nobody warned me.'

'We talk to Sarah on the telephone, but she says, much better leave it to tell you at the last minute. You make less arguments that way.'

Steve left it at that. He was feeling relaxed for the first time in months, years even, and if he was doomed to make an idiot of himself tomorrow – well so be it. At least it explained the pack of sailing kit that Sarah had wished on him.

The arrival of a world-famous athlete and a legendary yacht helmsman had drawn the attention of the whole street. Within half an hour a crowd had gathered and a photographer from a local paper appeared. Steve and Chris were pictured together in the front garden with the Hansens and half a dozen of the pushier neighbours.

In the hour or so before dinner, Steve walked with Chris to the yacht harbour and sailing club. It was a tranquil scene with the racing over and the last of a warm sea breeze blowing in from the Baltic. Within minutes Steve was cornered by Olle Morgensen, the rigger. Olle always insisted his surname meant son of Morgan, and that his ancestors were Welsh. Certainly his looks bore some of this out. He was a stocky bear of a man, with a dark complexion and curly black hair. He advanced on Steve with a loud whoop and slapped him on the back with his left hand while waving a large rivet gun in his right.

'Steve! It is good to see you. It has been a long time. Come and see – for tomorrow I have the perfect boat for you.'

'Do I really have to race tomorrow?'

'You bet your damn life you do. You turn chicken or something? You win everything once. Now you show dem kids you're not so old, eh?'

'Let's see this boat.' Steve sighed.

Olle led them along the lines of parked dinghies to a brand new Laser. She seemed to be straight from the showroom, her gleaming white hull unmarked, and with a pungent smell of new resin and fibre.

'There,' said Olle. 'We have set her up for you – everything tested. There is one hell of a good boat.'

Steve examined the Laser, going carefully over the hull, rudder and centreboard. All Lasers are identical, the product of one builder. With mast and sails also the work of one mass producer, customised sailmakers like himself were not involved. In the event, the sail seemed a workmanlike job and anyway the other competitors would be similarly equipped.

'All right, Olle. I'll have a go, but I'm not as fit as I was in the old days.'

'How you mean – fat?'

'No, fit! Oh God,' he remembered from way back. Fitness was a word with no Danish equivalent. 'I mean I'm just twenty bloody years older.'

'I guess you still show the young ones some tricks. I see you tomorrow – may your mast break and your keel fall off.' With a grin and a wave he was gone.

'That last bit wasn't very polite,' said Chris. 'Did you upset him?'

'No,' Steve laughed. 'In Denmark it's very bad luck to wish someone good luck. You must always say break your mast – it's old Viking lore.'

'I get it; same with actors in the theatre.'

They walked back to the Hansen house. It was early evening and with the days beginning to shorten it would soon be dark. Lights shone in the windows with an aroma from the kitchen that anticipated the meal to come.

The Hansens were the kind of extended family that would have delighted Hans Christian Andersen. Three generations lived under one roof in a straggling two-storey house with an extra apartment on the ground floor that the family let to visitors.

The Danes have a word, *hygge*, literally, comfort. It has no exact equivalent in English speech and tradition, unless it be the Australian, "no worries". The tradition, is to be with your friends in a warm room, with good food, good wine, no tensions or jealousies, and day-to-day worries banished. Steve and Chris absorbed this atmosphere with relish. If Steve had a worry it was the nagging doubt as to how he could tactfully broach his real reason for being in Copenhagen.

Two hours later, they were back in the living room, a memorable meal consumed, while Karl Hansen circled the room with a decanter of Cherry Heering. As Steve held out his glass, the old man caught his eye.

'I have a feeling,' said Karl. 'Perhaps it is just an old lawyer's intuition, but I think you are wanting to tell us something. Sometimes I am in the courtroom. I have a witness and I know there is more in him than meets the eye. Maybe I am just an old busybody, so tell me so, but I still think you have something to say to us.'

Steve took a sip of the delicious red nectar. He was startled but not entirely surprised. Karl, wartime resistance leader and cunning lawyer, was not one to trifle with. He was chastened though, to see how easily the man had seen through him.

He told them the events of the last few days; then, looking at his host, he said quietly. 'Karl, please help. What do you know about these Elgaads and the man Lindgrune?'

Now he had the hushed attention of the whole room. Karl had a strange quizzical look. 'I think I can tell you plenty. But believe me, with the name Elgaad there is a whole big can of worms.'

CHAPTER 5

Steve was worried he might have spoiled the party. He was relieved to see only surprise and anticipation on the faces of the others.

'Now,' said Karl to his family. 'What can we tell Steve about the Elgaads?'

'Nazis! To me that is what they will always be,' said Karl's wife Olga.

'I worry more about what they do now,' said Else.' 'They pollute the earth, and then they wave our Danish flag and say, "Look how many kroner we make for you". They think we should all be so thankful, but I say how many animals do you kill, and plants, and fish in the sea? I think nothing of these Elgaads – I spit on them.'

'Please,' said Steve. 'You've lost me. Until this week I'd never heard of these people. Could someone explain?'

'Yes of course,' said Karl. 'I think you see here the difference of generations.' He sat down in his armchair. 'The Elgaad family control the largest chemical company in Denmark. It is not a great concern like your ICI, but it is a big firm for Denmark. You see, our laws do not encourage large family-controlled companies and these Elgaads have not only built a big business, they have, I think, beaten the system.'

Karl replenished his brandy glass. 'The Elgaad company is an old concern. The grandfather of the man who is now its president founded it in the early years of this century. They make farm fertilisers, chemical sprays, cattle medicines. You understand I have nothing against Kaj Elgaad who is now the head of the company. I have met him many times and I think he is a good man. It was his father who Olga and I once feared and still perhaps cannot forgive.'

'He and his wife,' snapped Olga. 'She betrayed our people to the Germans, and he did everything they told him. All the stuff they make in that factory, where did it go? Straight to Germany.'

Olga's face was expressive with, anger, grief, and bitter memories. Steve knew it was hard for a Briton to fully comprehend the humiliation of those years of occupation.

Karl reached across and gently squeezed his wife's hand. 'But there is more to the story.'

He stood up, went to a glass-fronted bookcase and withdrew a leather-bound book with an embossed crest.

47

'Yes, I remember the case well and the references are all here.' He opened the book and sat with it balanced on his crossed legs, examining the pages through half-moon spectacles.

'After the war was over, I was one of a team assigned to bring cases against war criminals and the more serious collaborators. But with Eric Elgaad there is a problem. The doctors say Gerda Elgaad, his wife, is insane. She is not fit to plead and of Eric there is no trace. He has vanished and his little son with him. We questioned his daughter and son-in-law and it seems they knew nothing. There the matter remains on our files, until after some years we have an amnesty and this is one of the cases dropped.' Karl shut the book and laid it down beside him.

'Not long after this,' he continued. 'Eric and his boy appear again. He approaches our government and they give him permission to rejoin the board of his old company. It seems the family still have a large fortune overseas and he offers to invest it all if the government will wipe clean the slate. You must understand this is at a time when things are hard in Denmark and, I think, for you in England also.' He gave Steve another quizzical smile.

'So, Eric and Gerda Elgaad are long gone. Their son Kaj is now the president of Elgaad Chemicals, and whatever you may say, Else, they are great exporters for our country and they make many jobs. The family have sporting achievements also.'

'You mean the girl Schmitt,' sniffed Else.

'But she is good, I like her,' protested Pedar.

'I did not say that I did not like her,' said Else frostily.

'Uncle Steve, I show you.'

One of the younger Hansens produced a glossy sports magazine, which he thrust into Steve's lap. 'Here it is … Kirsten Schmitt … she is voted Sportswoman of the year.'

He pointed at a page. It contained a long screed in Danish and a picture of a windsurfer on a sailboard. The board was one of the ultra-light racing types with a transparent sail. It was three parts airborne and ridden by a figure of uncertain gender in a wetsuit and woolly bobble-hat.

'She is our top sailor now,' said Pedar. 'She the wins the European Women's twice.'

'That is so,' said Karl. 'The young lady is the niece of Kaj Elgaad. She keeps house for him now that he is divorced. But of course, I forget, you say you have found his son's body. But that is so sad, for his father will be a lonely man now. The boy's mother is American, but she left this Elgaad and it is said the son Per was unstable and had troubles with the police and with drugs.'

'What about the man Lindgrune,' said Steve. 'Have any of you heard of him?'

'Indeed,' said Karl. 'I have heard of this man but never met him. I have been told he is an Englishman, of Danish extraction, and that he is fluent in both languages. I think, Steve, you are wise to be cautious of him. I understand our police are also watching this man.'

'I know another thing,' said Pedar. 'The Elgaads have a big house and a farm near Naestved. They say there is an Englishman who stays there. In winter he shoots on the marshes. I think this man is called Lindgrune – I am sure that is the name.'

'Karl,' said Steve. 'Do you know why your police are watching Lindgrune?'

'I have no details except that there was an explosion on a ship in the dock at Esbjerg. The police were suspicious at the time, but I think your Lloyds insurers were the losers then. Also I have heard whisper of some frauds suspected here in Kobenhavn. Again the man Lindgrune was mentioned, but I must say I know nothing of his link with Elgaad.'

'There's one more thing you should know,' said Steve. 'The English police are treating Per Elgaad's death as murder. Of course, it doesn't follow it was Lindgrune's doing.'

'That is true,' said Karl. 'If the boy was involved with drugs in England, that could happen. In Denmark we have few murders, but in your country – I am sorry to say this, Steve – but, to us, it seems a dangerous place.'

'As an objective lawyer, you shouldn't believe everything you read in the papers.'

'Ah, touché,' smiled the old man.

That effectively ended the conversation and Steve sat back, relieved the talk turned to pleasanter and more mundane subjects.

At half past ten, Steve stood up. 'I've been hijacked into sailing this race tomorrow. I think I'd better have some sleep or I shall take to the water like a zombie.'

Downstairs in their shared room, Chris remarked to Steve. 'I'm glad I came here. That was a great evening and some dinner. I warm to these Danes – are there many like them?'

'Yes, thousands. Your Dane may look a dull fellow, but most of them are all right. Somehow you don't feel the aggravation here like it is in the UK.'

'By the way,' said Chris. 'That warehouse at Felixstowe I told you about. The company that used the premises was, surprise, surprise – Elgaad Chemicals.'

Steve was forcibly woken the next morning at six o'clock. Chris, already dressed in a tracksuit, had insisted he join him for a jog around the block. The ex-distance runner seemed as fit as ever and Steve's attempt to run level left him feeling inadequate and gasping for air. After a shower, he took the precaution of a high-calorie breakfast and then mixed himself a bottle of glucose and orange juice; today he would need all the energy he could muster.

The Laser race was to be the last start of the morning. Morgensen had told him this was to be a European qualifying event, with as many as one hundred and twenty boats. Steve was not too concerned, as big starts were his speciality. But how would he cope with a fourteen-mile course, in a forecast twelve-knot wind? He squeezed into the crowded pre-race briefing, which thankfully, was conducted by a race officer with a tolerable grasp of English.

The yacht harbour was alive with action. The sound of flapping sails, the excited chatter, the rumble of launching trolleys. A strange mixture of nostalgia and anticipation was beginning to wash over him; the adrenaline was starting to pump.

Steve rigged his boat, and made a thorough check of everything. Satisfied with the set-up, he sat on the ground and made a study of the course. It was to be two laps of a triangle with a final ellipse of a downwind run followed by a long windward leg to the finish. He checked the course on his own chart, a relic of the triumph of twenty years ago. He had smiled that morning when he discovered that Sarah had stuffed this item at the bottom of his sailing bag along with a lightweight dinghy suit.

The wind was forecast to blow from the north straight down the Sound. With no tide to speak of, only the wind shifts would need watching. He was aware that he was an overweight helm in a small dinghy and that shifting light winds had never been his forte. Even in his prime, at the height of his fame, he had frequently suffered humiliation at the hands of locals, on inland rivers, and places like Frensham Pond.

The other competitors were appearing now from several nearby harbours. Soon the horizon was filled with a mass of little triangular sails. He sat for a while taking in the scene. Another Laser passed within ten feet, its helmsman staring at him. He was a fat boy whose ample bottom was encased in yellow Bermuda shorts. His podgy round face was topped by a close cropped stubble of dyed blond hair. He circled Steve's stationary boat twice, the second time passing within a foot of his stern.

'*Bedstefader!*' yelled the fat boy with an insolent leer.

The word meant granddaddy. Steve knew enough Danish for that. Deep inside him flashed a spark of anger.

'Just watch it ... fancy-pants,' he shouted in response.

The insult came to him with a pleasing spontaneity and it cracked his last inhibitions. At that moment, whatever psychological block had been holding Steve back, vanished. He was going to give this race a go. If these sods thought he was finished, they could bloody well think again.

He steered for the start line and took a quick transit between the committee boat and a building on the city shore. He might need this if the mass start blocked out the line. The boat was equipped with a little steering compass on the foredeck. Three hundred and fifty degrees should be the lay line to the windward mark. Five minutes sailing was enough to confirm a growing hunch. The wind had shifted some ten degrees, creating a growing bias to the committee boat end of the line. Using his stopwatch, he made three timed starts outside the committee boat. Satisfied, he sailed back to the correct side just as the ten-minute gun fired. The wind had steadied on its new direction and was now around the forecast twelve knots. A typical, short, steep, Baltic swell was developing. It was the kind of sea that would stop the boat dead if not handled properly.

His mind now switched off to everything except the job in hand. He had reverted to tunnel vision. Timing was now all: the physical and mental harmony needed to bring the boat at full speed to the line as the starting gun fired. He could see a gaggle of forty or so boats with him at the committee-boat end; probably locals mostly, who like him, had sized up the conditions. Another group was gambling on the far end of the line near the buoy. The bulk of the fleet seemed to be making for the middle of the line in a huge crescent-shaped wedge. He knew the first five minutes would be do or die. He had to keep the boat moving and break away from the competition into clean air.

Fifteen seconds. He pointed at the line, locked in the mainsheet, and with his ankles under the hiking straps, sat his entire weight outboard with only his lower limbs in the boat. Had he judged it right?

She was moving fast now ... five seconds ... four ... three ... two

… one … zero – gun! Just one gun, no recall!

For five minutes he worked on boat speed. Nothing in the world mattered except to fight through to clear air. He squeezed every last inch of himself outboard and had a quick peep under the sail. At the moment, he was on starboard tack. He would have right of way over any boat crossing him on port. All clear, nothing to worry about. The whole fleet seemed to be settled on starboard tack, including a huge congested bunch of boats well to leeward of him, all engulfed in a babble of shouting. His back was hurting less now, although his calf muscles were torture, but the boat was upright, well balanced and really moving. He was, as the expression had it, in the groove. The crunch would come in a couple of minutes when he had to tack.

He had another quick look around. A crowd of port tackers was converging on him. Would they all see him in time to give way? Once more, he gave his whole concentration to the boat. He must keep her moving, upright, and in the groove. He felt a wave of elation; he was crossing the first of the port tackers with twenty metres to spare. A quick count – yes, he was among the leading twenty boats.

He made the windward mark in eighteenth place and picked up another four places on the two off-wind legs. He rounded the bottom mark fourteenth. The first twenty boats were well clear of the main fleet and Steve guessed he was now sailing among the star players. His legs still ached, as did his stomach and back. He knew he would have to avoid one-to-one tacking duels. He picked up one more place on the upwind leg and held it until the final downwind leg. Running with the wind astern is the most demanding of skills in a small dinghy and Steve Simpson was still one of the world's finest exponents. It enabled him to overtake four more boats. All that remained was the long windward leg to the finishing line. Now his blood was up. His aching body had been consigned to the subconscious. He was riding on a high such as he had not felt in years. He took stock of the other boats. One was now clearly ahead and had the race sewn up. That left ten other boats all grouped close to each other. The nearest was trying to work its way into a blanketing position on his weather bow. This boat appeared to be helmed by a valkyrie, or at least by a strapping blonde girl with a Norwegian flag sewn to her lifejacket. Steve tacked, gathered speed, and tacked again. The manoeuvre was enough to unsettle the other. She slipped into Steve's backwind and tacked to clear herself. He let her go. A large cruising-yacht, at least a fifty-footer, had caught his attention. She was running down the sound from Helsingor with spinnaker set.

Something had alerted him. Yes, the yacht was beginning to run by the lee; a dangerous position that could end in an unplanned gybe. Would the others read the clues? His advantage was that he had big boat experience, where these Laser boys and girl probably had not. At that moment the yacht gybed. It was a perfectly executed spinnaker gybe by a big crew.

Steve had no time for applause, he had seen enough. A dark shadow was snaking across the choppy Baltic water. Steve tacked and waited. The wind shift arrived within seconds. It not only lifted the wind speed another five knots, it also gave him a perfect lay line for the finish. The others reacted one by one but they were too late. Five minutes later Steve found himself in second place.

One well-placed opponent, a scarlet Laser, was sitting in his wind shadow some twenty metres away – the others were nowhere. As the wind backed to its original direction the other man tacked. Steve tacked to cover. The red boat tacked again. Steve covered; he still had half a mile to go.

Every muscle and joint in his body was screaming in protest. His ears were singing. A dreadful leaden fatigue gripped him. His chest hurt. His eyes seemed to half focus. His heart was pounding. All he knew was that he had to do it. Whatever the effort, whatever the pain; he must keep himself between the other boat and the finish.

The red Laser made six tacks and Steve covered every one, but he lacked the youth and fitness of the other man, and he lacked match practice. He knew one more tack would break him. He saw the committee boat anchored in her finishing position; only two minutes away. He took a gamble. He would ignore the other boat and throw everything into a desperate manoeuvre to lay the line on this tack. He must keep moving. He must punish his aching body that little bit more. Keep in the groove … in the groove.

The red Laser had tacked upwind and tacked again. She was well to windward now. He watched the buoy at the end of the line. If he couldn't make it he would be beaten. The buoy was dead ahead now on his bows and closing fast. Oh, God, he mustn't hit it. He threw the dinghy into a desperate luffing manoeuvre. The buoy slid by half a metre from his port side. He heard a gun and, a split second later, another.

He pulled himself inboard, letting the sail flap. He was trembling as he crouched in the cockpit hyperventilating; his heart pounding. His knees began knocking, to be followed by a racking cramp in his right leg.

'It's Steve isn't it – well sailed.'

Peering at him from beneath the boom of the red Laser was the grinning face of Sean Jeffries. Steve and Miriam had sailed against Sean's parents when Sean was a babe in arms. Now he was one of the Laser class rising stars.

'Heard you were racing,' said Sean. 'You know you beat me by half a boat length – really cool, man!'

'I dunno about that, Sean. You'd have got me if it had gone another five minutes – I was beaten.'

'Don't you believe it – you stretched me all I had. See you ashore – I'll buy you a pint of Special-Brew.' Sean waved and went planing away towards the shore.

Steve pulled in his mainsheet and followed. To his utter astonishment a TV crew and a cheering crowd greeted him. It was only then that the awful truth of what he had done dawned on him. At forty-five, he'd sailed a major international race. In doing so, he'd beaten the UK champion into third place and probably several other champions as well. All this from a Rip Van Winkle who was there by special invitation, and presumably was supposed to lose. An ecstatic Olle Morgensen was already waiting with the launching trolley.

'Hey, I tell you so! I know you show dem the way to sail.'

Olle was as overjoyed as if Steve had won, which he hadn't. He remembered the distant Laser that had received the winning gun. Olle told him the man was an American sailor, a former world champion.

'You not to worry about dat Yank. Now, what do you do in de afternoon race?'

'No!' said Steve firmly. 'Thanks, Olle, but for me there is no afternoon race. No way – understand! I'm shattered, kaput, finito. That was definitely the swan song of Steve Simpson.'

'OK, if you say, but I leave the boat for you. Sail her when you like.'

'Thanks, Olle, I'd appreciate that.'

'Steve, I nearly forget; there's two guys asking for you.'

'Who?'

'They not say, but they are not yotties, that's for sure.'

'What did they look like?'

'One was an Innuit – you know, Greenlander.'

'An Eskimo?'

'Sure, plenty of dem in town these days – they're OK.'

'What about the other one?'

'English guy by de way he talk. He looked like James Dean.'

54

'Eh?'

'Dat's right, but they are nosy parkers. They ask where you stay but I not tell dem.'

Steve found himself chuckling. He was well in the grip of post-race euphoria. He had a surreal, Pythonesque vision, of an Eskimo in fur boots and a long-deceased movie star, endlessly searching for him at dinghy meets. The absurd scene had him laughing out loud. Olle looked at him suspiciously but Steve did not explain. His sense of humour would be unlikely to appeal to a Dane.

'OK, Steve, you be around for prize giving – I see you.' With a wave, he was gone.

Steve watched the afternoon race from the comfort of the Hansen family Folkboat sailing cruiser. Ashore the prize giving was delayed for an hour while a race protest was heard. Steve wondered if he should go back to the Hansens and change, but decided against it. This was not a posh yacht club in the British mould: informality was the order of the day.

He sat on a wooden bench beside the marina at peace with himself, drinking in the scene. Lost in thought, he barely heard a polite cough behind him, followed by a cultured English voice.

'Mr Simpson, I believe? Excuse me; I hope I didn't startle you. May I introduce myself – I'm Kaj Elgaad.'

Two men stood there; the owner of the voice, with hand outstretched. Steve took it and acknowledged the greeting, but his eyes were fixed on the second man. It was Ken Lindgrune.

CHAPTER 6

Although fair-haired, Kaj Elgaad was not a stereotype Scandinavian. He was a slightly built man with sharp features, probably aged around fifty. He shook hands firmly and looked Steve up and down. His manner was friendly but he did not smile. Steve felt no particular sense of shock, nor did he feel embarrassed by the sight of Lindgrune, despite the small wound dressing and plaster above the man's right eye. Steve guessed these to be a relic of their encounter two evenings ago.

'I watched you race from my boat,' said Elgaad. 'My congratulations – you struck quite a blow for us older ones.'

Steve was puzzled by the voice, which had no Danish intonation. Elgaad spoke like a native Brit with a touch of lowland Scots.

'I made a special effort to be here today,' Elgaad continued. 'I only found out you were in Kobenhavn from the newspaper this morning.'

'That's right,' said Lindgrune. 'You were all across the gossip page. I gather you're staying in Hellerup?'

Lindgrune's manner showed no hint of their last meeting.

'Yes,' Steve confirmed. 'I'm staying with some friends for a couple of days.'

'Mr Simpson,' said Elgaad. 'I'll come straight to the point. I've been told you were the one who found the body of my son. I would be so pleased if you would come to dinner with my niece and I tonight. I know it must be awkward for you but we would be grateful. So ... please?'

Steve felt a strange mix of emotions. Instinct told him to make an excuse – any excuse. On the other hand, he might never have a better opportunity to learn more of the link between Lindgrune and Elgaad. What finally decided him was the expression on Kaj Elgaad's face. The man was gently pleading with him. Instinctively Steve knew this was a genuine invitation with no ulterior motive. An invitation he could not honourably refuse, and would not wish to.

'Thank you, Mr Elgaad. I'll be delighted.'

'Ah, good man.' Elgaad had a smile at last. 'I'll send a car for you around six o'clock. I live in the country a little way out of town. We'll look forward to seeing you. You know, my niece would never have forgiven me if I'd failed to bring you home. So you'll have done me a double service.' Elgaad gave another friendly nod. 'Goodbye for now. Dinner at eight o'clock.'

Steve watched as the pair disappeared into the crowd that was already gathering for the prize giving. He sat for a few minutes, his head in his hands trying to make sense of what had just happened. It seemed he had that newspaper reporter to thank for Elgaad and Lindgrune finding him. By all accounts they weren't the only ones searching for him; what about Olle's Eskimo? Nothing seemed to make sense. He felt a twinge of excitement; this coming evening could be interesting. A further confrontation with Lindgrune perhaps? But he was more than curious to learn about this mysterious Elgaad and his sporting niece.

The promised car, a Mercedes, arrived outside the door at six o'clock. The driver climbed out and leaned laconically against the bonnet, while half the small children of Gruntvigsvej peered through its windows and fingered the gleaming silver-grey bodywork. Steve, freshly showered and dressed in his blazer and best slacks, climbed aboard to a patter of applause from the bystanders.

Soon they were on the road out of town, and heading south, on the route to the ferry port at Gedser. Steve studied the driver. The man was a roly-poly individual dressed in a striped shirt over green moleskin trousers. His name, he said was Metvod. No, he was not a professional chauffeur, he was a farmer, but he did part-time driving for Herre Elgaad. It was soon clear that Metvod was not going to be a bundle of laughs. He was one of those deeply morbid and taciturn Danes, whose limited English contained no cheerful phrases. Farming, said Metvod, was no good. He was burdened by inheritance taxes, in hock for thousands of Kroner to the Land Bank, and pig prices had fallen six ore a kilo for the last five weeks.

Quickly disengaging himself from this fellow depressive, Steve looked out of the window. They were speeding through open country, very like the flat land between Chichester and Selsey. Only the red tiled barns and homesteads were different. Clearly the harvest was at full momentum, with combine harvesters working the fields and the roads filled with grain trailers and wagons of straw bales. It was a strange experience to sit in air-conditioned luxury and watch all this ant-like activity outside.

They left the main highway some fifty kilometres south of Copenhagen and entered a maze of back roads passing through several quaint medieval villages. Shortly afterwards Metvod slowed the

Mercedes and turned right into a long gravelled drive running straight between a field of grazing cattle and a railed paddock with six fine thoroughbred horses. At least Steve assumed they were thoroughbreds. He wished Sarah was with him, she could ride almost as well as she could sail. He glanced at his watch which said twenty past seven.

The Elgaad house was not a stately home in the English mode, but in its way it was impressive. The centre was a tall traditional farmhouse with a steep roof sweeping almost to the ground. From this main dwelling spread a series of single-storey wings built in the style of farm buildings. Beyond were similar structures clearly stables. The house and its wings formed three sides of a square around a paved courtyard and it was here that the car drew up, facing the front entrance.

The heat and dust struck him the moment he emerged, as did the background roar of harvesting. He looked up to see Kaj Elgaad advancing with hand outstretched.

'*Velkommen,* Steve, if I may. Welcome to our farm – it's not everyday we have a sporting celebrity to dinner. What do you think of this place?'

'It's magnificent; a little bit like a Roman palace – we've the ruins of a famous one in my home village of Fishbourne.'

'Indeed so – I know it well, but it's coincidence I'm afraid. I don't think the Romans did much in these parts – Barbarians, we were.'

Elgaad motioned him to follow and they walked to the front door.

Inside the house, all was deliciously cool and shaded. As Steve's eyes readjusted, he took in a pattern of white walls and dark timbers. The air wafted a pleasant aroma of lavender and beeswax, and while this entrance hall was sparsely furnished, the walls were decorated with a striking mix of Nordic woodcarvings and English watercolours, including one, which looked a genuine Constable.

'Steve, if we could have a quick word in private. Dinner will be in half an hour, or so my niece has just told me.'

Kaj Elgaad led the way up an uncarpeted wooden stairway to the first floor and then into a comfortable but not over-lavish room: clearly half office and private den. Kaj waved Steve to an armchair and offered him a whisky, though he poured only tonic water for himself.

'You see,' he smiled. 'I'm being careful. In northern Europe we like to think we're one great Scandinavian brotherhood. It's all phooey of course – we're just one great band of twenty million alcoholics.'

Kaj put down his glass and sat opposite Steve. 'Obviously you know why I want to speak to you. You and your daughter found my poor boy. I would be extremely grateful it you could tell me the whole story.'

The sad dignity about this man made Steve see his own troubles in a new light. Elgaad had lost his wife and son. He had nobody left now, unless it was this obscure niece. He tried to imagine how life would be if he'd lost both Miriam and Sarah; especially Sarah. Momentarily he was in his own nightmare. His stomach seemed to hold a block of ice. What were his troubles compared with those of this cultured, dignified man. Wealth, success and this lovely house could only mock Kaj Elgaad; in the real world he had nothing.

Steve told the story as simply as he could. It did not take long, and surprisingly Kaj was familiar with Chichester Harbour. He had a motor yacht, he explained, and twice a year he visited England, sometimes calling at Chichester. On the last occasion, Per had been with him and they had taken the ship's inflatable to Nutbourne to watch the wading birds. Tears were streaming down his face. Steve, knowing too well not to say anything, sat and waited.

Then without so much as a knock, the door of the study was pushed brusquely open and in came Lindgrune. Steve was still watching Kaj's face and for a fleeting second what he saw frightened him. Reflected in every muscle and deep in the man's blue eyes were expressions of hatred and fear, such as he had never witnessed before. It was only for a split second while Kaj was looking over him at Lindgrune, but Steve caught the full force of it. Something was wrong here. Kaj was in deep grief for the loss of his son and that was understandable; he was also frightened. Steve might not have the most alert imagination in the world but he knew fear when he saw it.

Steve stared at Lindgrune, mindful that this was the man he'd hurled through his front door and who might still bring a charge of assault.

He addressed Lindgrune directly. 'When you went to the mortuary the other day, you knew perfectly well that the man was Per Elgaad. Why bluff, and why try to implicate me?'

Lindgrune smiled contritely, as he raised an apologetic hand. 'Please, Simpson, let me explain, there are things you do not know. Poor Per was a troubled young man who found it difficult to come to terms with life. He'd had a breakdown plus a serious drugs problem, and, I'm sorry to say, a previous suicide attempt. I know it's difficult for Elgaad to talk about these things but I'm afraid they're true.'

Steve sat and deliberately watched Kaj's face. The expression was wooden but the eyes were blazing. A mixture of fear and rage was working inside the man and one day it would explode.

Steve addressed Lindgrune. 'So you're saying he committed suicide?'

Lindgrune shrugged. 'That's for the coroner, of course, but, for those of us who knew the boy, it seems logical.'

Kaj spoke quietly. 'I understand your authorities will be releasing his body next week. I shall be travelling by sea to bring him home for burial. It will be a sad occasion but I hope, Steve, that you will visit my boat *Kristabel* before we leave for home.'

Elgaad was regarding him with that same quiet dignity. Steve knew that he liked this man and respected him. Something was going on here that he didn't understand; only that Kaj Elgaad was a much-wronged man.

A new sound echoed through the house: the ringing of a deep and melodious ship's bell.

'Ah,' said Elgaad. 'Dinner is ready. Come along, Steve, you must meet my niece – she also is a sailor of some repute.'

Elgaad led the way downstairs and into a room beyond. Steve found himself in a cavernous chamber as high as the house, which, like some great church, had no ceiling, only the timber arches of the roof itself. High chandeliers hung from the crossbeams illuminating the polished floor and a long table gleaming with silver and glass. Steve realised he was in a latter-day Viking hall, a place resonant with the feel of older times.

By the table stood a group of women, the nearest of whom he recognised. She was Francine, Lindgrune's stepdaughter, and Sarah's friend, wearing an outrageous yellow jumpsuit that revealed every dimple of her plump form.

'Hi, Steve!' She called. 'How's things?'

'Hello, Francine.'

Changing times, he grumbled inwardly. When he was that age, one most definitely did not address one's best friend's father as Steve.

Francine had caught him by the arm and was introducing him to her mother, Trudi Lindgrune. Trudi was an even rounder and plumper version of her daughter. She greeted Steve and in a piercing stage whisper asked after Sarah. How terrible that she had found poor Per, she gushed. So distressing for such a nice sensitive girl. Trudi continued embarrassingly in the same vein, although Steve found her German/Swiss accent hard to follow. She was clearly a motherly and not over-bright lady. Gossip had it that Trudi's first husband had run off with a fashion model, and that Lindgrune had picked up both Trudi and her substantial divorce settlement along the way.

At last he was able to extricate himself, and Kaj presented him to the third woman in the group.

'Steve, I would like you to meet my niece Kirsten. She, as I have said, is like you, a sailor.'

So here was the wind surfer. Thirty years old maybe, she could never be described as beautiful, but she had a pleasing round face with long, jet black hair and a complexion darker than the average Dane. Her arms were a shade muscular, as one would expect, but something about her would have drawn his attention anywhere – she glowed. She glowed with the sexual magnetism of a mature woman. She glowed with all the latent energy of a trained athlete; just as her deeply tanned shoulders glowed above the line of her white strapless dress. Around her neck was a gold chain with a pendant and a single emerald that also glowed in the subdued light of the hall.

'Steve – *velkommen,*' the voice was soft and lilting. 'You must excuse me for not greeting you earlier, but Uncle has put me in charge of the arrangements tonight.'

The words were the near perfect diction of one with a well-learnt second language.

'I saw you race today,' she smiled. 'You beat that horrible Jens Olsen. I was so pleased!'

Although Steve had no idea which of his opponents was Olsen, he felt a warm glow at having won the lady's favour in this knightly way.

Kirsten smiled and excused herself while she supervised serving dinner, but a minute later she was sitting opposite him across the narrow table. She flashed another smile and as her eyes caught the reflection of the chandelier, they shone green to match the emerald nestling between her half-exposed breasts.

Steve suddenly realised he was hungry and that, apart from a plate of smoebrod at the yacht club, he hadn't eaten since breakfast, and on this the day of his first competitive dinghy race for nearly ten years. With a tremor of alarm he noticed tiny toasting glasses set beside each place. These, he guessed, were about to be charged with agavit, raw spirit to be knocked back in a single gulp at the call of one's host. The scotch he had just drunk was beginning to work on his empty stomach. He hoped, for the honour of England, that he would stay upright for the whole evening.

A trolley appeared and two women served bowls of a delicious fish soup accompanied by thin slices of the local black bread. Kaj then called for a toast to the Queens of Denmark and Great Britain. Steve drained his agavit in the approved manner while the room swayed, spun, and slowly refocused.

Kirsten was asking him about Chichester Harbour. She had been told this was where King Knut, or Canute to the English, had defied the tide.

Steve laughed. 'That's right; it's supposed to have been on the hard at Bosham. You know, every year, a dozen holidaymakers drown their parked cars there. Maybe they're trying the same trick.'

Kirsten was scornful. 'How typical of the English – as usual you have it wrong. You say Canute? He is that thick-skulled Dane who thinks he can turn the tide – Ha! Ha! Ha!'

She scowled at him in mock fury; then she smiled and he saw the green eyes sparkle.

She continued. 'We see it differently. Knut was a wise man. It was his English courtiers who came to him every day, saying. "You are the greatest. You have armies, navies – you are such a big guy even the winds and tides obey you". Knut gets tired of all this so he says. "OK, I sit in the sea and try it," and so he gets his feet wet. Then he says, "Why you give me all this bullshit? You know I can't turn the tide and I know it – so what you take me for?" Then all those English courtiers know not to try flattery because Knut is too big a guy to be conned.'

Steve grinned. He found the girl's enthusiasm infectious and her soft, lilting Danespeak, a delight.

Kaj intervened. 'Another toast. To that great and much mis-understood gentleman King Canute, who ruled over both England and Denmark.'

Steve drained his second glass of agavit and gripped the table as it laid its fiery trail down his throat.

He could not help but notice that Kirsten was completely ignoring Lindgrune sitting on her right. The man made one attempt at conversation to which she replied in Danish and clearly none too politely. This puzzled him, for the girl seemed cheerful and uncomplicated by nature; bubbly would be the modern term, and someone like that would not be rude to a guest at her table.

Francine on his left was clearly the worse for agavit. She eyed Steve lecherously, replied incoherently, and collapsed in giggles when her mother snapped at her in German. Kaj, at the far end of the table, said and ate little. He remained a courteous host, but seemed deep in some world of his own. Like his niece, he ignored Lindgrune.

The conversation became increasingly unreal and stilted, and Steve could hardly miss the tensions in the room. He began to feel as if he were an actor in a play, but with the disadvantage that everyone in the scene knew their lines but he.

The talk turned to economics and Europe. Steve ventured that Britain was fortunate by geography to have escaped the trauma of invasion and occupation, and that might make her insensitive to the problems of countries like Denmark who had suffered. He had made this point a dozen times before when abroad, mainly because it sounded profound and went down well. This time a shadow seemed to fall over the room and he knew he had blundered. Nobody looked at him and for three seconds total silence ensued. Kaj stared nervously at the table and then across to Lindgrune who muttered something in Danish. Then Kirsten spoke also in Danish although Steve recognised only one word.

'*Gerda er dod ... dod!*' She slapped the table angrily.

Dod meant dead, but who was dead – Per? Well they all knew that, but what on earth had it to do with his reference to the war. Could there be something in Karl Hansen's story that the Elgaads were German sympathisers? He found that hard to believe because there had been relatively few collaborators in Denmark. The country had the most honourable record of all in that respect. Everyone knew the story of how the country's Jewish community had been smuggled out to Sweden under the noses of the Germans. Hundreds of ordinary people had played a part but no one had betrayed. He glanced across the table to Kirsten although, despite himself, his eyes were fixed on the emerald resting against the coffee brown cleavage.

'Have I said something wrong?' he asked quietly.

'No, of course not – don't worry about it.'

The conversation was beginning to pick up again. Kaj was lamenting the high rates of taxation, echoing much of what Metvod had said earlier.

'You see,' he sighed. 'Our company is the nation's third largest single exporter. We bring in millions of Kroner in foreign exchange and do we get recognition?

'This year we've launched a new product. Decodon is set to become Europe's, top-selling, pain reliever. The product was developed wholly in our laboratories. My poor Per worked on the programme you know.' His voice tailed away. Steve saw the grief on his face and felt embarrassed.

Fortunately a diversion was at hand. Francine announced to the company that she was going to be sick, and she was hustled from the room by Kirsten and Trudi. The three men were alone. Coffee was brought and Lindgrune lit a cigar. Steve took stock of the other two.

What was he to make of all this? Elgaad and Lindgrune were supposed to be business associates but they were hardly on speaking terms. Lindgrune, for all the hostility shown to him, seemed completely at ease. Kirsten obviously had no time for Lindgrune. She had treated him with downright rudeness. Elgaad had been polite but Steve would not forget the man's reaction in the room above. Between these two was no mere business disagreement, something was desperately wrong. If Kirsten was open in her contempt for Lindgrune, Kaj could not conceal his fear.

But who was Lindgrune? In Chichester, he was merely another uppity millionaire trying to exploit the boating scene. Yet, here in Denmark, he seemed to be, a Dane; or at least he spoke the language well. Easterbrookes' manager in Kiel, Wolfgang Bartels, had told Carol that Lindgrune had been making unpopular waves in Denmark. Karl Hansen had confirmed this, and the detective Matheson thought the whole answer to the riddle was in Copenhagen. He wished there had been time for him to have met Matheson before he started this quest.

Steve found to his consternation that Lindgrune was staring at him. 'Simpson, I owe you an apology.'

Steve stayed silent, on his guard.

Lindgrune exhaled a plume of cigar smoke. 'No need to look like that – you should be honoured. This is only the second time I've apologised to anyone in my life.'

With an effort, Steve gathered his faculties and met the eyes of the other man. If this was to be a further confrontation, he had none of the advantages of last time when he was on his own ground and definitely sober.

'You see,' continued Lindgrune. 'My organisation has grown so big; these days I spend my time surrounded by grovellers and sycophants …'

'Like King Canute,' Steve interjected.

'Possibly, but I do not set out to employ court flatterers. I hire the best and I pay well. But I have my ways of doing things and as my employees need to keep their jobs they bend to those ways. Then I come across you, a technocrat. Skilled technicians are usually the least of my worries. I pay well, I leave them alone with their specialities and everyone is happy. I only ask that their skills are profitable.'

'That's not what you said the other day. You said loyalty to you should come before decent behaviour and principle.' Steve was beginning to be angry again.

'That's why I want to apologise. I've been living in a very competitive world for a long time. Perhaps somewhere along the way I've lost something and that's why I misjudged you.'

This attitude from Lindgrune was certainly unexpected and Steve was far from convinced.

'I know this sounds trite to you but I just like doing the things I do, and a lot of money isn't going to make me any happier if I've lost my integrity.'

'Integrity,' said Lindgrune. 'The man would stake all for his integrity? Extraordinary, but you really mean it. I'm enough of a judge of character to see that. All the same, I wish you'd consider my offer – a little integrity would be quite a novelty in my world. What do you think Elgaad?'

Kaj, wooden faced, said nothing.

'You see,' said Lindgrune. 'Elgaad is a man who struggles with his integrity, but I think he has rather more to lose than you.'

The voice had hardened. The tone was spiteful and vicious. Steve, watching Elgaad's face, saw once again the expression of suppressed hate, but it was only fleeting. Kaj's composure returned. 'Perhaps we should rejoin the ladies.'

He led them to the main living room. This was not a formal drawing room, but a comfortable well-furnished place, with bookshelves, pictures and a television. Above the fireplace was a large framed photograph of a woman cradling a small baby. She was striking, with flaxen-hair, sitting in a cane chair and by her shoulder stood a girl in her late teens; tall and solemn staring at the baby with puzzled wide eyes. On the white mount of the picture the photographer had signed his name: Ernst Klammer, Muenchen. Muenchen was Munich, so the portrait taker must have hailed from there.

'That is my grandmother,' said a soft voice behind him.

It was Kirsten. He hadn't noticed her approach, so intent had he been on the picture.

'The baby is my Uncle Kaj, and the other lady is my mother. That picture was taken just before the war when my grandparents lived in Germany.'

'Were they in Germany during the war?' he asked.

'No, they came home just before the outbreak, but it is such a sad picture. Only Uncle is alive now. My grandmother died just after the war and we lost my mother last year, and my father too. He died in an air crash in the States ten years ago. So with poor Per dead, only Uncle and me are left.'

'I'm sorry,' said Steve. 'I didn't mean to be tactless, but I know so little about you, and I'd so like to know more.'

He smiled at her in approval. Whatever his troubles, Kaj had a golden asset in this girl and he could not but make comparisons with himself and Sarah. He looked at his watch; it was nearly half past ten.

'I think I should be going soon,' he said.

'I know,' she smiled. 'I think Bent Metvod is getting impatient. Poor Bent, he is always so miserable. I am not sure he likes me – Per and I used to play tricks on him when we were young.'

Steve shook hands with Kaj and Kirsten, but it was Kirsten who insisted on taking him out to the car.

'I need to talk. I have spoken to your daughter.'

'Eh?' Steve couldn't comprehend.

'Yes, on the telephone; Francine rang her earlier.'

They were in the middle of the paved courtyard, when she stopped and faced him.

'Sarah has told me about Lindgrune and the sail-loft. She tells me to tell you that she has again spoken to the policeman Matesen.'

'Matheson?'

'Yes, look, I cannot stay here long but I will tell you this. Lindgrune brought men with him from England. They were in Hellerup today and they are watching you and your friend.'

The Mercedes had appeared again, gliding towards them.

'Steve, I must talk to you in private. I know Morgensen has left you his boat again, so will you go sailing tomorrow?'

Yes, I was going to anyway.'

'OK, midday tomorrow. Head north past Skoshoved towards Helsingor.'

'And then what?'

'You wait.'

'Wait for what?'

'Just be there and you'll see.'

CHAPTER 7

Steve dozed intermittently during the return journey, his sleep eventually broken by a sharp dig in the ribs.

'You home now,' said Metvod.

Steve mumbled his thanks and staggered into the street to find himself outside the Hansens'. The house was in darkness apart from a single light in the room he shared with Chris. He knew the Hansens had gone to a wedding, and that Chris had been to an athletics dinner.

He was surprised to find Chris outside in the garden waiting for him.

'Somebody's been in there nosing about.'

'How d'you know?' Steve was sceptical and suddenly very tired.

'Cigarette smoke; it's fading now but it was strong when I came in ten minutes ago.'

'Maybe one of the Hansens was in there earlier.'

'No way – none of that lot smoke except old Karl with those Havanas. The rest are all eco-freaks. Anyway this was fresh.'

Chris turned back to the house. 'Come inside, but don't talk until I say; I've got a professional intuition about this.'

In the rooms Chris, began combing behind the beds and furniture.

'Aha, here we go!'

He bent down, removed a two-way adapter from a power socket, fumbled with a pair of scissors, and undid a retaining screw. The fitting fell apart, revealing a small condenser and a maze of wires. Probing further, he pulled out a tiny battery and then hurled the whole thing into the furthest corner of the room.

'Jesus Christ! If those idiots really thought they'd fool me with a Mickey Mouse piece of kit like that. I'd like to stuff it down Lindgrune's throat.'

'Chris, what was it?'

'Electronic surveillance device – bug to you. Probably a short-range transmitter. Whoever's on the end won't be far away – come on.'

Chris strode to the door, switching off the light as he went. The street was deserted, apart from a dumpy vehicle parked under a lime tree fifty yards away.

'Let's, go for it!' he yelled, taking off down the street with the élan of a sprinter.

Chris reached the parked car in less than eight seconds and thumped angrily on the rear window. The occupants were clearly startled. Steve heard the engine start, and with gears crunching, it sped off down the road towards the sea. It seemed the driver had forgotten or did not realise that he was in a cul-de-sac. The wall at the end of the Vej loomed, and brakes screamed as the car did a U-turn, before racing back up the road. Steve, who had been rooted to the spot, had enough presence to try and read the number plate. He was incensed at such driving in a suburban road, that in daylight, would have been crowded with young children. The number was a blur, but in the light of the street lamp, he caught an instant photographic impression of the driver.

Chris jogged back; he was carrying something and Steve saw he was smiling.

'Did you see anything?' Chris asked.

'Range Rover – couldn't see the number but I reckon I'd know the driver again. It was Olle's Eskimo.'

'Who?'

'Today at the Yacht Club, Olle Morgensen said there were two characters asking about me.' Steve paused and broke out laughing. 'He said one was a Greenlander and the other was English but he looked like James Dean.'

'That's not a bad description,' said Chris. 'So he saw an Eskimo and a young lad with a fifties' haircut and a leather jacket. There you are, Watson – how's that for deduction?'

'Pretty useless, I should say. For a start Copenhagen's full of Greenlanders – they're the colonial ethnic minority.'

'Well there were certainly two persons in that car and they had a nice little antenna on the roof – have a souvenir.'

Chris held up an object that looked like a table-weight with a piece of cable and a wire shape on top.

'Magnetic on the bottom – you stick it on your car roof and tune in. But I tell you, they were amateurs, a couple of real bumblers. That gadget they left indoors stood out a mile. For heaven's sake, I'm reasonably observant. I knew there was no fitting in that power point when I went out tonight. What's more, none of the pros have used clumsy gear like that in years. As for puffing away on a fag end...'

Chris led the way back into the house. He shut the door, walked into the bedroom, and fell back on his bed, staring at the ceiling.

'You know, I'm fairly certain they were Lindgrune's men. Those buffoons were all of a kind with that dumb security firm he uses.'

'I agree,' said Steve. 'Lindgrune definitely has men watching us. I learnt that tonight.'

'Did you now. What else did you learn?'

'Not much, just a whole lot of new riddles. Elgaad's OK though, he seems a very decent guy and he's shit scared of Lindgrune.'

Steve awoke next morning after seven hours of dreamless slumber. Chris had already gone to another athletics function, so he would be left to his own devices until the grand Olympic reception that evening.

Something was teasing him; he was supposed to go sailing. Then he remembered. Last night, that Kirsten woman, had told him to take the boat and head north up the Sound where something would happen. Who on earth would plan an assignation in the middle of the Baltic? It was ridiculous, but he had hours to kill; he would go sailing and see what happened.

A change in the weather was evident, the fresh breeze of yesterday was gone. The temperature was already in the eighties and the sun beat down through the heat haze that covered the water. He launched the Laser, and sailed slowly out into the glassy waters of the Sound.

Within half an hour the ghost of a sea-breeze began blowing from seaward towards the shore. Force two at most but enough to breathe life into the little dinghy and let him sit comfortably on the weather deck. The coastline had become a vague blur in the haze. It was to be one of those scorching hot late summer days that occasionally visit the northern latitudes. Now that the regatta was over few craft were about. Steve saw a scattering of yachts on passage, and a ship he recognised as a Russian cruise liner. Inshore from him, some water skiers cavorted, but he could see no other dinghies; or were there? He shaded his eyes against the glare. Yes, he could see it now; a tiny craft catching up fast. It was a sailboard, one of the lightweight competition types. He could see its sail. Transparent microfilm with Dacron panels; expensive and state-of-the-art. The board was now less than two hundred metres away. His concentration on his own course began to lapse as he stared with mounting astonishment. The board was beautifully trimmed and expertly sailed. Its rider was a girl and she was stark naked.

Not that this was unusual. Naturism was common in these parts he knew, and caused no hang-ups for the Danes, although it embarrassed the British profoundly. The wind-surfer was close now and about to pass to leeward. He narrowed his eyes against the blinding glare. One

69

thing was certain. This girl was no buxom Nordic Bruhnhilde, she was an enchantment. It was as if the Little Mermaid had put to sea with the body of a trained athlete. He could see the muscles and sinews of her legs and arms working in perfect harmony with the board as it slipped gently through the water.

Above all, he was mesmerised by her colour; every inch of her was tanned a rich golden brown. It was a colour that told of other skies than the Baltic. It was resonant of the Mediterranean and the beaches of Australia and California. Steve had lost his embarrassment, he was staring openly. He knew he was looking at human perfection of a rare quality.

The sailboard passed through the lee of the Laser and as it cleared his bows the girl turned and looked at him, seemingly holding the sail boom with one finger. He had already guessed who she was and recognition was instant; she was Kirsten.

'Steve!' she called, 'follow me – OK?'

Steve raised his arm and nodded. He could think of nothing to say; he could only rejoice in his good fortune.

The competition board was a good deal faster than even a modern dinghy like the Laser and Kirsten deliberately slowed enough for Steve to keep pace. The wind was still around force two and the sun was becoming even hotter. Kirsten was heading towards the shore whose details became clearer as they drew closer. They were to the north of the built-up areas and the shoreline was open with beaches and little outcrops of rock. The board was leading straight to a little islet topped with a pair of stunted pine trees. Steve looked nervously over the side and pulled up his centre plate as high as he dared. He could see the bottom and a particularly jagged weed stained rock not far from his starboard side.

'Follow me, Steve,' called Kirsten. 'It's OK if you follow me.'

He obeyed apprehensively. He began to wonder to what potential shipwreck this lovely siren might be leading him; he was aware that this was not his boat. As he concentrated on the wake of the craft in front he smiled. It was not every mariner who was sent a pilot as alluring as this one.

He could see more rocks, both port and starboard, with the port hand line ending in a long ledge of rock from the islet. He followed the board round one more outcrop with straggling bushes on its summit. Now the islet was clear ahead with a cove and a long shelving beach. Steve raised the centreboard and grounded the Laser on the shore a few feet from Kirsten. She stood there facing him, unabashed in all her glory.

'*Velkommen* to Wildcat Island.' She smiled.

'Where?'

'Wildcat Island. You are English. Surely you know Arthur Ransome?'

'Of course I do,' he laughed. 'I can still recite whole chapters if you try me.'

'When I was a kid, I was not so good at learning English at school. My mother would read me Arthur Ransome. And then I would read the book myself and I would dream dreams.'

She looked proudly around her little domain. It was a tiny islet, maybe no more than an acre, and separated from the shoreline by another fifty metres of water.

'Arthur Ransome.; he was a Baltic sailor, did you know that?' she asked.

'Yes I know. He had a boat called *Racundra.*'

'Quite so.' Kirsten nodded. 'Me and my friends, long ago we find this place and so it becomes Wildcat Island.'

Kirsten picked up her board as if it was weightless and ran up the beach. Steve pulled the Laser above the waterline and followed. The girl's feet must be as hard as leather, he thought. The sharp stones were biting into his bare toes and he regretted leaving his footwear with the launching trolley on the dock. He trod gingerly up the slope to where Kirsten was sitting on a patch of mossy grass. Her lightly-oiled brown body gleamed in the sunlight. She made no move to cover any of herself and this was making him nervous and embarrassed again.

Some of this must have communicated to her.

She laughed. 'Oh, you English – you are so funny.'

She untied a plastic wrapper from the deck of her board and withdrew a long-tailed, white cotton shirt. Steve watched with a mixture of relief and regret as she pulled it over her head until it covered all of her above the knees.

'Is that better?' She smiled mischievously.

'What is so funny about us?'

'You are ashamed of your bodies. Modesty is an admission of your own imperfection.'

'That sounds like a quotation.'

'If so, I expect it was said by an Englishman.'

Steve sat down beside her, at ease now, as they both stared at the sea. Not a word was spoken for five minutes. Eventually it was Steve who broke the silence.

'Last night you said you'd spoken to my daughter and that you had something to tell me.'

Kirsten said nothing as she watched a handful of sand trickle through her fingers. When she spoke it was with a question of her own.

'What did you think of us last night? I guess you like my Uncle Kaj and that you do not like Lindgrune. Am I right?'

'I think that's a fair supposition. I did like your uncle and I've got my own reasons to mistrust Lindgrune. By the way, his men searched our rooms last night when the house was empty.'

'I thought he might do something like that, but please, we did not invite you to dinner to set you up for Lindgrune. Uncle was telling the truth. He wanted to talk to you about Per, but I have wanted to meet you, again, since I was nine years old.'

'Again?'

'That is so. You came here and won the Finn Gold Cup. After the presentation you signed my book for me, but I do not suppose you remember?' She looked at him almost pleading.

Steve grinned and shook his head. 'It was twenty years ago and it's all a blur now, but I'm sure I was flattered to be asked.'

'I know,' she sounded wistful. 'I still have that book.'

Steve tried to move the conversation on. 'Last night a lot of things seemed wrong. Everything went quiet when I mentioned the war, and why is your uncle frightened of Lindgrune?'

Kirsten looked pleased. 'Steve, you have a good nose for these things and you are right. I would be happy if you would listen to the whole story and tell me what you think.'

She turned away from him and sat with her arms hugging her knees. Exactly the posture that Sarah adopted when something was troubling her.

Kirsten began to explain, speaking slowly, sometimes faltering and picking her words with care. Steve guessed this was a taboo subject in her family.

She told him how her grandmother, Gerda Elgaad, had been a zealous follower of Adolf Hitler. Gerda had joined the Nazi Party when she and her husband Eric were living in Munich in the nineteen thirties. Gerda was an actress whose stage career had had only mixed success. But in Germany she had been offered film parts in propaganda movies. Always emotional and unstable, Gerda had swallowed the entire Nazi creed.

Gerda and Eric returned home just before the outbreak of war. A few months later came the German occupation and Gerda had been one of the tiny vociferous minority of Quislings and fellow travellers. Eric had never supported his wife's views, but quiet and introverted, he was no match for the domineering Gerda. Throughout the war, the Elgaad factory had supplied the Germans to order, although resistance saboteurs had destroyed machinery and wrecked the plant's railway link. The Germans had made reprisals, and this had further isolated the Elgaads in the eyes of their fellow Danes.

At the liberation, Eric had gone into hiding with Kaj, then aged six. Kirsten explained that neither her grandfather nor her uncle ever talked about these events. Subsequently they had settled under an assumed name with a Danish friend who lived in Scotland. Gerda had been arrested but never tried. Six months later, she had died, insane.

Steve broke in to confirm that Karl Hansen had already told him this.

'Hansen is a good man,' said Kirsten. 'They say he's a great lawyer – sometimes our Queen consults him.'

She lay back on the grass, stretching her lovely brown legs. For a while she was silent.

'I now come to the point of this story. The man my grandfather and uncle lived with in Scotland was Alfred Lindgrune. I know nothing of this Alfred, except that he was married to a Scottish lady, and they have a son. It is this man who is Kent Lindgune, or Kenneth as you call him.'

Suddenly her voice hardened. 'Lindgrune is a blackmailer. He has destroyed my Uncle Kaj and broken his marriage. Now Per is dead, and Francine and Sarah say Lindgrune killed him. That also is what I think, but I have not told Uncle. You must help me. I want to come to England; I have things to tell the policeman Matesen. Steve, please … you will help me?'

The words poured out in a torrent and there was no doubting her bitterness. Suddenly he was alarmed. Blackmail; certainly that rang true. The explanation was so obvious. It explained everything about Elgaad's attitude to Lindgrune. He looked at Kirsten. He must be firm with her; his problems with Lindgrune were his own. He liked both her and her uncle and was desperately sorry for both, but help them, how could he? If he became involved in the Elgaads' troubles he would be in deeper waters than he cared to think.

'What is this blackmail?'

'I do not know,' she said miserably. 'Lindgrune is blackmailing

Uncle about something long past. I think it is something to do with the war, but not those things I told you. They are common knowledge. It is something else. Something that has been hidden very deeply and neither Per nor Uncle would tell me.'

'Then how can I help?'

'I am coming to England with you. This morning I spoke on the telephone with Sarah. She has invited me to stay with you both, while I talk to this Matesen.'

Kirsten had stood up and was staring down at him defying him to argue. Steve said nothing, knowing he had been out manoeuvred. Things would have to wait. Tomorrow was another day, and with luck this amazing girl would have had another brainstorm and a change of plan.

Kirsten's face broke into a smile as slowly she peeled off the white shirt, folded it carefully, and without warning flung it in his face. By the time he had scrambled to his feet and limped down to the boat she was already sailing. Steve followed, concentrating entirely on the rock-strewn channel.

In open water he turned to chase the sailboard, but this time Kirsten was not waiting and the gap between the two craft widened steadily. Within a mile of the marina, a large white motor yacht lay at anchor. Kirsten turned towards this ship, dropped neatly alongside her landing platform. She secured the board, then ran up the steps to the deck. She stopped by the stern rail for a second, waved to him and vanished. Steve passed the yacht's stern and read her name: *Kristabel.*

Steve strode into the flat in a cheerful mood to find Chris already changing for the grand function that evening.

'Cast your professional intuition over that.'

He tossed Kirsten's overwrap across to Chris, who took it with a startled expression.

'Cotton,' he said. 'Worn by small lady or large midget. Smell: coconut oil – posh perfume – sweat. Christ what have you been up to?'

'Learning things, surprising things. Ever have a naked woman stand before you telling her life story?'

'Not since my honeymoon, no. Go on, man, tell me; something happened today – you came in grinning like the Cheshire cat.'

Steve told him about his encounter with Kirsten and her revelations about her family.

'So, your little ladyfriend reckons Lindgrune's a blackmailer which, frankly, surprises me not one bit. It'd be par for the course for a bastard like that.' Chris peered into the mirror, adjusting his tie. 'Right, what are our tactics tonight?'

'You advise me.'

'OK, we've both got legitimate motives for asking about Lindgrune. I'm going to corner the brewery boss. I've met him before and he's shrewd, as you'd expect.' Chris reached for his jacket. 'You concentrate on the Elgaads – find out what you can. We'll meet up to compare notes after the speech making.'

Steve and Chris were collected by car, and driven into the city to arrive promptly at seven-thirty. The formal reception for the Olympic veterans was taking place in an ornate, eighteenth century hall. With hundreds of others, they crowded like children around detailed models of the planned stadia and Olympic village. Steve was shown drawings of the proposed yachting venue. It was at this point that he spotted Wolfgang Bartels, his German colleague at Easterbroke Sails.

Carol had told Steve that Wolfgang was due at this bash, and he had been watching out for him.

'Steve, good to see you. Any news from Sam?'

'Not yet, Boston say Sam's in Tokyo. Come on, let's get some drinks and we'll swap news.'

Wolfgang was the oldest of the Easterbroke managers and had lived a more colourful life than any of them. A former U-Boat crewman, he'd been captured aged seventeen and spent two years in a Midlands POW Camp. He had accepted the experience philosophically and used the time to learn excellent colloquial English. After the war this skill had landed him a plum job in his hometown of Kiel, where the British forces had employed him to maintain the captured Luftwaffe training yachts. Sailing had become an obsession for Wolfgang, culminating in a keelboat class silver medal in the same games where Steve had won his gold.

Wending their way to the bar, Steve fixed them each a glass of Schnapps.

'*Prost*! Mastbreak,' grinned Wolfgang.

'*Prost*!'

'OK,' said Wolfgang. 'I understand you've met this Lindgrune – tell me the worst?'

'I've met him at home and again yesterday evening, and he's left a bad taste each time.'

'I've not met the man and I'm not sure I want to. But we had one of his sidekicks around the Loft a couple of weeks back.'

'Who was that?'

'A guy called Dan Larsen; said he was a Swedish-American. Easterbroke told me to co-operate and show the man the works.' Wolfgang shrugged.

'Funny that, I only found out about this take-over four days ago.'

'I think,' said Wolfgang, 'that your Carol has suspected something, but she says you have not been too well, my friend.'

'That's true, but I'm fine now and I'm spoiling for a fight. Now, Wolfie, does the name Elgaad Chemicals ring a bell?'

'Danish firm, they make a medicine to make pigs sleep.'

'What?'

'It's true. My brother Joachim is a farmer. He says the stuff is brilliant, Stops all the little piggies beating seven bells out of each other. It's called Elgaadine. Jo stuck some in himself by accident – laid him out for hours.'

'Well, you learn something every day.' Steve laughed. 'Anyway, last night I had dinner with the head of the firm, Kaj Elgaad, and his niece. I was invited because it was Sarah and I who found the dead body of his son in the sea off Chichester. The police think the boy was murdered and today I've learnt that Lindgrune has a blackmail hold over the Elgaads.'

'This is news to me, Steve. I know Lindgrune throws his weight about, but blackmail...?'

'That's what I was told today, and on top of everything I've seen, it adds up. Next point, the blackmail is something to do with the war. Kaj Elgaad's mum was an actress called Gerda Elgaad. It seems she was a bit too sympathetic towards you lot and they've got a skeleton in the cupboard because of it.'

'Oh now!' Wolfgang was alert and excited. 'Of course – Gerda Elgaad – *Mein Gott* I remember her.'

'What d'you remember?' said Steve sharply.

'OK, OK, cool it. Unhappily I never met the lady but I saw her in the movies when I was a kid.'

'Yes, her granddaughter told me about that. She said they were propaganda.'

'Yes, true, but they were clever work.' Wolfgang stretched out an arm for two more glasses of Schnapps. 'You see, at the time all we young ones were carried away by the ideal of a Greater Germany; me too – I didn't know any better.' Wolfgang downed his drink. 'Not Hitler though. He never cut much ice with us seafarers from the north-coast. The man was always ranting in that Austrian accent – sounded like a country bumpkin. It was different if you met him, I'm told – there was a power there.'

'But the films were good. Goebbels' people made them and they were clever. Always good yarns about the old days. The propaganda was there but they were subtle with it.'

'What about Gerda?'

'Oh yes, she was a lovely girl. You see, as well as racial purity, Goebbels wanted to sell Nordic solidarity. Elgaad used to be cast as the Queen of Sweden or a Viking Princess; that sort of thing. She had some fan club, I can tell you. Then she just faded out; plenty more films but no Elgaad.'

'She came home to Denmark before the war started. But it seems Lindgrune knows something pretty damning about her and her family.'

'How does all this help us, Steve?'

'I'm not sure yet. Our police say Lindgrune's a villain and everything I've heard points that way. I want some solid evidence to put before Sam Easterbroke as to exactly the kind of man he's thinking of selling out to.'

That was all Steve was able to say to Wolfgang before they were separated and swept away to meet other guests. By the time the proceedings ended at midnight, he knew, by his own standards, he had, eaten too much, and talked too much. His voice was going and in the whirl of events he had almost forgotten his quest for news of Lindgrune and the Elgaads.

Reunited with Chris, he felt relieved to walk into the outside air and await the car. On the return journey, Chris said little and cut Steve off sharply with a finger to his lips and a sideways nod in the direction of the driver. Once again they found themselves outside the Hansens' house. One other car was already parked under the street light. Chris strolled across to inspect it.

'BMW Z1 – Nice motor – wouldn't mind that myself.'

'There's a light on in our rooms,' said Steve.

Chris spun round. 'Good God, I don't believe this – those bastards are trying it again.'

They both stared at the window. The curtains were drawn and from behind them came a soft glow.

'Come on, Steve, let's sort this out once and for all.'

Chris ran lightly across the grass and tried to peep through a crack in the curtains. He made his way back to the shadow of the bush where Steve was standing.

'It's no good, I'm sure there's somebody in there but I can't see a thing.' He darted a quick glance up and down the street.

'Got your key?'

'It's here,' said Steve.

'OK, I'm going in through the bathroom window. I left it open a crack to ventilate the place. You go straight in the front way when you hear me yell.'

Chris disappeared round the house to the right, while Steve, holding his latchkey, walked the dozen steps to the door. He was becoming increasingly dubious about this adventure, and doubtful of the wisdom of it. What the hell was he supposed to do should six of Lindgrune's heavies charge out.

'Now!'

Chris's voice sounded with a roar from within, followed by a frightened squeal. Steve swung open the door and ran through the tiny hallway and into the bedroom. Chris was standing in the bathroom door. Sitting curled up on the settee was a startled and woebegone Kirsten.

'Who is this?' said Chris icily.

'It's all right. This is Kirsten – the young lady I told you about.'

'Indeed, and how did she get in here?'

Chris shot a cool glance at Kirsten. He was a formidable sight as he stood glaring down at her in a none too friendly way. Kirsten, composed now, stared back. Steve was impressed. The girl must have had a real shock when they charged into the room; now she seemed prepared to give as good as she got.

'Steve, Herre Hansen said I might wait for you. He and his wife wished to go to bed and they did not know how long you would be away. It surprises me that you did not awake them with your stupid noise.' She glared at both of them.

'That BMW outside is yours?' asked Chris.

'Yes.'

'Hmm, nice car – I suggest you get back in it and go home.'

'You can say what things you wish,' she flashed angrily. 'I know nothing of who you are. I come to talk to Steve.'

'Go ahead then – don't mind me.'

Kirsten shot him another grimace and then, ignoring him, spoke to Steve.

'This afternoon I phone Herre Nielson. He says I may have a

ticket for your plane tomorrow if you, Steve, will speak for me?'

'You're still dead set on talking to Matheson?'

'Yes, I must.'

'Nielson's the PR man for the brewery,' said Chris. 'Why should he offer her a ticket? I don't believe a word of it.'

'Kirsten is special. She's their TV Sportswoman of the year. She's a household name, so of course he'll give her a ticket.'

Steve glanced at Kirsten. She was sitting upright on the settee with her hands folded in front of her. She wore a striped Rugby shirt over designer jeans and Reeboks. Somehow she seemed even more alluring than in her expensive gown of last night or her nakedness this morning.

'So,' she said. 'Tomorrow, will you ring Nielson and say it is OK for me to travel with you?'

'I suppose so. Yes all right, I'll do it.'

'Good,' she smiled. 'I will go now. I hope that soon I will know your friend better, and he will find we are both on the same side.'

Steve saw her to the door and watched until her car was out of sight.

'Phew! That's a cool customer,' grinned Chris. 'I came crashing in here all fourteen stone of angry male and within seconds she's turned me inside out and mentally knocked the stuffing out of me. What a woman, are there many like her in your game?'

'Yes, quite a few.'

'Well, I wish we had more like her.'

'Did you learn anything tonight?' asked Steve.

'Not sure. I might have a line on this Elgaad secret but it'll need research back home. As for Lindgrune – they don't like him, but there's nothing positive against him, just rumours. What about you – did you find out anything?'

'Not much. Only that in Hitler's time, Gerda Elgaad was something of a Kraut sex symbol.'

CHAPTER 8

'Steve, I'm going to ask a few questions and do a little digging on my own account,' said Chris, as they stood among the crowded arrivals at Gatwick

'I'll be in touch when I've got something to report. So long, old mate, and you watch out with that new lady friend.'

Chris disappeared into the throng. Steve looked around for Kirsten; seconds later she appeared with their luggage trolley.

'Come on,' he said. 'Give me your bag; we've a ten-minute walk to where my car is.'

'I carry my own bag, thank you,' she replied. 'I am younger than you and just as strong.'

She picked up both her bag and his, leaving him to carry his sailing holdall.

They walked the quarter of a mile to the garage, where Steve recovered the car and set off for home. They reached Fishbourne to find Sarah's Mini already parked.

Sarah gave her father a joyful kiss and then swept Kirsten away to show her the room she had prepared. Behind its closed door Steve could hear their laughing, animated girl talk.

He made himself a cup of tea, kicked off his shoes and sat back contentedly in his own armchair; simultaneously as the telephone rang.

'Good evening, Mr Simpson, I'm Frank Matheson from Portsmouth. We spoke a few days ago; you remember?'

The ex-policeman's voice was gentle and cultured with a leavening of a country burr.

'Hello, Mr Matheson, of course I remember. In fact, I've been active on your behalf the last couple of days. I've brought home a young lady from Denmark who's very anxious to talk to you.'

'I know, Miss Schmitt, your daughter told me all about her. Look, Mr Simpson, I'm sorry to ask this at such short notice, but could you and the lady meet me tonight, in Portsmouth?'

'Yes, I suppose so,' said Steve uncertainly.

'I'd be mighty grateful if you could. You see, things in my business don't wait and tonight I've had a stroke of luck. I've a man coming to see me who actually saw young Elgaad abducted. I'd like us all to hear him and then you can brief me on what you know about our mutual friend?'

'All right, I'll come. I can't speak for Kirsten but I expect she'll be there. She's mad keen to meet you.'

'That's fine. Now my witness won't come to my office, he'll only talk on neutral ground. So I've fixed the meeting at a friend's place. He's Johnny Xjiang and he runs Xjiang's Restaurant, in Rookway Street, Milton. That's in the new development just south of the football ground. Can you find it?'

'No problem, what time?'

'Can you make it sevenish and I'll see Torrents, he's the fellow we're talking to, is kept happy until you come.'

Xjiang's was a smart restaurant on a new estate, with a parking lay-by opposite. Steve locked the car while Kirsten looked around. Across the rooftops came a puzzling noise like the sound of distant surf on a shingle beach. The noise culminated in a crescendo – 'ahhrr-oooh.'

Steve laughed. 'That's Fratton Park, our local football ground – must be an evening match.'

The girl's lovely green eyes sparkled. 'In Kobenhavn we have two teams, sometimes I go with my boyfriend.'

'Boyfriend?' It was absurd that he should feel this pang of jealousy.

'Not my friend now. He's a no good bloody Norwegian – pissed off to America.' She waved a hand disdainfully.

They crossed the road to the restaurant. Inside were dim lights, wall tapestries and garish lanterns. From the gloom emerged a Chinese man wearing a dinner jacket.

'Mr Simpson? I am Johnny.' He held out a hand. 'Mr Matheson said to expect you, he is waiting – please come.'

Steve and Kirsten shook hands with Johnny who then led them upstairs into a spacious sitting room, mostly furnished in English style, but with Eastern overtones. In a corner sat a bulky man watching television. He stood up to greet them. In height and build he was not unlike Ken Lindgrune, but thinner in the face, with sparse sandy hair. His suit was an untidy baggy tweed and in a different context Steve would have placed him as a farmer. His age he would guess was a well-preserved sixty.

'Mr Simpson? I'm Frank Matheson, and this, I guess, is the young lady from Copenhagen.' The big man had an infectious smile as he shook hands. 'Lovely country, Denmark. I took my missus and our two boys there a few years back. We went to Legoland.'

Kirsten smiled politely.

'Right,' said Matheson. 'To business – where's Torrents?'

Mr Xjiang grinned. 'My girls have been filling him with chowmein and Newcastle Brown. I think he is now one very happy fellow.'

'Good man, could you fetch him?'

The restaurateur departed; Matheson looked in turn to Steve and Kirsten. 'This Torrents saw Per Elgaad abducted and he's identified two of the parties involved. I've questioned him briefly and so have the lads at HQ. We think he's telling the truth.'

Matheson sat down with a lugubrious sigh, and stared at them both intently. 'You're going to hear Torrents for yourselves, but you'd better understand that he's an unsavoury character,' he looked uneasy. 'I don't want to shock the young lady.'

Steve shook his head. 'Kirsten is a Scandinavian, I'd say she's unshockable.'

'If you say so. Torrents has given us good information in the past. He listens a lot, and people don't notice him. But first, you should know he's a poof. In his early days he was on the game, what the press call a rent boy, but in my book he sold his arsehole.'

'Good God!' Steve was genuinely horrified; Kirsten sniggered.

'Right,' said Matheson, his eyes narrowing. 'I know this is a wicked old city in some ways, plenty of queers and tarts, and you Sussex folks look down your noses at us. But, I ask you, who controls the prostitution down here, or two thirds of it anyway?'

'How should I know?'

'Has Foxy ever mentioned Councillor Terry Yapplington?'

'Yapplington?' said Steve, totally nonplussed. 'I thought he ran a garage? Good heavens! He races yachts – I've made sails for him.'

'I know, I know, don't take it to heart. Fox said you'd led a sheltered life. Just remember, old son, never take anyone at face value – that's my code.

'Now, Yapplington is no longer my concern, but Kenny Lindgrune is. I gather Fox told you the gist of what happened?' Matheson looked at Steve questioningly. 'Lindgrune cost me my career. I know I disobeyed orders and took a chance, but that rat is still loose. He's unfinished business and I'm going to follow and harass him until he does something that can't be covered up. I don't know who it is that's protecting Lindgrune, but however high and bloody mighty, I'll get them too, and time is no object. I'll take as long as it takes.'

The room had gone very quiet, Steve could hear the chatter in the restaurant below. He felt cold – Matheson: genial, dedicated, ex-copper, had suddenly revealed the steel within.

The door opened and the restaurant owner reappeared, with another, presumably Torrents. Steve looked with interest. Torrents was small and thin, with a sharp face and dark, well-groomed hair; he wore an immaculate pinstripe suit with a carnation buttonhole. Steve thought he had the look of a bank clerk on his way to a wedding.

'Hello, Ronnie,' said Matheson. 'Come and sit down, lad – how's you today?'

'Very well thanks, Mr Matheson.' The voice was nasal, with a Portsmouth accent, but not overtly camp.

'Now, Ronnie,' Matheson continued. 'This lady and gentleman have come from overseas to hear you. I know you've been through all this before, but I want you to tell it again, for me, and for these good people.'

'Of course, Mr Matheson – only too pleased to help you.' Torrents made himself comfortable in an armchair.

'Right,' said Matheson in the tone of one calling a meeting to order. 'We go back to last Tuesday night, the fourteenth. It's eight o'clock and we're in The Golden Daffodil Club. That place is fairly new by the way; it's down the road in Southsea.' He looked back to Torrents. 'Ronnie – spin us the yarn.'

'Well, gentlemen and ma'am. I was in the Daffodil, when in comes this bloke Pierre. I don't know him personally but he's been around. None of us really knew him, except that he was a quiet sort of boy, and he was Dutch.'

'Danish,' said Kirsten, 'and his name was, Per, not Pierre.'

'If you say so ma'am. But that night the lad was full of himself, and he had money, a big wedge – could have been a whole grand in readies. Not surprising he got hit on the head.'

'We think there's more to it, but you keep that to yourself, Ronnie, or you may be the next.' Matheson wagged a warning finger. 'Right, what happened then?'

'Pierre started shouting, "Drinks on me everyone", so, as you can imagine, he collected quite a crowd. But he was acting weird. If it wasn't booze, then he was high on something. He kept yelling about how he had the answer to world peace, and he was going down in history – all that sort of crap.' Torrents grimaced. 'And he kept on buying rounds, and of course the boys loved it. They kept egging him on, and by that time Pierre'd gone completely bonkers – he didn't make any sense.'

Torrents looked shyly round. Having a captive audience hanging on his every word was apparently a new experience.

'Go on,' said Matheson.

'Well, Pierre'd been making a prat of himself for about ten minutes, when in comes this other bloke, who none of us had seen before, at least not in the Daffodil.'

'Meaning he was straight?'

'There's no need to be like that, Mr Matheson,' Torrents had an air of injured dignity. 'Well, this one looked an evil bastard, and when Pierre got sight of him he clammed up. I saw his eyes and he was scared – I swear it.' Torrents paused for effect. 'The man walks right up to little Pierre and he says, "That's enough, you're coming home", and out they both goes.'

'Were those his exact words, Ronnie?'

'They were, Mr Matheson. I was only a few inches away and he spoke slow and clear. I tell you something else. That bloke was a Yank.'

'You mean he spoke with an American accent?'

'That's right.'

'Then you followed him out – why?'

'To be honest, Mr Matheson, I didn't like the look of it, so I thought I would tag on but not too close. Tell the truth, I thought there might be something for you.'

'Yes I know, and I pay you for good info. Now tell us the rest.'

'When I got outside the club it was dark, of course, and five past nine, because I checked my watch. Pierre and the Yank were about twenty yards in front heading for the underpass. The man had hold of Pierre's arm, then, just by the steps to the underpass I see the other two, and I knows them. Now before you asks, I'll tell you. I could see them because they were standing under that orange light by the steps.'

'Good, well observed. Now tell us about them?'

'Well, one of them I don't exactly know, except he's called Reg, and he's a Corkhead off the Island.'

'What's that?' asked Kirsten.

'He means the man comes from the Isle of Wight,' Steve whispered.

'But the other – I knows him – it was Kuo.' He sat back and looked around in triumph.

'You really are certain about that?' said Matheson. 'Sorry, Johnny, no offence, but I hardly know one Chinaman from another.'

'Not so, Mr Matheson. I'd know Kuo anywhere.' Torrents was emphatic.

'Yes, I reckon you would and all.' Matheson nodded. 'Now, the rest?'

'All of them crowded round Pierre and hustled him down the underpass, and I wasn't following them down there – no way!' Torrents shook his head with vigour. 'But the road was quiet, so I just ran across and waited for them to come out the other end. Half a minute later, out comes Reg and he opens up this Cavalier estate that's parked. Then the other two comes out and they pitch Pierre in the back. That Reg gets behind the wheel and off they go.'

'Registration number?'

'Sorry, Mr Matheson, it was dark and they didn't switch their lights on until they was out of the close.'

'Well done, Ronnie, have a drink.' Matheson slipped Torrents a fat brown envelope.

'Thanks, Mr Matheson. I'll be off if there's nothing more.'

'Please, Mr Torrents, a minute.' It was Kirsten.

'Yes, ma'am?'

'Per Elgaad was my cousin, we grew up together. You say he was shouting strange things – what things?'

'I'm sorry ma'am, but I don't really know. You see none of it made any sense. But when that Yank came into the club, Pierre was yelling something about gerbils – you know, the little furry creatures. He said all his gerbils had bad blood, but he was going to make up for it by saving the world.'

Torrents left the room with Johnny Xjiang.

Matheson sat deep in thought. 'Did your cousin keep gerbils, or did he mean laboratory animals?'

Kirsten shook her head. 'No, they never use animals in our labs. Uncle does not allow it, and Per was a vegetarian. We had a dog once, a Yorkshire Terrier, but never gerbils.'

'Not a very promising line of enquiry. Anyway, I understand there's something you want to say to me. So here I am, all ears.'

'Mr Matesen, the man Lindgrune has been blackmailing my uncle for two years, but I do not know what the secret is, only that it is something to do with my grandparents.'

'Well, well,' said Matheson. 'I hadn't associated Lindgrune with blackmail before, but it doesn't surprise me. Now, your cousin Per. I don't want to distress you after what we've just heard, but can you tell me something about him?'

Kirsten glanced at him nervously. 'Per was a mixed-up kid. He was into drugs – hallucinating drugs. He played around, experimenting in the lab. You see, I think I know what Torrents meant just now. Per was always saying that one day he would make the perfect safe drug. Then all the world would take it and no harm done. He called it his Peace Drug. He said young people would take it all over the world and then there would be peace. OK, I know all this is bloody crazy but that is the way he talked.'

Her voice faltered and Steve could feel her distress.

'It's all right, miss – take your time,' said Matheson.

She dabbed her eyes with a tissue and went on. 'Two years ago Lindgrune came to my grandfather's funeral, and it was after that he began to blackmail us. I tell the truth when I say, I do not know what it is about. But Per knew because Lindgrune told him.'

'If you weren't told anything, we can presume there was nothing to be gained by telling you,' said Matheson. 'Blackmail only works when it's a secret between the blackmailer and his victim, but if the victim comes to us at the very beginning, we can nearly always protect him and put away the blackmailer. Which makes me ask why hasn't your uncle gone to your police? It would've saved him all this grief, I can tell you.'

'Because he is weak and Lindgrune works him like he is a puppet. No, maybe that is not fair. Because, you see, this secret is something very terrible. Only three people were told by Lindgrune. My uncle, his wife Julie, and Per. Julie leaves my uncle the next day and she has never been back. Per had a breakdown and for a while we think he may die. Then, when he is getting better, he did try to kill himself.'

'You say you and Per were close,' said Matheson. 'You must have tried to talk to him?'

'Yes, several times I tried, but it was no good. He cried all the time. All he would say was, "if I tell you – you will hate me." You see, Per and I, we grow up together but we are different. Per had a clever brain and he lived for his science. Me, I am not so clever but I live for my sport. And it is true what Torrents has said; Per was gay – but me – I like men.'

Kirsten made this last statement with such triumphant finality that Steve grinned despite the tension.

Matheson stared at her sharply. 'No, there's something that doesn't add up. What on earth could your grandparents have done, that was so bad, it comes back as a curse to haunt you young ones? Secondly, they were your grandparents as well as Per's, so why aren't you involved?'

Kirsten shrugged. 'I have never thought of it like that, but you are right, I do not know what Gerda could have done that can still hurt us.' She sat frowning at the floor. 'I will tell you something. I have never believed my grandmother was an evil person. She was deluded and a little crazy, but once she did something good and brave. May I tell you about my father?' She looked intently at Matheson.

'Yes of course. Tell us anything you think will help.'

'My surname is Schmitt. That is my father's name. He was a German but he met my mother when he worked for our company in Denmark. They married during the occupation. Then, one day, the Gestapo find out my father is half Jewish and they come to take him away. But my grandmother Gerda defies them. She goes to the telephone and rings Berlin. She keeps talking until, in the end, she reaches someone so big that he orders the Gestapo men to leave my father alone. So, you see, but for Gerda, I would not be here today.'

Matheson nodded. 'Strange things happen in war. Nobody is all bad and sometimes unlikely people are the bravest. By the way, how widely known is all this you've just told us?'

'About my father, I do not know, but about Gerda, well that is common knowledge.'

'So the blackmail is something different?'

'Yes, but I'm sure it comes from something that happened in the war.'

'If Lindgrune is blackmailing your uncle there must be a price – does he pay money?'

'I don't think it is money, they are both rich men anyway. I would say there is something else goes on – I only wish I knew.'

Johnny Xjiang had returned to report that Torrents was safely off the premises.

'Johnny,' said Matheson. 'Breaking necks is Kuo's speciality, I gather?'

'I guess so, Frank. It wouldn't be the first time.'

'Agreed, he was the one who killed our Mandy I should say, and one day he will pay for it, and so will Kenny Lindgrune, if I can only tie it to him.' Matheson's voice had an edge of ice.

'But Johnny,' he continued, 'There is something we need to straighten out. Young Elgaad was into drugs. Bluntly, I would guess he was a pusher on a fairly large scale. If Kuo killed him, could it be nothing to do with Lindgrune? Would your lot do it, Triads or whoever?'

Johnny shook his head. 'No way, Frank! Those people would never mix it with the indigenous English. It's family only; all that Bruce Lee stuff is hogwash.'

'Yes, I thought as much. What about the American Torrents saw – any idea who he is?'

'Sorry, never heard of him.'

'Nor have CID. They can't find Kuo or Reggie Thropping either. The ground seems to have swallowed them.'

A knock on the door was followed by two women pushing a tea trolley. Steve guessed correctly these to be Mrs Xjiang and daughter. The younger girl muttered a couple of sentences in Chinese, and pointed out of the window.

'Mr Simpson,' said Johnny. 'My daughter, Mary, says there has been trouble at the football match. One of our customers says Pompey have won, two-nil, and the Millwall fans are rioting. She says there are many police. You are welcome to stay here until it's over.'

'That's kind of you, sir, but I'll chance it. I've been on the go for the last seventy-two hours and I want to get home and catch some sleep.'

They said goodbye to the Xjiangs and Matheson walked out to the car with them.

'By the way,' he said to Steve. 'Miss Schmitt's talking about the war has jogged my memory. Do you know two brothers, name of Fieldman? They're big in your game of yachting.'

Steve was surprised. 'Ross and Dave, of course I know them. They sail a Fourteen. I make their sails myself.'

'Fox sent them to me a few weeks back. They had some crazy story about Lindgrune protecting a war criminal in South America. I'm afraid I was a bit short with them. Told them I was a copper, not an inhabitant of Fantasy Island. However, in view of what we've just heard, I'm wondering if I wasn't a bit hasty. Would it compromise your business if you had a little chat with them; off the record of course?'

'Yes, I'll do that,' said Steve. 'I'm due to meet them any day now.'

It was dark, and Steve's watch said nine-fifteen. There was no sign of any riot, all seemed peaceful, though the glare of the Fratton Park lights lit the sky only a few blocks away.

'Go out by the Eastern Road,' said Frank. 'You'll probably miss the worst.'

CHAPTER 9

The side roads from the restaurant were surprisingly quiet. Then they came to the junction with Milton Road. Three motor coaches were parked near the turning, and close to them stood two statuesque police horses. Steve turned right and headed for the junction with Eastern Road.

They passed two police cars and a police van parked by the kerb. Seconds later Steve saw figures on the road running towards them. Cursing under his breath, he stood on his brakes and sounded the horn. The car came to a halt and the group divided, hurtling by on either side. He was surprised to see the runners were all teenage girls, about a dozen of them, wild-eyed and breathing hard. Clearly they were avoiding trouble, not causing it.

He started the car again, moving slowly forward up the street. He could see another much larger crowd ahead. Steve closed the electric windows and ordered Kirsten to lock her door. A compact mob was sprinting towards them. They came within twenty yards of the car, stopped, turned, and hurled a fusillade of milk bottles, beer cans, and other missiles away from them up the street. Ignoring the car they also divided and surged past. Steve had a good look at them. He was left with a jumble of impressions. All were young men with sweaty faces, bright eyes, jackets, jeans, and Millwall colours.

Steve groaned with impatience. 'That lot are the visitors. I suppose this is what's called a strategic withdrawal.'

The road ahead was blocked, awash with a huge crowd filling its entire width. Steve looked for a way out. He had passed the last turning on the right and on the left was a public park. He contemplated a rapid u-turn but already it was too late. A vast surge of humanity had engulfed them. With a sigh of resignation he switched off the ignition and addressed his passenger.

'My apologies. You are about to witness the great English football supporters first hand.'

He flinched as Kirsten gripped his forearm, digging her fingernails into the flesh. In her alarm the girl clearly had no idea of her amazing strength.

'Steve, I have heard the most terrible things about these people. They say the English are animals, they will kill us!' Her voice had risen a pitch in fear and Steve sought to reassure her.

'Don't believe everything you read in the papers. Look, this lot; they've no quarrel with us. This is a private war, a sort of tribal rite. I'll tell you what's worrying me. This isn't a company motor; it's all mine, the most expensive motor I've ever owned, and it's nearly new. These silly sods are going to scratch it to hell.'

He could hardly blame Kirsten for feeling scared. The crowd was frightening in its sheer size, though on the whole it was good humoured. Steve suspected rightly that the trouble was coming from a small minority on both sides. Passing them now was a mixture of ages and classes, but mostly young men in their twenties, some with wives and girlfriends. Among them were older men with children, presumably sons or nephews. All were noisy, but happy. Occasionally a section of the crowd would break into a rendering of the *Pompey Chimes*, a doleful chant to the tune of Westminster Bells. As Steve predicted, nobody seemed much interested in them. A few faces loomed at the car windows, some leered suggestively at the frightened girl, while Steve winced as passing hands thumped on the roof, and his car-phone antenna vanished into oblivion.

Steve might not have noticed the change, had he not been alert and concerned for Kirsten. His gaze was drawn to a small boy leaning against the bonnet of the car, every detail of him caught in the glare of an overhead light. He was clean and smartly brushed and not a day over fourteen. Everything about him spoke of a secure home and a fond mother. Then Steve caught his face in the light, and what he saw sent a frisson of alarm through him. The expression was void and empty but the eyes stood out, staring and dilated. Then the boy moved and the vision was gone. For the first time, Steve was worried. They were in the middle of another group of passers-by: teenagers, mostly boys, but with a sprinkling of girls. There must have been between seventy and a hundred of them in a solid block. He looked at their expressions with increasing bafflement. They were sullen faces, almost robotic. They stretched for yards on either side, surreal in the eerie street lighting. Even more surprising was the lack of sound, just the slapping of hundreds of pairs of training shoes.

For ten minutes the crowd rolled by, tightly packed and hardly moving. Kirsten was still nervous and, for the moment, there seemed little hope of escape. Steve pushed a CD into the car stereo, and turned the volume up full. The music, Mozart's *Marriage of Figaro*, had a soothing effect on both of them and their tension eased. Outside, the crowd slowly began to thin.

Then Steve, watching the street saw a familiar face, and without

90

warning flung open his door. Kirsten gave a squeal of alarm as he jumped out into the street and roared the single name.

'*Darren!*'

A denim-clad teenager, with tattooed arms and a shaven head, turned and shambled up to Steve, a sheepish expression on his face.

'What are you doing here, and what the hell's going on?' Steve shouted.

'Hi, boss,' said the skinhead. 'I've been to the match and it's my own time anyway – I can do what I like.'

'Not if you bring the firm into disrepute, you can't. You keep out of trouble. And what's wrong with that bunch up ahead, they're like bloody zombies?'

'A lot of 'em's high on Drifters, whole pocket-fulls of 'em selling at the ground. I don't touch 'em, don't fancy the stuff. See ya', Boss.'

Darren vanished into the crowd.

Steve climbed back into the car and started the engine. Slowly he edged forward through the last of the mob. Coming up behind the stragglers were two more police horses, both dark and rather sinister, with their helmeted riders. Steve wove the car through the gap between them, and thirty seconds later, they had an open road.

'That Darren,' said Steve. 'He's a trainee sail cutter with the Loft. He came to me on a government scheme. He looks odd, but he's a good boy at heart.'

Kirsten's voice still shook. 'Steve, you frighten me when you get out of the car. They might have hurt you.'

'No they wouldn't, I told you, it's a private fight – we're not involved. All the same they'll have to do something about the yobs, they're killing football and they're getting this country a bad name.'

'That you can say again!' was Kirsten's tight-lipped reply.

Steve laughed. 'Did you know I was a footballer once?'

'No, I didn't. You mean a proper one?'

'I suppose so. I played for Saints youth team, before I got hooked on boats.'

'Who are these saints?'

'Nothing religious, they're the Southampton Club. My God, you know we could've been in trouble back there – real trouble if Darren had opened his mouth. He knows all about my time with the Saints.'

'Why should that matter?'

'Local rivalry; I guess it's a bit like Copenhagen and Malmo. I'm told you sort of love each other.' Steve teased.

Kirsten bristled. 'What is this? They are all bloody Sweden men.

Come over on the ferries Saturdays – go home pissed as farts. We hate them!'

'There you are, that makes my point – nuff said.'

A few cars still travelled the road as they came to the Farlington flyover with its bright overhead lights. To the south the moon shone on the marshes, and the wide expanse of Langstone Harbour. Kirsten stole a sideways glance at Steve, his features lit by the passing headlights.

'Sarah has told me about your wife, and that you miss her so much.'

Steve made no response and for a moment Kirsten worried that she might have blundered.

'I think we all miss her,' he said. 'She was a lovely person, every-one liked her.'

They continued in silence. Kirsten tried again. 'Tell me about sailing. Twenty years ago you win everything. Then suddenly you vanish and we never hear of you again – why?'

'I hadn't a choice. I smashed myself up in a motor accident. It took eighteen months to recover and when I tried the boat again I wasn't the top man anymore. There were a dozen who were fitter and better.'

'You've never tried the big boats?'

'Not seriously. I've done a bit of offshore stuff, but mostly I was there to monitor the sails, and then there was the seventy-nine Fastnet.'

'That was the big gale?'

'That's right, I was taken along, allegedly as navigator-tactician, on a boat with this loony French skipper. Kirsten, are you religious?'

'No.'

'It's a funny thing, but there were times that night when I thought we were all going to die. I did some praying then, I can tell you.'

Steve lapsed into silence and this time Kirsten let him stay there.

Her memories of twenty years ago came flooding back. Danes are by nature, fatalistic and phlegmatic, but Kirsten had always been a person of tempestuous loves and hates. She put this down to the legacy of her German-Jewish father. It had led her to fall in love, at the age of nine, with Steve Simpson. The *Gold Cup* was being raced for in the Sound. This Englishman had not been everybody's favourite person, but that week he had dominated. She remembered standing in the crowd at the prize-giving as Steve went up to receive the trophy, his long blond hair flowing in the breeze. His wife had been standing in front, pretty and bulging in her maternity dress. Steve had walked back with the cup and kissed her, while Kirsten had looked at the woman with a deep and jealous loathing.

She remembered and felt ashamed. Miriam's fate had been to die an agonising death and the baby she carried that day was now Sarah, her new-found friend. As for Steve himself, it appeared he was nothing like the fantasy figure of her childish dreams; away from his boat and his sailmaking, he seemed quiet and reserved.

Then, there had been the Laser race, three days ago. Steve seemed to have no idea what a sensation he had caused. The other competitors might have been half his age and fully trained, but it mattered nothing. Steve had out-thought them all with the finesse of a chess master. Beaten: the other Englishman, Jefferies, all the Germans and French, and that shit Olsen, and that fat lump of lard, Gudrun Sundertsen. She smiled at the memory with malicious satisfaction.

Oh how she wished she could get through to this enigmatic thick-skinned man. She knew enough to see that this was someone who needed to pour out his troubles, and in doing so, leave them behind forever. She had given him an open invitation and what had she got? His only reference to Miriam had been casual, almost throwaway. She wanted to talk properly about sailing. She also had fought her way to the top. The boardsailing press rated her at number six in the world. It was a position she had held for three years and she wasn't prepared to settle for it. But Kirsten was nearly thirty. True, she felt as good as ever she'd been, but commonsense told her she was running out of time. What did it take to reach the pinnacle? Steve had been there, perhaps he could help her reach it as well.

Was it Lindgrune, who was putting this wall between them? Surely it should bring them together; they both stood to lose everything should Lindgrune win. Had she made a mistake, by riding the board that day naked? It was plain that he was uneasy and embarrassed. Kirsten was proud of her body, and might have felt offended, had she not remembered how incredibly prudish were the English. It was something she hadn't thought of at the time. On a day like that, she always wanted to be in total harmony with the wind, the board and the water.

'Nearly home now,' said Steve. 'You know, I almost wish we'd stayed at Xjiang's for a meal. I'm just beginning to feel starved. Perhaps you and Sarah could whistle me up some supper?'

'Steve – you are a male chauvinist.'

'Only when I'm hungry.'

Indoors, that problem was solved. Sarah had obviously heard the car, and was already making omelettes. Steve fell on his with enthusiasm.

'I had a talk with Francine tonight,' said Sarah. 'You know she's left home?'

'What does her mother think of that?'

'I don't know, but she's not gone far – she's staying in Bognor with the Ripleys.'

'The hell she is.'

'She's told me lots more about Per. I think some of it will interest Mr Matheson.'

'Such as?' said Steve through a mouthful of food.

'Francine says that when Per was in England he spent most of his time in a new-age hippie commune not far from here, and he was pushing Drifters by the sack full.'

'Drifters? I've heard that word recently.'

'They're soft drug pills. They've been circulating everywhere.'

'The whole world seems to be drug-crazed. What's this poison made of?'

'The doctors were talking about it the other day,' said Sarah. 'There's a paper in the current *British Medical Journal*. The thing about drifters is they seem to be a mixture of a veterinary sedative and a mild hallucinogen. They're not really addictive and they don't seem to do any physical damage. They're not like any other recreational drugs, and no comparison with the hard ones.'

Steve disagreed. 'I've just seen the results of these drifters, and they're nasty enough for me, thank you.'

'Where was this?'

'About an hour ago, outside Fratton Park, after the match. I've never seen anything like it. Ask Kirsten; some of them looked like the living dead in mass hypnosis. Then we saw young Darren Stokes. He told us the crowd were on Drifters. I couldn't make head nor tail of what he was on about, but I see it now.'

'That's it,' said Sarah. 'It fits; drifters kill aggression. The subject goes into a pleasurable dream world. That's the reason the police are turning a bit of a blind eye. A hundred youths on drifters are easy to handle. The same ones on the lager would be big trouble.'

Steve looked at Kirsten. 'I think we'd better face it. This sounds exactly like the poison your Per was playing around with – his peace drug.'

CHAPTER 10

Steve awoke next morning feeling better than he could remember in years. He found Sarah and Kirsten in the kitchen in deep conversation.

'We rang Mr Matheson,' said Sarah, 'but he wasn't there. His wife says he left for the airport an hour ago on his way to Italy; but he's left us a message. He says he'll be in Naples for a couple of days, and it's to do with our business.'

'Naples?' Steve was not at his best first thing in the morning, and he found the idea bizarre. 'What the hell's he after?'

'I think I can guess,' said Kirsten. 'My uncle's ex-wife, Julie, lives there.'

'Did you tell Matheson?'

'No.'

'Then it can hardly be that.'

'Mrs Matheson was quite definite,' said Sarah. 'The message is, he's following a line in the Elgaad affair.'

Sarah left for the surgery, and following breakfast Steve invited Kirsten to come and see the Sail Loft.

In the office, they sat down for a further cup of coffee. Carol cast a sharp eye over Kirsten, while Steve explained what had happened in Denmark, and in Portsmouth the night before.

Steve had to admit that a week away from the Loft had caused no crisis that the staff had been unable to cope with. He took Kirsten on a tour of the workshops which she turned into something of a royal progress. The hours flew by and at half past twelve Steve suggested lunch.

'We'll go down the road to Itchenor,' he said. 'As it happens, I've a new sail to deliver to the Fieldman boys. They rang up earlier and it seems they're there now.'

'I've heard that name,' said Kirsten, puckering her face.

'You heard it last night. They're the two who went to see Matheson. Claimed Lindgrune had connections with a war criminal. Matheson thought it was rubbish and I must say it sounds odd to me too.'

The twins were on the Hard at Itchenor with their boat.

'Thought you was overseas,' was Ross's greeting.

'Just back, and here I am complete with one asymmetric spinnaker,' said Steve holding up a sailbag.

'Well done, mate. Shall we give it a workout?'

'That's why I brought it.'

During the car ride, Steve had told Kirsten something of the story of the Fieldmans. The brothers were identical twins in their early thirties, macho in looks and both confirmed jokers. They were Jewish, spoke with authentic cockney accents and seemed to have endless funds. What had drawn this unlikely pair into yacht racing was unclear, but they knew the business like no others. This year they had yet another new boat and Steve had designed, cut and tested their sails himself.

Steve and Kirsten watched as the brothers bent on the new sail. Steve showed the workings of the boat to Kirsten. The dinghy was an International Fourteen – the sailing equivalent of a Formula One racing car.

'Ever been in a Fourteen?' Steve asked her.

'No, I have seen them in Denmark, but I have never sailed one.'

'We'll have to put that right.'

'Look Steve,' Kirsten pointed at the name embellished on the port quarter. '*Bendy Wendy* – what a lovely name. What does it mean?'

'Ask them,' said Steve, grinning.

Ross had told him once that the original Wendy was a madam, with a discreet house in Camden Town.

Bendy Wendy, with the twins aboard, powered away down harbour against wind and tide. Steve and Kirsten moved on to the pub for lunch. When they returned to the water it was to see the brothers planing towards them through the yacht moorings. Dave exchanged places with Steve who had already donned a trapeze harness. For half an hour Ross planed the dinghy across the harbour, while Steve, at the end of his wire, checked every panel of the new sail. On return to shore they found Kirsten waiting dressed in an ill-fitting wetsuit.

'Ross,' yelled Dave. 'You gotta' take this one next.'

'You sure?' said Ross doubtfully.

'You betcha, this is Kirsten Schmitt, you've read about her in the boardsailing mags.'

'Of course – thought I'd seen you before somewhere, darling. Hey, board sailors do it standing up – ha-ha-ha – I like it.'

Ross convulsed with his own wit while Steve helped Kirsten into the harness.

She scrambled aboard and Ross steered away down harbour.

Within a minute they saw her lithe figure at the end of the wire.

'That your bird then, Steve? 'scuse me saying but it's about time.' Dave watched his fast disappearing dinghy.

'I don't know, Dave. To be honest she's a great girl, but she's sort of in this country on business, certainly not a health cure'

'Well you think about it, mate. Were I not a happily married man myself, I'd be in there.' Dave rubbed his hands together speculatively.

Steve was not sure if he was more flattered than embarrassed. All these people seemed to assume he'd picked up this exotic Danish girl on his travels and brought her home for keeps. He knew he would have to be careful. Kirsten's smouldering sexuality was transparent, and linked to a personality unlike anyone he'd ever met. It wouldn't take much for him to fall for this girl; already the memory of Miriam was beginning to fade. He would have to be sensible, if he was not to make a fool of himself. Kirsten had not the slightest reason to be interested in him. They were of different backgrounds, different nationality, and he was fifteen years older. She had her own problems with the mystery surrounding her family: her Uncle Kaj, burdened by some horrendous shadow from the past, and her young cousin a suspected drug dealer. Kirsten was vulnerable too. Beneath the exuberant, happy-go-lucky exterior she showed to the world, he suspected lay a deeply troubled inner self. If he could rescue her from whatever trauma lay in her family's past, then together they might make a fresh beginning.

Kirsten returned, bubbling with excitement. She leapt ashore, gave both brothers a kiss and flung her arms around Steve. Her lips and hair had a rich tang of salt spray.

'How about a drink?' said Ross.

'No good,' said Steve. 'Pub's closed.'

'Never mind the pub. We've got our trailer.'

'Lead on – good thinking.'

In the car park was a thirty-foot white Mercedes lorry. It had started life as a racehorse transporter, before the brothers acquired it. At the rear was a workshop with housing for a dinghy. At the front were living quarters and a galley. It was to this part that Steve and Kirsten were shown. They sat on full-length settees, while Dave poured drinks from an oak-topped bar.

'Orange juice for me,' he said. 'I'm the one who's gotta drive this old tank home.'

Steve accepted a lemonade shandy. A relaxed feeling of well-being began to wash over him.

'Is Lindgrune going to get control of your shop?' asked Ross.

Steve came back to the real world with a bump.

'Not if I can help it.'

'Well I hope he doesn't, because if he does, you've lost us; I think you ought to know that.'

'I'm not sure I'll be working for him anyway. He's got reason not to like me.'

'Good,' Ross looked pleased. 'You see we know things about that geezer. Things that'd surprise you.'

'Such as?'

Ross looked dubiously in the direction of Kirsten.

'You can say what you like in front of Kirsten. She's her own grievance against Lindgrune. Frankly, that's why she's over here.'

'All right, but what I'm going to hint at is a matter that's confidential within our own people.'

Steve was puzzled.

'I mean us of the Jewish persuasion.' Ross's tone had hardened. The comic veneer, his usual trademark, had vanished.

'Steve,' said Dave. 'I don't want to be personal old mate. Tell me to mind my own business if you like. Your missus that's dead, she was Miriam – that's a true-blue Yiddisha name if ever I heard one?'

Steve shook his head. 'Miriam was Catholic. I was brought up one as well, but she really believed it.'

'OK, just wondered.'

Kirsten spoke. 'My grandmother, my father's mother, was Jewish, but I never met her. She was murdered in the war and my father only just escaped, as Steve here knows.'

'Then you at least will have some idea of why us two are watching Lindgrune.'

'Watching?' asked Steve.

'Ever hear of Simon Wiesenthal?' Ross threw the question at both of them.

'Yes,' said Kirsten. 'He is the man who searches for old Nazis.'

'That's the guy. He's why we're keeping an eye on Lindgrune.'

'Hang on a minute!' Steve spoke urgently. 'Look, I've no reason to defend Lindgrune, but he couldn't possibly be a war criminal. He's no older than me.'

'I know that, but it's not what the man did. It's what he knows and who he's protecting.'

'Ross, for heavens sake, man. I'm now totally confused – can't you start at the beginning?'

'Yes please – I need to know!' Kirsten's green eyes were shining as she rotated the glass in her hands.

'All right, if we're sitting comfortably, I'll begin.' Ross's face showed a trace of a smile and then froze again.

'About the one thing you can say for old Hitler, is that he always intended to sink with the ship. That's more than you can say for some of the others and it's them others we're concerned with.' Ross took a long swig of beer.

'In the late nineteen-thirties quite a few of Hitler's mates started taking out a bit of insurance. That is, numbered bank accounts in Switzerland, with tidy little sums salted away. Now, I don't know much about Swiss banks, only that the accounts are coded and no one outside can pry. In other words anyone, even the great train robbers, can keep their loot concealed. I don't know when or how, but it seems Israeli Intelligence did get hold of twenty or so of the key codes to these accounts. It seems they had people placed throughout the banking system all through the fifties and sixties. The plan was to wait until an account was accessed and then track the money to Paraguay or wherever. In a couple of cases it worked. It got them a line on Mengele, but the bastard was always one jump ahead.

'Then, sometime in the late fifties, one of these accounts was emptied. It was one of the big'uns, real mega-bucks. But this time it was different. The man who pocketed all this dosh was a Dane called Alfred Lindgrune. Mossad, or whoever, ran a check on this Lindgrune and got nowhere. It seems he was a businessman resident in Britain, no Nazi form as far as they could trace. Also, he hadn't got the money anymore. He's laundered the whole lot for someone else and very cleverly. There weren't sight nor sound of it. Yes, love?' Ross was looking at Kirsten who'd let out a suppressed gasp.

'This man Alfred was Lindgrune's father.'

'That's it exactly.'

'I assume this Alfred Lindgrune is dead?' said Steve.

'Yes, but his son lives on, and we've been asked to keep an eye on him, or rather an ear to the ground. That's because we're in the sailing scene and Lindgrune's a big wheel in these parts.'

Steve was still dubious. 'Is there any reason to think he knows what his father was up to? If it was in the fifties Ken Lindgrune couldn't have been more than a schoolboy.'

'That's not what our people say, Steve,' it was Dave speaking. 'The buzz is that Lindgrune's protecting somebody with a past history. Someone the Israelis want to get their hands on.'

Steve sat in silence trying to absorb this information, which on the face of it, made perfect sense. Ross drained the remains of his drink; Dave seemed lost in thought. Kirsten was trembling, deathly pale beneath her sun-tanned face.

Steve spoke. 'If I'd heard all this from anyone other than you two, I'd have said it was a wind-up. Now it's my turn to come clean. One of the reasons I came today was to talk to you about Lindgrune. Last night, we met a man in Portsmouth called Matheson…'

'Not that thicko copper?' said Dave contemptuously. 'Typical Bill, couldn't see further than his own flat feet.'

'Yes I know, but after Kirsten told him a thing or two, I think he began to change his mind about you. He admits he was a bit off-putting, but now he's beginning to see your story in a new light. He's asked me to have a chat with you, and so, here we are.'

'Will the law be able to pin anything on Lindgrune?' asked Dave.

'Not easy, I gather. The gist of it is, that he's suspected of bribery, the police think he's involved in at least one murder, and we know he's a blackmailer.'

'Bloody hell,' said Dave. 'You've gotta' hand it to the man, he works hard.'

'And,' Steve continued, 'Sam Easterbroke knows nothing of all this, but when he does he'll hit the roof. So I hope you'll still buy from me with a clear conscience.'

Even as Steve was speaking, he felt Kirsten stir beside him. She stood up trembling, visibly distressed.

'Please,' she said. 'I must have some air.'

With a wan smile she walked to the door and jumped down on the grass outside. Steve gave the brothers an apologetic glance and followed her. She was standing face into the wind breathing heavily. He placed an arm lightly on her shoulder.

'I'm OK now,' she said. 'I wanted to breathe.'

'It's something they said in there isn't it?'

She made no reply.

'Kirsten, trust me. Have you really told me everything about your uncle? Is there anything else you want to tell me?'

'I have said everything I can say,' she muttered.

He heard the words and knew she was lying.

CHAPTER 11

Boselli was waiting in the crowded arrivals area. Matheson saw him standing, unobtrusive as ever, against the far wall.

'Good to see you, Frank. Pompeii comes to Pompey, that's what we said last time.'

The little man was clearly delighted to see him and the feeling was mutual. Matheson clasped the outstretched hand.

'I'm in good form I hope, Toni. Good of you to spare the time, and I believe we're going to have a better result than the last one.'

It was four years since Matheson had worked with Boselli. There had been an Italian-registered coaster in the Camber dock. Four hundred kilos of cocaine and a dead seaman with a cut throat. The drug haul had been welcome but the trail had run cold.

Certainly Boselli looked the same, though his flat East Anglian accent sounded incongruous here among his fellow Neapolitans.

'Frank, this is unofficial. I can't take you to Headquarters, but I've got all the paperwork at my place. It's not far and you can put your feet up while we have a cappuccino.'

Matheson squeezed his bulk into the passenger seat of the Fiat Uno.

'If you weren't so bloody incorruptible, Toni, I guess you'd have a swankier car by now?'

'Could be, Frank, but this little one suits Napoli, so I'm happy.'

'If you say so. I think it makes us look like Laurel and Hardy.'

The view from the Boselli family apartment was spectacular. On the shaded balcony Matheson looked out over the huddled, noisy streets of the city to the blue sweep of the bay. Toni Boselli was sorting through a stack of files. This little room was Toni's private den, off limits even to Signora Boselli and her brood of dark-eyed children. The room reflected Toni's consuming passion for sport and sporting records. The walls were covered in posters. Athletes, the football stars of Napoli and Italia 90, and framed in black and white, the team photo of Peterborough United 1955. Toni, though a native-born Neapolitan, had spent his formative years in Northamptonshire's Italian comm.-unity. He was the archetypal new Eurocop; conversant in six languages and completely fluent in two: an Italian in Italy and an Englishman in England.

'Toni, you know anything about yachting?'

'A little, I know the Italian scene.'

'Ever hear of either Kirsten Schmitt or Steve Simpson?'

'Schmitt, yes, she's the windsurfer. Won the women's event out there in the bay, only a couple of months back.'

'And Simpson?'

'Olympic gold in dinghies, but that was nearly twenty years ago.'

'Spot on.' Matheson was impressed.

'Not so difficult, Frank. You Brits didn't win much else at those games. You usually under-achieve; no self-belief. We Italians are different.'

Matheson smiled. The little man was visibly swelling with machismo.

'The girl Schmitt is the niece of the Danish industrialist, Elgaad. It's Elgaad's ex-wife I've come to see.'

'Julie Grossman,' Boselli nodded. 'She lives among the aristos' in Posilipo. I'll take you up there presently.'

'Good man. Now what's this you say you've got for me?'

Toni pushed over a sheet of paper. 'This is from our files. It's got a security classification, so I'm taking a risk showing it to you. This is an English translation. My typing I'm afraid.'

'Thanks old son. Don't worry, you can trust me.'

Matheson adjusted his reading glasses.

FEDERAL BUREAU OF INVESTIGATION.
WASHINGTON DC.

To Colonel. A. Boselli.

At your request. Profile: Daniel Larsen.

Daniel Larsen: Born Seattle, 10th February 1946 – third generation Swedish American. 1959 – expelled from high school for threatening a teacher with a gun. Psychiatric report warned Larsen has psychopathic tendencies. 1970 – Larsen sentenced to five years in Wyoming for theft of drugs from a hospital. Acquitted of murdering an associate when a witness failed to testify. 1977 – Larsen enrolled in US airforce as civilian paramedic with forged qualifications, under the name Daniel Lomax. 1979 – Larsen/Lomax sentenced to twenty years for supplying cocaine to US bases in Germany. Released after nine years in July 1988.

Our current information is that Larsen is based in England, under his real name, and purports to be manager of Winterbirch Security.

This is a branch of Winterbirch Real Estate, the group controlled by Kenneth Lindgrune. In Denmark Larsen is also linked with the activities of Kent Lindgrune. We understand that Kenneth Lindgrune and Kent Lindgrune are the same man.

The British police are reticent concerning Lindgrune. One senior police officer has already been dismissed for probing too deeply into Winterbirch. We suspect Lindgrune has graft in high places, probably political. This makes it difficult to monitor Larsen's activities now he is in Britain under Lindgrune's protection.

Dario Giacheri. Lt. U.S. F.B.I.

Toni was grinning. 'It seems your fame's spread to Washington, Frank. I assume you're the senior officer referred to?'

'Too right I am. Another thing, Toni, these Yanks know more than we do. I've never heard of Larsen. Tell me more'

Toni sighed. 'We've got a problem. Manufactured chemical soft drugs. We've had them around of course, but mostly a passing fad with rich kids. It's the hard drugs that are killing the youngsters in this city. Now we've got this other stuff. The whole country's flooding with it, thousands of kilos. The Camorra run the distribution but it's not made here. It's being shipped in from elsewhere but how, we've got no idea.' Toni shrugged and spread his hands, 'We can't prove a thing, it's all circumstantial, and rumours, and snippets we pick up from our own intelligence among the Camorristi. The only thing we've got, is that Larsen is the supplier. He's an outsider, you see. He stuck out like a sore thumb, but I can't touch him, not enough proof and the Camorristi have prime lawyers.'

'Well, well,' Matheson had a trace of a satisfied smile. 'Toni, this could be your lucky day. Up until yesterday I couldn't have helped you. Understand we've the same problem. However, in the course of my own investigations I've learnt something. I think I know the man who concocted these drifters. Trouble is he's dead. Someone broke his neck and threw him in the sea a week back.'

'You mean Julie Grossman's son. The one you told me about.' Toni was staring at him intently. 'Good work, Frank. You're right, we do have something to share.'

Matheson was thinking fast. 'Toni, you're watching Larsen? Any idea where he was on Tuesday the fourteenth of last month?'

'No, but I can check. That's assuming he was on my patch that day.'

103

'You do that, because I'll lay good odds he wasn't. Not in Pompeii, he wasn't. He was in Pompey that night. Get me a mug shot and a description and when I'm home I'll prove it.'

The road to Posillipo was uphill and winding. As they came in view of the bay again, Boselli stopped the car.

'How about that then?' he said, pointing.

The view was stunning. Far out into the Mediterranean, with the whole city spread out below, and the brooding bulk of Vesuvius glowering over the scene. Symbolic, thought Matheson. Like Sodom and Gomorra, this crazy, dirty city was living on borrowed time.

'See Naples and die, eh?'

'*Vedi Napoli e scappa*, more like,' grinned Toni. 'I don't really mean that. She's a shithole, but I love her.'

Boselli turned and pointed inland. 'That's it, over there - Villa Mimosa.'

Five hundred yards away up the slope was a fringe of pines partly concealing a white wall.

'That's where Signora Grossman lives,' said Toni. 'That's why I jumped up and down when you rang me. You see, Larsen called on her a month back. We know because we've had a tail on him. He's been twice more but each time he's been turned away. Now the Camorra are watching the place round the clock, and we're watching them.'

Toni picked up a pair of binoculars and focused on something away to the right. He grunted and passed them to Matheson. 'See that old Citroen parked by the tree?'

'Got it.'

'Two metres to the left you'll see the driver. He's Marco Pedroni, small time Camorristi. There's half a dozen of 'em – watch the place in shifts.'

Matheson was put out. He hadn't expected this.

'Don't worry about it.' Toni turned to look back down the road. 'Good, here come my lads.'

Another Fiat came round the bend; this time a grubby delivery van. It pulled over and parked in the shadow of a bank of earth. Two men climbed out, both wore casual, but stylish clothes; Toni went to meet them. Matheson couldn't follow what was said but the body language spelt orders. The two nodded respectfully and vanished up a track to the right.

Toni rejoined him. 'They're going to put the frighteners on that little creep. Give 'em five minutes and then in we go.'

The villa was completely surrounded by the wall, broken only by one large wrought iron gate. Boselli marched up to it and rang the bell. Two minutes followed, then a guard appeared, glaring through the bars. Boselli, showing his ID, snapped at the man. His manner was brusque to the point of rudeness. Matheson couldn't understand a word but the meaning was clear enough. The guard swung open a wicket gate and they went through.

The house stood in the middle of the austere formal garden. It was a small, but beautifully proportioned Mediterranean villa, cool and white in the heat of midday. An elderly woman dressed from head to foot in black met them at the door. Boselli showed his ID again, though this time he exuded charm. The woman received him frostily, and without a word, led them inside.

The room was delightfully cool. Matheson, who'd been perspiring in the heat of the day, put on his jacket again. The decor was wholly Italian; plainly furnished with highly lacquered pieces, some white, some dark red. The floor was gleaming marble, though a bright oriental rug covered it near the white leather sofa on which he and Boselli were sitting.

'This is better,' he said, mopping his brow.

There was no sign of the housekeeper who had departed with their message.

'Nice houses these in the summer,' said Toni. 'Can be really chilly in winter though. Rather have my own place then, any day.'

'Gentlemen?'

A voice close behind them made them start. A woman had come into the room unnoticed. Both men stood up, embarrassed.

'I'm Julie Grossman. You are Colonel Boselli? Perhaps you would introduce your friend?' The accent was cultured New York.

'Signora, this gentleman is Frank Matheson. He's a former colleague of mine from the British police, though he's retired now.'

'If he's retired, what interest does he have in me?'

Evidently a cool customer, thought Matheson. She was small, mid forties, long permed, dark hair, and wearing a full-length yellow housecoat. Her hands, face, and bare feet, were all heavily tanned.

'I'm a professional private investigator. Yesterday I had a visit from your niece, Miss Schmitt.'

The woman's face registered a flicker of displeasure. 'If this is some olive branch from my ex husband, then you're wasting my time and yours. He knows what he is. There's no more to be said.'

'I've never met Mr Elgaad,' Matheson stared steadily back, eye-to-eye. 'It's your niece who called on me. Your former husband is being blackmailed by a British criminal. I want you to help me catch him. What's more,' Matheson paused for a full five seconds. 'What's more, I think I can prove he's the same man who killed your son.'

'My son – you mean Per?' she looked puzzled. 'Has he been killed?'

Matheson felt a sudden hollow in the pit of his stomach. 'You've not been told?' he said awkwardly.

'No, when was this?' The woman seemed bewildered.

'I'm sorry, madam. I assumed that you'd been informed. I'm sorry it's been my lot to bring you the sad news.'

'Hardly sad. You, whatever your name is, English cop, you're asking me to help catch the man who killed him? Forget it! I'm glad he's dead, it makes one less…'

Matheson was aghast. 'I don't believe I'm hearing this,' he found himself spluttering.

'You're surprised – huh?' The woman had a grim defiant smile.

'I'm not only surprised, I'm appalled!' Toni was speaking.

Matheson was startled for a second time. Toni was blazing with fury. He guessed the Italian's reverence for family and children had been deeply affronted.

'I cannot see how any civilised Christian mother could rejoice in the death of her child.'

'I'm hardly a Christian person, Colonel, but I hope I'm civilised. At least I'm more civilised than those who destroyed my family. I expect Per will have a fine funeral. But I think of my grandparents, my aunts and uncles and their babies. Do you know how they died? And what grave they have now?' She was more than matching Toni's cold anger.

Matheson was not wholly impressed. 'My contacts in New York tell me that when you married Kaj Elgaad, his mother's Nazi back-ground was common knowledge. They say none of your family objected to your marriage on those grounds.'

The chips were well and truly down now.

'I didn't know it all when I married Elgaad,' she stared back cold-eyed. 'Do you know what the book says. They shall be cursed even until the third and fourth generation…'

'There's no evidence that Gerda Elgaad did anything other than act in a couple of Goebbels' films,' said Matheson.

'Huh, that's all you know then.'

'Mrs Elgaad, what of your niece? I've met her and her young man, and I think highly of both of them. I suppose you wish her dead as well?'

'No, not Kirsten. No!'

Her whole attitude had changed. Now she was weeping, all restraint gone. She flopped down on a white leather chair, head in hands sobbing uncontrollably. The men sat where they were, watching, waiting.

Slowly she looked up. 'You shouldn't have said that, it was cruel. Kirsten's a great kid – just let her alone.'

'Pardon me, Signora,' said Toni. 'As I understand it from my friend here, your niece has a different father, but she shares the same grandmother as your son, this Gerda no less?'

The woman made no reply.

Matheson joined the attack. 'Funny, Mr Lindgrune isn't black-mailing her as well? It seems she knows nothing about it. I believe her, and, as I've said, I've a high regard for that young lady. So, madam, you'll have me to reckon with if anything happens.'

He was standing now, glaring down at her. For the first, time he felt distaste for his role. Like everything to do with Lindgrune, this affair was a maze of riddles and obscurities. He had no relish for a bullying interrogation of this deeply disturbed woman.

She looked up. Her face was wet with tears but she was controlled again. 'I told you, Kirsten's a great kid. None of this is her fault. She's no part in it. Let her alone.'

Matheson sighed. 'Mrs Elgaad, I don't give a damn what this blackmail is about. That's your secret and you're welcome to it. I'll come to the point. The man Lindgrune is a highly dangerous criminal. He's killed your son, probably because he knew too much and he'd outlived his usefulness. He'll certainly kill your niece to make things neat and tidy whether she knows anything or not.' Matheson was leaning forward, his voice little more than a whisper. 'But, before he kills young Kirsten, he's going to kill you!'

They were outside the gate again. Matheson was sweating and not just from the heat.

'Toni,' he said wearily. 'I want something. Get me two tickets on the next flight out for London. I'll pay whatever it takes. Oil the palm of the Grand Dragon of the whole bloody Mafia if you like. Just get that stupid woman and me on a plane out of here.'

CHAPTER 12

A cloud had settled over both Steve and Kirsten. They said goodbye to the twins and set off home to Fishbourne. Steve made no attempt to speak to her, or she to him. His memory was ranging back over the things he'd just heard. Kirsten was upset. Something had been said back there by one of the twins, something that had struck a chord and frightened her.

It was five o'clock before they were home and indoors. On the table was a note from Sarah. She was going to spend the night with Francine and her friends in Bognor. Steve screwed up the note irritably and dialled Matheson's number. Mrs Matheson answered. She confirmed that Frank had flown to Italy early that morning on urgent business. No, she could not say when he'd be back. Steve repeated this to Kirsten, whose face seemed to mirror in turn disappointment then relief.

She vanished into the kitchen to appear a few minutes later with a pot of tea, and a dish of Danish smoerbrod that she had contrived from the contents of the fridge. She smiled wanly at Steve who grinned back and sank his teeth into the bread and tuna.

'Steve, I am sorry about just now.' She eyed him again with the same worried smile.

He said nothing and waited.

'Please, Steve, can you not trust me?'

'I want to, but you're holding out on me. There's something you haven't told me. It seems it's you who does not trust me.'

'No, I trust you. More than you think. Maybe more than anyone in the world. It is just that, back there, those two boys, they say things that woke memories and I think I am frightened.'

'You know what they say in our country. A trouble shared is a trouble halved.'

His hurt and irritation of an hour ago was gone. Kirsten didn't shy away from his gaze, though a whole mix of emotions flittered across her expressive face.

'It was something I once overheard. I was eavesdropping, I think that is your word.' She sat with her hands in her lap staring at the plate in front of her.

'It was the day Julie walked out on my uncle Kaj. I couldn't help overhearing. They were shouting and they both have loud voices.'

'Julie's your aunt?'

'Yes, she is American, she was Julie Grossman before she married Uncle. They met in New York when he was representing our company there. It is so sad, they were really happy, until Lindgrune comes with his poison.' Kirsten's voice had sunk to little more than a mumble.

'That morning I heard them. Uncle is saying, "I did not know – they never told me – how could I have known?" Then Julie screams, "I don't care, that man killed my grandmamma, my grandpa, my aunts and uncles and all the kids, little babies too, every one of them. Don't come near me, don't touch me, you are evil!" Then Julie storms out of the room and an hour later she is gone.'

'Have you any idea who she was talking about?'

'No,' she shook her head helplessly. 'I have no idea.'

'Do you think Mr Matheson's gone looking for her? You said she was living in Naples.'

'Could be, but how does he know that? And why go in such a hurry?'

'Because she knows the blackmail secret, that's my guess. If he finds her, what'd be her attitude to you?'

'Oh I'm sure she'd be OK. When she went she hugged me and she was crying. Whatever this is about it was between her and uncle. She did not blame me.'

'You must tell Matheson what Ross and Dave said. Tell him as soon as he's back. He might be able to clear up this thing once and for all.'

He smiled as he saw her woebegone little girl lost expression, so different from her usual brash self-confidence.

'How about a drive in the country?' he said. 'Lets find Per's hippie commune.'

Kirsten sighed with relief. Suddenly she was her own happy self again.

'You trust me now?' she said.

'I trust you.'

Ten minutes later they were on the road north heading for the Downs.

Steve drove through Petersfield and took the winding road into the wooded hanger country beyond. They passed the last of the beech woods and once again they were in open country.

'Francine told Sarah the hippies live near the Fox and Goose pub,' said Steve.

He turned down a side lane and there beside the road was a dilapidated red brick building with a fading sign. 'This is it. We'll ask directions inside.'

Steve parked the car, climbed out and stretched his legs. 'We used to come in here sometimes when we were looking after Sam Easterbrooke's daughter. She went to school at Bedales, just down the way. Did you know Sam had an illegitimate daughter?'

'That's the way you English say it when you mean a love child?' Kirsten smiled.

'There never was much love for poor Sophie. Staying with Miriam and me was the nearest she ever had to a proper home.'

Steve stood with his hand on the handle of the pub door. 'By the way, a warning. This could be a bit of culture shock.'

She gave him a questioning look, but Steve only grinned. The interior was dark and austere. Around the walls huddled half a dozen figures. The rumble of conversation ceased abruptly as the locals eyed the newcomers warily.

'This is just like a village Kro back home,' whispered Kirsten stifling a giggle.

Steve walked to the apparently unmanned bar. 'Hello – house?'

'Wait your fucking turn,' boomed a disembodied voice.

Steve, far from offended, gave Kirsten a wink.

A man emerged from under the bar and stood facing them belligerently.

' Hello, seen you before haven't I ?' He said staring at Steve.

'That's right, I used to come in here three or four years back.'

'Oh my God, you're the one who sailed a "yort". Fellas,' he announced to the room. 'Here's the great yortsman.'

The locals stared at Steve with blank disinterest.

'Perhaps we could have a half of lager each?' said Steve.

'Help yourselves.' The barman pointed at an ice bin on the bar top. Kirsten peered inside.

'Look,' she said. 'There are all sorts here, Danish, German, Dutch.'

'Oi,' said the barman. 'What are you: Kraut or a Swedish nightingale?'

'I am Danish,' she replied stiffly.

'There's a Danish boy comes in this place sometimes.'

'Who is he, what does he look like?' The urgency in her voice surprised Steve.

'I dunno as I ever hear his name. Little short-arsed bloke with fair hair.'

Kirsten fumbled in her shoulder bag and produced an envelope with a photograph.

'Is this him?'

'Yeah, that's him, and you too I reckon.'

She passed the picture to Steve. It showed Per and Kirsten, both maybe a year or two younger, sitting on a sofa.

'He was my cousin, but he's dead now.'

You don't say – he came in here only a couple of weeks back.'

'Did he ever say much about himself?' asked Steve.

'Not really. You need to talk to Dennis and his new-age lot. That's where he used to hang out.'

'Hippies you mean?' said Steve. 'Where can I find them?'

'Easy, go up the hill, turn right, second left and down the track. Look for the old bangers.'

Ten minutes later Steve turned the car down the dirt road as directed.

'Steve,' asked Kirsten. 'What are old bangers?'

'In this context, old cars, wrecked but still running.' He winced as the steering hit a pothole. 'Trouble is, it's getting late. I don't know what sort of reception we'll get from these people. They're bound to be a weird lot.'

Two hundred yards on as they rounded a bend they saw the cars.

'It's a motor museum,' said Steve in wonder. 'I haven't seen one of those in years.'

He was looking at a 1950's Jowett Javelin, wheels missing, and blocked up on railway sleepers. Its bodywork had been re-sprayed an excruciating purple and yellow. There were other decrepit vehicles, and a battered horse-box. Steve drove on, looking for signs of life. Through a gap in the hedge he saw a house, or to be exact, a vintage 1940's Prefab. Lights shone in the windows and wood smoke poured from a stovepipe chimney. By the gate was a girl seated on a stool milking a tethered goat.

As the car stopped she looked up and flashed a friendly smile. She was dressed in a red ankle-length skirt and a cashmere shawl. A cascade of unruly blonde hair tumbled over her shoulders and back. Not bad, thought Steve giving her a second covert glance.

'Hi, I'm Glenda,' she said.

'Hello, I am Kirsten, and this is Stephen. I think you are friends of my cousin Per.' She held the photograph for Glenda to see.

'Oh yes, we all know Per. He usually comes to us when he's in

111

England.'

'He won't be coming,' said Steve. 'He's dead.'

'Dead!' The girl looked horrified. 'But how – what happened?'

'Did he jump, or was he pushed?'

A man's soft voice from behind made them spin round. A figure had emerged from the shadow on the other side of the track.

'What do you know about it, and why should it have been either?' said Steve.

He studied this newcomer and, despite his prejudices, he was impressed. The man was tall and commanding, probably in his late fifties, with grey to white shoulder length hair. He wore overalls and wellingtons and carried a log-splitting axe.

'I don't know anything about it. You tell me, friend.' This tall man, if not actually menacing, was clearly not to be trifled with.

'Just as I've said,' Steve replied. 'He was found in the sea. The police say he was murdered on land. This lady is his cousin, and all we want to know is where he spent his time, and who were his enemies?'

'Why should he have enemies?'

'I was hoping you'd tell me.' Steve was beginning to wonder if this conversation would ever get much further.

'Dennis, they're not accusing us,' cut in Glenda. 'These are Kirstie and Stephen. They're OK – good vibes!'

'Please,' Kirsten pleaded. 'Per was my cousin. I think we are all friends. Can you not tell me about him?'

'That's for my family to say,' said Dennis. 'Come and meet them.' He indicated to follow him down the garden path.

Steve was puzzled. Dennis was not his idea of a dropout; he had a certain aura and presence. His voice was commanding but cultured, and for all his advanced years he was clearly in peak physical condition. Steve was to learn later, that Dennis, in previous incarnations, had been a Royal Marine officer, and later a teacher.

'Dennis is OK,' whispered Glenda. 'You go on, I'll come when I've finished here.' She inclined her head towards the now restless goat.

On the left of the path was a well-tended vegetable patch. To the right was a large dewpond, almost full after the recent rains. Ducks rippled its dark surface. Standing astride the path was a large white goose that hissed and stuck out its neck at Steve, its tiny blue eyes flickering with malice.

The prefab was one of a pair; the second tucked in behind the one

112

visible from the road. Dennis led the way into the first, a long room almost bare of furniture, except for a wooden refectory table. Steve was relieved to see the room was spotless and the table scrubbed.

The place started to fill with an assortment of people drifting in from outside and from other parts of the house. A young couple with Irish accents introduced themselves and invited Steve and Kirsten to eat with the family.

'That way you can be telling your story to all of us,' said the girl.

Steve accepted as politely as he could manage. He wondered what strange vegetarian concoctions these hippies fed on.

It seemed Dennis read his thoughts. 'We eat in a minute, friends. We're waiting for Cyril.'

Waiting For Godot, thought Steve. Miriam and Carol had dragged him to Chichester Theatre to see that play. Its dialogue and characters would have fitted this place exactly.

Cyril, the others explained, was a travelling horse farrier and the only one of them to work regularly on the outside. Presumably, the only one who did any work at all, thought Steve. Two minutes later, Cyril arrived in person. He was a large rotund man with unkempt hair and a bushy black beard. He carried an insulated picnic box, which he dumped in the centre of the table. Glenda removed the lid to the unmistakable aroma of fish and chips.

The girls distributed the contents of the box and it was they who insisted on sharing their portions with the guests. Communal sacrifice, it seemed, did not extend to males.

With enormous gravity Dennis silenced the gathering.

'We thank the divine life force for these gifts of earth and sea,' he said in the manner of a Victorian patriarch saying grace. Steve sensed Kirsten was making an heroic effort not to giggle.

The meal was finished and cleared away. Dennis turned to address them.

'Friend,' he said looking at Steve. 'If you're to hear what we know of Per, you must first tell our family what you know of him and how he died.'

Steve was ready for this. He explained the finding of Per's body and the opinions of the police that he'd been murdered. He then nodded to Kirsten, who gave a surprisingly frank account of Per's troubles with his personal life and the blackmail.

'Good,' said Dennis. 'You are certainly the cousin Per told us of, and you are telling the truth in so far as you know it. Now, Glenda.'

Glenda explained that she had known Per when both of them had been fellow students at Reading University.

'Per got honours in agricultural science, and at Reading that means something. Then about a year ago I saw him again. He was backpacking up the A3 and I gave him a lift. When I began to talk about the college, and the old times, he broke down – cried like a baby. He was distraught – kept saying something about a newspaper girl – said he'd told her too much.

'I couldn't just pitch him out on the road, so in the end I brought him here. That night he told Dennis and I his secret. So we know he was being blackmailed and we know what his secret is. But as things are I don't think I can tell you.'

Dennis spoke. 'When people come here in good faith with their secrets, we respect their confidence.'

'Please,' said Steve. 'Kirsten and her uncle are being destroyed by whatever this secret is. People are being murdered because of it.'

'Then, it's not a healthy secret to share,' said Dennis. 'If it's any comfort to you, girl, this blackmail does not touch you or taint you.'

'So everybody says,' she replied angrily. 'But how can that be? We are family; same grandparents – it must hurt me too.'

'As I say, I'm still bound by Per's confidence. I can only say again you are not involved, be thankful for that.'

The room had suddenly hushed, even the children were no longer chattering. Dennis' scholarly voice was quieter now almost as if he was in prayer.

'I can tell you this. It is a terrible secret, for one of my generation it seems a horrendous thing. I would not care to carry such a burden.'

He paused, the room was still silent. Every eye was on this man's face.

'I don't believe in inherited evil. I do not believe Per was born evil. But I reject inherited wealth. Per had that in plenty and it helped destroy him. So, sister, see it doesn't destroy you.'

Steve felt Kirsten tremble as her hand stretched out and closed over his.

'Please, one more question,' he said. 'Per was involved with drug dealing. May we assume that had nothing to do with the blackmail, or with his murder?'

For the first time Dennis laughed; a happy melodious chuckle.

'No, nothing to do with Drifters. Very proud of those concoctions was Per, but they don't appeal to us.'

'Anyway,' said Glenda. 'We grow our own grass.'

Kirsten spluttered and broke into helpless laughter; he knew she'd caught sight of his baffled expression.

It was nine o'clock, and Steve had had enough; he desperately wanted to go home. The mystery of the Elgaad family seemed impenetrable; he desired nothing more than a night's sleep in the hope that tomorrow would be another day and maybe all would be clearer.

He whispered to Kirsten. 'I want to go home – get us out of this.'

'Friends,' she said. 'We are very tired and we would like to go now. May we come another day?'

'You're welcome,' said Dennis.

'I'll light you to your car,' said Glenda, picking up a torch.

Outside, was a pitch dark moonless night. Coming from the bright lights of the house, Steve eyes did not adjust instantly, and the torch battery was clearly exhausted. Tired, and not really concentrating, he walked a foot or so behind the two girls. A stinging pain shot through the calf of his left leg. A white apparition was clinging to his trousers. The shock almost made him cry out, before he recognised the dim outline of the goose. He tried to kick the creature away, only to be caught a vicious blow from its outstretched wing. Caught off balance, he slipped, tried to recover, only to stagger and fall his full length in the muddy water of the pond.

He surfaced and groped for the bank, spitting out a mouthful of brackish water, far fouler than the seawater he experienced in capsizing dinghies. Red-faced with the indignity of it, he crawled ashore. In the subdued light of the torch he could see Kirsten shaking with laughter.

Glenda was all concern. 'Oh this is an awful corner – you're the third person to do that.' She addressed the goose. 'As for you, Toby, how could you do that to our friend Stephen?'

She aimed a kick at the goose who backed off with a raucous cackle of triumph.

Kirsten appeared with a blanket that someone had brought from the house.

'Into the car and wrap this round you. I will drive.'

'Have you got a licence for our roads?' he asked anxiously.

'I have an international ticket for heavy lorries,' she said, reaching over to set the seat belt. 'You are a crazy man and ... I love you!'

The words sounded completely sincere, but with Kirsten you could be certain of nothing. Perhaps she was still laughing at him. From being elated he began to feel depressed again.

Kirsten's driving was competent and unspectacular and, beyond directing the route, Steve left her to it. Home at Fishbourne, the bungalow was in darkness. Steve fumbled with the front door key before stumbling, damp and bedraggled, inside.

'A hot bath for you,' said Kirsten bluntly.

She went to the bathroom and he heard her running the taps. Steve tiptoed to the sitting room and poured himself a whisky.

'Steve,' she called. 'Bath is ready, get in and I will come and wash your hair.'

He shuffled to the bathroom, leaving damp muddy footprints on the carpet.

'Hey,' shouted Kirsten. 'This place feels sad, how about some music?'

'Record player's in the sitting room,' he called. 'CDs and tapes in the cupboard on the right.'

'What music do you like?'

'Whatever you fancy, I don't mind.'

He undressed, flinging his sopping clothes to one side, and climbed into the bath. He lay back and let the luxurious hot water work into every pore. Just down the passage Kirsten was fumbling with the music player. He winced as he heard a cascade of CDs scatter on the floor. Seconds later the treacle tones of Phil Collins singing "In The Air Tonight", began to pulse through the house. Steve shut his eyes as sleep and the languor of the hot bath began to wash over him.

He heard the bathroom door. It was an ill-fitting door that scraped across the carpet; he had been meaning to re-hang it for ages. He opened his eyes and sat transfixed, every trace of tiredness gone. The music was louder now, flooding down the passage and through the open door. Kirsten was in the room, once again naked, as she had been that day on the sailboard. In the subdued light of the bathroom she glowed from every pore of her golden bronzed skin as she walked soundlessly on the thick carpeted floor.

She had her most mischievous smile as she said, 'I also would like a bath, and I think it's more friendly with two.'

She stepped lightly into the water and stood looking down at him. Then she knelt facing him only inches away. Spontaneously he lifted his hands and placed them gently beneath her firm breasts.

CHAPTER 13

Steve woke at three-thirty; or so said the red digital display on the bedside clock. The sleeping girl lay in his arms, and as he snuggled against her he could hear her heartbeat and her steady rhythmic breathing. The duvet had slipped to the floor as they lay, naked and uncovered, sharing each other's warmth.

It had been one great glorious release to make love with this sensuous, uninhibited girl. As a shy sailing star, Steve had been an easy target for the predatory groupies who attached themselves to the competitive scene. He'd half a dozen torrid affairs that had left him miserable with guilt. The devoutly Catholic Miriam had been hurt but always forgiving. Her death had left Steve, shattered and distraught, to two years of blameless celibacy.

Now all that was ended. Tonight, in his arms lay Kirsten, this wonderful vibrant girl, and he loved her. For days he'd suppressed the thought; driven it out of his mind. Now there was no going back. He loved this girl, and he knew he'd loved her from the moment she had shared her secrets on the little island by the Baltic shore.

'Steve, are you awake?' Kirsten whispered in his ear and began to run her tongue over his face and neck.

'Mmmm … awake now.' He could feel the full strength of her arms as she pressed against him.

'Thanks, Kirsten,' he said, adding lamely. 'You were wonderful.' Curse it, he was becoming tongue tied again and as usual saying all the wrong things.

'Why do they always say the English are bad lovers?' she murmured.

'Who says?'

'I think it is all the girls who have never tried one,' she nuzzled her face against his chest. 'I think it is an untruth that is believed … there is a word.'

'A myth?'

'Yes, a myth – that's it.'

She slid her lips over his, thrusting her tongue into his mouth. They kissed and cuddled contentedly.

'From now on I sleep with you,' she said.

'Hey wait a minute,' Steve said in alarm. 'Sarah gets back tomorrow.'

117

'So what?'

'It's embarrassing of course, what'll she think.'

'If it is so embarrassing, I will ask her to stay away another night.'

'Do you mean what I think you mean?' Steve was grinning now.

'Just so; Sarah and I have just met, but already we are good friends. We agree she will leave the field clear for me. She says it is time for you to forget the past. She told me I would be good for you.'

Steve was shaking with happy laughter. 'You know, I was just thinking, I seem to be putty in the hands of women.'

'That is because we know, what for you, is right.'

Steve slid his arm around her and slowly traced his forefinger down the line of her lovely back, unfolding his hand to gently caress her buttocks. Kirsten gave a gurgle of pleasure and sank her teeth into his neck. Then with a sigh of contentment she slowly stretched and unrolled onto her back.

As they came together for the third time that night, he remembered the words: "forty-five-year-old arthritic cabbage". They were his own a week ago in another life.

Kirsten was first up at daylight. Slipping silently out of bed, leaving her partner still sleeping, she showered, dressed and made a pot of coffee. Steve awoke to see her sitting on a bedside chair, sipping her cup.

'Any for me, my love?' he asked.

'Here.' She smiled and passed him a mug.

The bedside telephone shrilled. Kirsten leant across and answered it. Steve closed his eyes and sank back in languid contentment.

'Steve,' she called urgently. 'There is one Fox here to speak with you.'

'Oh yeah.' He yawned. 'Which one – Uffa, Edward, or Samantha?'

'He says he is No Man Fox,' she replied with a puzzled look.

Steve laughed. 'Pass him over … Hello Norman, you're early.'

'Got to be in my line. I've heard you were busy in Copenhagen. Carol likes your girlfriend by the way – full seal of approval.'

'I'm glad to hear it. You didn't call to tell me that though.'

'No, but I've had a call from Frank Matheson. He's arriving at Gatwick mid-morning and he's bringing Mrs Elgaad with him – mother of the dead boy. She's agreed to make a statement but not until she's talked to your Miss Schmitt. Frank says he'll see you in Pompey this evening, same place as last time.'

'This is great news, Norman. Are we getting somewhere at last?'

'Could be, but we keep our fingers crossed. Everything depends on what this Mrs Elgaad chooses to tell us, or more like what your girlfriend persuades her to say. Is she really your girlfriend by the way?'

'Yes,' said Steve looking across to Kirsten, 'I think you could say that.'

'Well, that's good news, hope it all works out.'

Steve said goodbye and told Kirsten what had happened.

'Anyway,' he said, 'there's nothing we can do until this evening. We'll have to be patient and in the meantime, my darling, I've got a job to go to.'

He leant across and kissed her.

She knelt beside him on the bed, her arm around him. 'I want to come with you.'

'OK, we'll spend the morning at the Loft, and then if the wind's right, I'll take some sails up to our test rig.'

'What's that?'

'I've got some masts at a place up on the Downs. It's not quite the same as a boat but it's a good testing ground in the early stages.'

Kirsten was looking puzzled again. 'How can we be up and down...?'

'No, Downs, that's our local name for those hills we crossed yesterday. You'll like it; there's a cracking view: right across to the Isle of Wight and then way along towards Brighton.'

'This bridge crosses the motorway. It's for a farmer to move his cattle and sheep,' said Steve. 'They haven't got round to fitting the safety rails yet but it's all right for motors.'

It was three o'clock in the afternoon as they rode in the car, with a full load of sails. Ahead of them was a tall spur of the South Downs and a long dirt road leading to the summit. This was wild country, five hundred feet above the fertile grainlands of the Chichester Plain. Here sheep grazed the short downland turf, interspersed with anthills and small thorn bushes. Kirsten was entranced. She made excited noises at the sight of the sheep and shouted with delight as a small herd of roe deer ran in front of them.

'Steve, that bird, look, hovering like a helicopter.'

'Kestrel,' he said. 'There he goes, straight down, bang! One nice fat vole for dinner.'

'Oh, that's cruel.'

'All part of nature. You should get a good sight of the sea by now.'

She turned and looked back. 'Yes, I can see the Isle of Wight, and the town, and all the harbour.' She paused, shading her eyes. 'Steve, there is another car on this road, but not over the bridge yet.'

Steve glanced in the mirror. 'Yes, you're right, but it's a long way back. Probably the shepherd – there's no one else comes here much.'

Five minutes later they reached the summit. Beside the track was a flat area of mown grass surrounded by a stock fence. Within it stood a garden shed and three concrete plinths. On a wooden rack was an assortment of dinghy masts.

'This is it: the Stephen Simpson top-secret research-base. Tell you something, they used to have the gallows up here in the old days?'

'Steve, stop it! I do not think that is so funny.' She glared at him.

'Not so funny for the condemned man, but most entertaining for the spectators. Half the town used to troop up here, or so that historian bloke at the museum says.'

'I think I not like this place so much. Why we come here?'

'Because I live in the present, and I've got this mainsail to test and...'

He was interrupted as echoing from far below in the valley, they heard a long muffled explosion. A column of oily black smoke rose slowly, drifting lazily away from the site of the bridge. Steve reached in the car and took out a pair of binoculars.

'There's a vehicle on fire on the motorway. It looks nasty. Wait here while I go and have a look.'

He climbed into the car, at the same moment as Kirsten resumed her passenger seat.

'Hey, I said you'd better stay here.'

'No way – I come with you.'

There was no time to argue. He turned the car and bumped back down the track as fast as he dared. By the bridge he stopped, jumped out, ran to the edge and looked over.

The blazing car lay upside down on the road surface. To Steve's relief he saw they were not the first. A group of roadmen, in Day-Glo' jackets, had dragged a limp figure from the wreckage and were carrying it to the grass verge. They stood staring at the prostrate form for a few seconds, before a burly bearded man slowly covered the head and shoulders with a coat. Evidently he was the foreman, because this done, he directed the others in the gang to cone off the accident scene, while he began to angrily wave on the slow-moving column of voyeuristic drivers. Steve scrambled over the fence and ran down the slope to the road.

'All right! That'll do. Keep back – there's nothing to be done here.'

The foreman, a giant of a man, was bellowing at him in a strong Irish accent

Steve raised his hand. 'I was working on the hill when I saw this. Look, I've got a phone in the car. Can I send for help?'

'Thank you, but it's been done. The emergency services are on their way, but 'tis too late they'll be. The poor woman's stone dead. Holy Jesus, what a mess.'

'What happened?'

'She fell from the bridge, she did; drove right off the edge. I never saw such a thing, and I'll be telling you, I hope to God I never do again.'

'But I don't understand, I've just driven over that bridge. I know the barriers are missing but there's a curb. Even if your steering failed you'd stop in time.'

'It was stopped she was,' said the Irishman. 'The boys and me saw it. We were five hundred yards back that way but we saw the car stopped on the bridge along with another one. Not that we were taking much notice, mind you. We were doing our work, then the next thing we know she's driven straight over the top. Good boy there that Donal, he pulls her out, but she's a goner, poor woman. Her neck broken – may her soul rest in peace.'

In the distance they could hear the scream of sirens, then blue lights flashing on a police car, followed by a second and a van. The occupants put up notices and cones while chivvying more gaping motorists past the scene. Two minutes later a fire appliance arrived. It took the fire fighters less than thirty seconds to extinguish the blaze, leaving the burnt-out shell on the road. Last to appear was an ambulance that pulled over to the pathetic draped remains of the casualty.

Steve looked around for Kirsten. She had followed him down onto the road, but he'd lost her while he spoke with the road foreman. There she was, over by the covered body. He saw her take a quick look at the advancing ambulance team, then deftly, she bent down and lifted the jacket from the dead woman's face. She dropped it instantly and slowly walked along the hard shoulder away from the crowd and the noise. Steve ran after her, caught up, and put his arm around her.

She turned and faced him and he noticed her rapid breathing and a tinge of green beneath her sun-tanned face. She caught his arm, and dug her fingers in painfully.

'We must go away from here.' Her voice had an edge of desperation.

'I can't yet, love. I'm not a direct witness but they may want a statement.'

'Tell them you will go to the police station. Tell them you will talk to this No Man.'

'That's not a bad idea, I'll see what they say.'

'Steve?' Kirsten's voice was little more than a mumble.

'Yes, love?'

'There's something I must tell you. Down there I had a shock.'

'I can understand that. So did I.'

'No, listen! The shock is not what you think. I have seen such accidents before. I take things as they come. It is life...' She paused. 'This woman had a ring on her hand, it is a special setting and I know it. I tried to think maybe there are other such rings in the world, but it is stupid to try and kid myself. No, I had to see her face...'

Her words trailed away into silence. Steve had a terrible sense of foreboding.

'Steve ... ohhh...'

The dam of self-control burst. She was shaking and crying unrestrained. He put his arms around her and she buried her face in his sweater.

'I must talk to the police. That woman is my Aunt Julie.'

CHAPTER 14

Steve extricated Kirsten and himself from the accident scene, and drove straight to the police station. Fox was off duty, but another sergeant saw them. He took their statements and then left the room. Sometime later he returned with a woman inspector who took Kirsten away to the mortuary. She was a kindly, middle-aged woman who explained that the body had already been identified from documents found on it. It would probably be enough for Kirsten to confirm the name via a video of the face. Steve wanted to come with her but was advised that this was not allowed. Instead, he went out into the fresh air, walked over to the old canal basin nearby, and gazed down into the black waters below.

A cold shadow was settling over him. It seemed as if some malignant force, beyond his control, was waiting to smash his new-found happiness and drive him back into darkness. A week ago he had no other thought than to protect his livelihood. Now it seemed he'd stumbled into some evil twilight world. Not only was his job in jeopardy, but also their lives were in danger. Not his perhaps, for plainly he knew nothing. If Julie Elgaad had been murdered, almost in front of their eyes, it was because she knew too much and someone had known she was about to spill her secrets. Had she really been murdered? The Irish road man had told of two cars on the bridge, and Steve had seen one himself in the rear mirror, at least ten minutes before, but which one? Was someone waiting for Julie? The roadman had said her neck was broken, the trademark of the man Kuo. Were there really Chinese gangland killers? Yes, it could have been an accident, but everything in his being and his commonsense was screaming otherwise.

If these people had killed before to protect their secret, they would do so again and again. How safe was Kirsten? He was convinced she knew nothing, but what if Lindgrune and his men suspected she knew more than she did? He stood staring into the turgid waters of the canal. His thoughts were of the two people in the world that he loved: Kirsten and Sarah. If needs be, he would tell Lindgrune that he would support his bid for Easterbrooke. Pride did not come into it. He would protect his own.

He was woken from his reverie by a voice behind him.

'They told me you were over here, I think I'll join you, if I may.'

It was Matheson. The big man had walked up on him unnoticed.

'Yes of course.' Steve gave him a weak smile.

'I came as soon as I heard. That stupid American woman gave me the slip at the airport this morning. If only she'd waited a few more hours she'd be alive and we might've been on our way to cracking this thing.'

'You think she was murdered?'

'Bloody certain she was. She was on her way to find your Miss Schmitt. I knew they were watching her in Italy, but they must have been waiting for her here as well. We're up against some clever people.'

'Lindgrune's men?'

'Yes and no; Lindgrune is the blackmailer, and he's used Kuo to frighten people before – that I could prove. I know he's used Kuo to kill as well; my little girl Mandy for one, as well as young Elgaad. Trouble is there's more to this than meets the eye. From what I learnt in Italy, I'm beginning to wonder if Lindgrune's the number one driving force behind this business. There's something else going on that I don't understand.'

'Mr Matheson, do you think Kirsten, Miss Schmitt that is, is in danger? You see, I brought her here and I feel responsible for what happens.'

Matheson gave him a sideways look. He's guessed about us, thought Steve.

'If she really knows nothing, I doubt if they'll touch her. All the same, I'm going to put pressure on the force here, to give her protection. Yes … all right … wait!' Matheson held up his hand to silence Steve, who was about to interrupt. 'I know what you're thinking; some clumsy PC listening at the keyhole. What I mean is, a watch on your house at night and your office by day. You will keep the young lady close by you through twenty-four hours. Now that won't be a hardship, will it?'

Steve agreed rather sheepishly and changed the subject. 'I'm sorry about Mrs Elgaad. You worked bloody hard on this, you deserved better luck.'

'Not bad luck, bad management I'm afraid. She slipped me at the airport and hired a car. I'd spent an hour drumming into her the danger she was in and I thought she'd twigged.' He sighed.

'I found out a little anyway. I didn't have too much trouble tracking her down. I got hold of an American contact and he faxed me back within two hours. It seems Julie's family, the Grossmans are well known in New York. Julie's father escaped from Germany in the early thirties. They weren't orthodox Jewish and it doesn't seem there was any opposition to Julie marrying Elgaad, despite the Nazi connection. That was well known, by the way. Then I had a real lucky break. My contact found out that Julie was living in Naples. Well, believe it or not, the police chief of Naples is an old mate of mine, he's half English, and I've worked with him before through Interpol. I rang him up and he went bananas. It seems this Julie had contacts among the ungodly of Naples, or at least they were watching her house. What got my mate, Toni, excited was that one of these contacts is the drug baron who's pushing the drifters in those parts.'

'Was Julie Elgaad involved in Per's drug dealing?'

'No, I'm certain she wasn't. You see, when I questioned her about Per Elgaad, she was completely indifferent. She told us she was glad he was dead.'

'She said that about her own son!'

'She did, and she meant every word. I've seen most things in my time, but I don't mind saying it shook me.'

'How did you persuade her to come back to England?'

'I laid it on the line. She was privy to the blackmail secret, the only person apart from her ex-husband who knew it, as far as I know. I think Lindgrune miscalculated when he told her in the first place. He never expected her to walk out on Elgaad. From then on she was a real danger to him. I explained all that to the woman and she agreed to talk, but only after she'd spoken to Miss Schmitt.'

'I take it you won't want us at Xjiang's tonight?'

'No point now. You know, I had such high hopes of this meeting, but no, it seems we're back where we started.'

Steve looked at the ex-policeman and felt a wave of sympathy. The big man's shoulders seemed to sag, and his tired face was almost haggard. He could think of nothing to say that would be remotely comforting. Together they walked back to the police station to rejoin Kirsten. She looked controlled but solemn, as she greeted Matheson. Steve hustled her into the Volvo, and they set off for the Sail Loft.

Steve told Kirsten what Matheson had said. She sat in silence for a minute.

'Steve, why should Julie be so angry and bitter?'

'I don't know; I wish I could make some sense of it. I tell you something though, Matheson's wrong about one thing.'

'How so?'

'Julie Elgaad isn't the only person who knows the blackmail

125

secret – there's Dennis and his girlfriend.'

'Did you tell him?'

'No, it slipped my mind. I was so uptight about what's just happened, but I'll give him a call later.'

In the office, they broke the news of the tragedy to Carol.

'Steve, you'll look after Kirsten, won't you?' she said. 'You know, Norman is more worried about you two than he lets on.'

'I'll look after her. Nobody's going to harm Kirsten!'

He surprised himself with the vehemence of his reply. He saw Carol and Kirsten exchange surprised glances.

Carol changed the subject. 'Kirsten, this fax came in an hour ago. It was sent to Steve, but it's really for you.' She passed the paper to Kirsten who read it and handed it to Steve.

> MV Kristabel.
> Wednesday 1450 hrs
> On North Sea passage.
> Arriving tomorrow. ETA Chichester Bar 0800 GMT
> Kaj Elgaad

Kirsten was clutching his arm again. 'I think we should meet them at sea.'

'How?'

'In your boat – Sarah's *Glorfindel.*'

'Why, he'll anchor in the harbour anyway.'

'No, you do not understand. It will be our only chance to talk to Uncle without Lindgrune around. Uncle has spent three days at sea. If we are ever to break him free of Lindgrune, this will be the time … believe me, I know!' She gripped his arm and angrily tapped her foot on the floor.

'I'm not sure Sarah will want to go alongside a ship that size in a seaway,' he said doubtfully.

'No problem. There are boats aboard *Kristabel*. He can come to us.'

'OK, you talk to Sarah tonight.' He was already looking up the tide tables. '0800 GMT isn't as bad as it sounds – you've got to add an hour for British Summer Time, so it'll be around nine am, which is just about low water. He'll have to anchor outside anyway.'

It was five o'clock when they arrived home. Sarah was cooking herself a meal before her stint at the surgery. Steve had no wish to alarm her further than was necessary and tried to pass Julie's death off as a road accident. Sarah made no comment but the perceptive look she gave him was enough to show he hadn't fooled her. She sat quietly for a minute, then looked at him, her expression troubled.

'What do we do now?'

He explained Kirsten's plan to intercept the *Kristabel*.

'Great idea, Dad, count me in.'

'It'll mean a six o'clock start.'

'On present form that should worry you more than me. Kirsten will get you up on time, I've no doubt. You did sleep with her, of course?'

Steve reddened and looked furtively around as if they might be overheard.

'Well yes, but we were alone … and she was … I mean she's lonely and as she says you two get on well…'

'Oh, Dad, forget it. It's what I want for you and I'm sure Mum wouldn't have minded, not after two years. Anyway, Kirsten's great – you'll be a fool if you don't stick by her. She's nuts about you, and I'm not jealous. I think she'll be a super new mum.'

'Thanks, love,' he said quietly and incredibly his eyes were moistening. 'What you've just said means a lot to me. Now it's up to you to find a good bloke yourself. I rather fancy teaching my grandchildren to sail.'

In his joy he gave her a hug that lifted her clean off the floor.

'Hey, you put that little girl down, you nasty big gorilla man,' said Kirsten.

She was standing in the kitchen doorway smiling happily. Steve caught her hand and drew her unresisting into the room. For a moment he stood ecstatically, an arm around each of the girls.

The wind was cold next morning, but a steady force three. With a strong ebb beneath her, *Glorfindel* sped down the main channel towards the harbour entrance. Sarah was steering, while Steve and Kirsten sat on opposite sides of the cockpit, working the jib winches. Steve knew they were all apprehensive about this meeting with Kaj Elgaad. There was the additional unhappy task for Kirsten, who would have to tell her uncle about Julie's death.

Steve refused to be downcast. To him, this trip had deep significance. It was the first sail for all three of them as a family, an important bonding experience.

Kirsten spoke. 'Will you show me the place where Per died?'

'We're not there yet,' said Steve. 'But I'll show you, I promise. Remember, though, he could've been put in the sea anywhere within ten miles. The tides are fierce in these channels.'

'Like Commander Crabbe,' said Sarah.

'Who?' Kirsten looked mystified.

Steve explained. 'He was a crazy fellow who was around when I was a kid. He was a Navy underwater sabotage expert. Some Russian warships were visiting Portsmouth. Crabbe went down to have a look underneath them and was never seen alive again. Weeks later his body turned up in Thorney Channel, just over there.' Steve pointed towards the bleak, depressing sands of Pilsey Island, a quarter of a mile away to the north.

The ebb was fiercer than ever. With wind and tide together they were going to be early. As they sailed past the entrance beacon, Steve touched Kirsten and pointed at the sea.

'It was here,' he said quietly.

'Poor Per, will we revenge him?'

'I hope so, but the truth may not be comfortable for you.'

'I know.'

She sat small and solemn, until she caught his eye, and gave a half smile.

By nine o'clock the sun was well up, lighting the land behind them and sparkling the sea. Immediately they were all feeling better.

'That's her,' shouted Kirsten, '*Kristabel*.' She pointed at a large vessel coming in from the Owers to the east.

'How do you know?' asked Steve.

'I know her anywhere.'

'Give her a call then.' Steve passed her the radio mike.

Kristabel's professional skipper answered at once. He directed Kirsten to an intership frequency and a five-minute conversation followed in Danish.

'Uncle will come over as soon as they see our boat. They ask if we have a signal lamp?'

'No we haven't,' Steve said.

'OK, I tell them I stand on the bows and wave.'

Kirsten scrambled to the front of the boat and climbed onto the pulpit safety frame while hanging onto the forestay with one hand.

'Dad, shift your weight back to me,' said Sarah. 'She's un-balancing the boat horribly.'

Even in these tranquil conditions, the confused swell of the sea on the bar had a hidden menace. They watched the approach of the huge motor yacht with awe. *Kristabel* seemed even more impressive to Steve than the last time he'd seen her. They watched her slow down some two hundred yards away and then release her anchor in a depth of nine metres.

A flurry of activity could be seen aboard as a rigid-inflatable-boat, a RIB, was lowered into the sea from the davits on her stern. Seconds later, it sped towards them, bumping across the waves in showers of spray. A seaman in a white Arran sweater sat in the control seat, and in the bows was the distinctive figure of Kaj Elgaad. The RIB dropped expertly alongside and Kaj scrambled aboard *Glorfindel*. He had a brief word with the helmsman in Danish, then the RIB spun round and departed back to the *Kristabel*.

'I've told him I'll travel in with you people if you'll have me,' he said. 'Jesper says he can't move into the Harbour for at least three hours.'

'Uncle, we have some bad news.' With a set expression Kirsten told him of Julie's death. She spoke in faultless English in what was clearly a carefully rehearsed speech.

For a few seconds Kaj said nothing. He sat still staring at the horizon.

'Poor Kirstie. You and Julie were so close, why did you have to be the one to see her dead?'

'Uncle,' Kirsten hesitated before continuing. 'I think you should know that she was murdered and the police say it was by the same people who killed Per.'

'I know,' his voice was barely audible above the sounds of the boat. 'It's no good, Kirstie, there's nothing I can do. I'm trapped in this thing. Now they have only me left to kill, but they won't dare do that, because I'm the key to their schemes, and I'm only useful alive.'

'You mean you will let an evil shit like Lindgrune destroy us, without you even try to fight.' There had been an awesome change in Kirsten. She was blazing with passion, all restraint gone. 'You are a coward!' She stood up, leapt across the cockpit and struck her uncle across the face with the full force of her arm.

She stood over him glowering in fury before launching a tirade in Danish. Steve and Sarah exchanged glances of horror and embarrassment. Kaj sat, head bowed, nursing his bruised face, a figure of defeat. Kirsten's anger subsided as quickly as it had begun.

'I have told him he is a coward,' she said grim-faced. 'He has disgraced our name. He has no honour. I tell him he is not my uncle anymore. I have finished with him. You are my family now, Steve my lover, and Sarah my friend.'

Kaj slowly lifted his head. 'Kirstie, I wish I could tell you the truth but if I did, you would be trapped as well. Then you would have real reason to despise me. As for Lindgrune, all his life he's borne this grudge against me. His father was a good and brave man, I idolised him, but Kenneth is different. I believe he's a regression, a terrible throwback. You know his mother's name was Armstrong, it's their house that the Lindgrunes inherited. It's where I grew up as a boy. Long ago that family were Border reivers, cattle thieves. It all sounds very romantic now, but in reality they were gangsters, protection racketeers, no different from the worst today. That's what makes me say that Kenneth is a throwback.'

He sat brooding and silent, sad but dignified. Steve felt the same liking and sympathy as he had at their first meeting.

Kaj went on. 'I think I could have handled this if it'd just been Kenneth working out his spite. But that man has overreached himself. There are other people involved now, and, believe me, they are to be feared. I'm not worried for myself, death is the only escape I have. If they kill me, too bad. But I fear for all of you, Kirstie, and you, Steve and Sarah, and little Francine and her fat mother.'

Hardly a word was spoken aboard *Glorfindel* during the return trip. Kirsten was completely subdued and Kaj sat silently, more dejected than ever. At Itchenor, Steve went forward to pick up the mooring buoy and, as he came back to the cockpit, he spoke.

'Mr Elgaad, will you be staying on your ship or would you like to come with us? We've room for you at my place and you'd be very welcome.'

Kaj shook his head. 'It's no good, I shall have to stay with Lindgrune, I've no choice. I see your dinghy is here, would you take me ashore?'

'Must you go, Uncle?' asked Kirsten; there were tears on her cheeks.

'I must, I've no choice.'

Kirsten flung her arms around him, weeping uncontrollably. Kaj pushed her gently away, kissed her lightly on the cheek, and climbed into the yacht's dinghy. He sat in the stern while Steve rowed the short distance to the jetty.

'Steve, at the risk of seeming impertinent, I see you and Kirsten have become very close.'

'To be honest with you, yes. We've only known each other for a week, but this business has thrown us together. It's almost as if we've been together for years.'

'That's a very good thing. I still see her as little Kirstie of long ago, but of course she's nobody's fool. I don't expect you to realise that she's always idolised you. Did she tell you about the time you gave her your autograph?'

Steve smiled. 'Yes, she did, but it's awkward because I can't honestly tell her that I remember when I don't.'

'And why should you? She was only a child.' For the first time Kaj's face had a flicker of a smile. 'The important thing is that she knows you properly now. The idol matches the dream when she might have found he had feet of clay.'

Steve steadied the dinghy as Kaj climbed onto the steps of the jetty. He turned and looked down.

'I think Nemesis is about to call me to account and, sadly it's for another man's sins. I'm a pariah, an untouchable, but little Kirstie is unblemished by all this. I commend her to you. She's a good girl and I predict the two of you will be happy and deserve to be. As for myself, I will not be around much longer.'

CHAPTER 15

Steve drove to the sail-loft. The encounter with Kaj had left him badly shaken, while Kirsten and Sarah, were understandably subdued. Sarah left for the surgery, while Steve and Kirsten walked to the workshops. The first person they saw was the boy Darren, busy packaging sails.

'Hi, boss,' he said. 'Did those two Yanks find you yesterday?'

'Yanks?'

'That's right, just after you left. There was a woman in a blue Vectra, wanted to know where you was. I told her you'd gone up the hill. She goes, and a few minutes later, there's another one.'

'Another American?'

'That's right, a proper Yankee doodle – I didn't like the look of him one bit. Vicious little sod; not the sort I'd reckon as one of our customers.'

'What did the woman look like?'

Steve sucked in his breath as Darren gave a fair description of Julie Elgaad.

'OK, and the second one, the man?'

'He was a short-arsed, little bloke, and nasty; sort of looked as he'd as soon smash your face in as talk to you. He was in a Range Rover with two others and the one driving, I fancy I've seen before. Youngish bloke, my age, with a fancy red leather jacket – bit of a poser.'

'And the third one?'

'Dunno, boss. He was in the back seat and I didn't rightly get a look at him.'

'All right, Darren – a word of advice. Don't say too much about this, and secondly, I'm afraid you'll have to repeat what you've told me to the police.'

'Oh bloody hell – the Bill?'

Yes, and for your information the woman you saw was the one who was killed on the motorway yesterday, and the Bill, as you call them, think it's murder.'

They departed, leaving a thoughtful looking Darren behind. The boy clearly had no relish for an interview with the law, even as a detached witness.

The speaker-system rasped a message. It was Carol at her most imperious, recalling Steve to the office for an urgent call. He ran through the workshop, nearly tripping on a coil of rope, and picked up the phone on his desk.

'Hello, Steve mate,' Chris Bainbridge's voice boomed as unmistakable as ever. 'I'm passing through Chichester and I've got some information for you. Can we meet for lunch?'

'Yes of course.'

'Good, where'd be a handy place?'

Steve thought quickly; better to stay out of town with Lindgrune's men around.

'Chris, go to Dell Quay. It's just south of the town, off the old A27. You'll find it on the map.'

OK, got it – see you in half an hour. Just one thing, on your own please, no lady friend. Is she still with you, by the way?'

'As it happens, yes. Anything you've got to say to me you can say to her, right?'

'Keep your hair on,' Chris was laughing now. 'Sounds like she's got you round her little finger already. Never mind, you can tell her later if you really think it's wise.'

Steve was not pleased. He rang off abruptly and began to search for his car keys.

'That man! Why he not like me?' Kirsten's voice made him jump.

He looked up to see her, the extension phone in her hand, glowering at him.

'Likes doesn't come into it. He's a security man, by nature he doesn't trust anyone he doesn't know. He's a good guy though; we go back a long way. I won't be long, you can keep Carol company.'

Steve was the first to arrive at Dell Quay. He parked his car by the Crown and Anchor, went in and bought himself a beer. He carried it out to one of the garden tables, with its spectacular view down the upper reaches of the harbour. Ten minutes later he saw Chris arrive and waved to him. Hardly giving his visitor a chance to sit down Steve told him about Julie's death and its implications.

Chris looked around and chose a table well away from other drinkers.

'Nice spot this,' he commented. 'It's discreet – we won't be overheard.'

'Any danger of that?'

'Could be, it's obvious now that we're up against some evil people and they're clever with it.'

133

Chris set down his document case on the table and took out a single sheet of paper. He handed it to Steve. It was a typed letter on headed paper from the University of East Anglia.

J.H. Heppel. MA.. Lecturer Twentieth Century European History.
Dear Chris,

Hereby my reply to your questions. I have spoken with my colleague Dr Phillip Rowe of our Department of Agriculture, and with, Prof Jens Lungstorm of Copenhagen. There is no record of the Elgaad Company producing anything other than fertiliser and basic farm chemicals during the period concerned. The bulk of this production went to Germany from 1944 onwards. It was intended to make good losses due to Allied bombing. In the event much of it was sidelined due to the chaotic state of the German railways. The Elgaad company's diversification into pharmaceuticals dates from the middle 1960s with the emergence of Eric Elgaad as the Company's president.

Gerda Elgaad, and her role in German propaganda, is more in line with my own field and I must say throws an interesting light on Goebbels' film making. Gerda played leading roles in three films. Eagle of the North. The Quest Of The Vikings. The Great Christina.

This last film was her one starring role. Apparently no complete copy survives, but it was a lavish production in which Goebbels took a personal pride, visiting the set daily. Although the film was a popular and critical success, Gerda never acted in movies again.

The rest of the letter was a greeting to Chris, apparently this professor was an old running friend.

'It's interesting,' he said, handing back the letter. 'But that stuff about the films is the same as Wolfgang told me the other day. There's nothing new.'

'I know,' said Chris. 'It's all negative, but still useful. You see, it seems to rule out Gerda as the cause of the blackmail. Therefore, it's got to be something that Eric and Kaj were involved in jointly, and much more recent than the war. That's the main reason I wanted to talk to you alone without your girlfriend. I'm sure she's honest, I just think she's got this thing all wrong.'

'Why were you so interested in what the factory was making?'

'That was a long shot. You see it's known that the chemicals used in the gas chambers were made by a German company I.G. Farben. I just wondered if the Elgaads had been sub-contracting.'

'I take your point about Kirsten, but you haven't heard the half of it.'

He told Chris about Torrents, the Fieldman twins, and of Kirsten's eavesdropping on the row between Kaj and Julie.

'We think that's why Julie Elgaad's dead, murdered for certain. She was looking for Kirsten. Matheson says she'd agreed to talk but only after she'd spoken to Kirsten. Whoever wants this kept secret got to her first, and Kirsten and I nearly saw her killed. It's hit Matheson hard, but Julie told him one thing.'

Steve fell silent. The truth was that he didn't want to think about the murder, let alone talk about it.

'What did she tell him?' Chris prompted.

'She told Matheson she was glad Per was dead.'

'She said that about her own son?' Chris was incredulous.

'Just that. One thing's certain, this must be one hell of a damning secret.'

'You can say that again.' Chris sat for a moment in deep thought. 'Let me think this thing through. Julie Elgaad was Jewish-American by birth. It seems she lost close family in the Holocaust. She would grow up to be virtually paranoid about all things Nazi. That's understandable. Your friends, the Fieldmans, say Lindgrune's protecting a war criminal. Just suppose the Elgaads were involved – never mind the reason – just suppose. If Julie were true to her heritage, she'd walk out as soon as she was told and quite right too. But having done that she'd go to the authorities, swear an affidavit, tip off the Israelis. She'd want that war criminal caught.'

'She didn't do anything. She was living like a recluse in Italy.'

'That's what doesn't add up. She was living with a time bomb, keeping the secret to herself. I'm not surprised she's been killed. Something like that was bound to happen. To be safe she only had to talk – so why didn't she?'

'If she was in danger because she knew the secret, she's not the only one.' Steve spoke more prophetically than he knew.

The Landlord of the Fox and Goose had just opened his doors for the midday session. He looked across his car park with mounting irritation. There in full view of the passing traffic was a 1960s Volkswagen camper van. Its side windows were curtained, and its bodywork was painted a lurid mauve, with white scallops and yellow flowers. New age travellers; a bigger turn-off for trade would be hard to imagine.

135

An individual with long black hair and wearing mechanic's overalls stood by the driver's door. The landlord was no shrinking violet, indeed he relished his reputation for abusive surliness. He was well aware that people travelled long distances to sample his unique atmosphere. It was a game of love and hate that both sides enjoyed. Hippies were another matter. Rightly or wrongly, they frightened visitors and made his regulars aggressive.

He was not one to waste words. 'Oi, you, sod off!' he yelled.

The hippie raised a hand and walked across.

'You heard me, I won't serve you – sod off!'

To the landlord's chagrin, the man kept walking towards him. In the past, strong men had quailed before such a reception and secretly he was impressed. The man was surprisingly polite. No, he didn't want a drink, but could he be directed to the camp of his friend Dennis.

Relieved, the landlord gave directions and watched the van drive away up the hill.

'That's odd,' he said aloud. 'I've never known one o' them scruffs take care of how he looks.'

Dennis was behind the bungalow splitting logs. He used a heavy splitting axe with a hardened ten-pound head. He swung the axe rhythmically, splitting logs for the kitchen range. Most of the commune had gone to Alton for the morning. By the roadside Cyril was trimming the hooves of a small pony that had been led down from the village by Charlotte its fourteen- year-old owner. Dennis's girlfriend Glenda held the pony's head, while Charlotte watched. They could hear the engine of a vehicle bumping down the rough track, and Charlotte turned round in anticipation.

'They're travellers like you,' she said.

'Could be,' said Glenda. 'But I've never seen that van before.'

The Volkswagen came level with Glenda and she smiled and waved a greeting. The smile faded and she looked puzzled. The interior of the van was dark. She could make out some shadowy forms, but no one waved back.

The van drove past, stopped and turned round in a field gateway. It moved back slowly to stop next to them. The doors on the far side opened and they heard the sounds of feet jumping to the ground. Glenda, though curious, could not let go the pony's head. Cyril continued oblivious to all else. He never saw or heard the shot that blew his head to a bloody pulp.

136

The gun was a pump-action shot gun. The gunman was a short squat figure, in dark dungarees, his head concealed with a full-face balaclava with eye holes. Charlotte and Glenda screamed, while the pony reared. Glenda, staring in horror at the dead Cyril, failed to see the second armed man as he walked round from the van. He aimed and fired. The shot was for Glenda, but it missed its mark by inches. The pony, its brains blown apart, fell twitching to the ground. Glenda screamed, let go of the bridle, and rushed at the gunman, trying to tear his face with her fingers. The gun fired. Glenda fell to the ground, blood gushing from her chest, and from the vicious exit wound in her back. The gunman fired again. She lay still.

Dennis, hearing the shots and screams, instantly made the right connection. Somewhere in his subconscious and in his darkest nightmares he'd expected this. He'd known they could be at risk from the moment they'd taken in the boy Per, and listened to his secret. Dennis picked up his axe and ran across the paddock into the ash copse. He faded into the trees and began to move stealthily towards the danger. A change had come over the man. The mystic pacifist was gone. Fifteen years had rolled back. Dennis was once again the Marine Commando, trained to kill, and do so, if need be, unarmed.

The bodies of man, girl and horse lay where they had fallen. Charlotte knelt on the ground, clinging to her pony's flanks, whimpering. The gunmen ignored her, and moved into the garden, dividing to circle the bungalows. Dennis, seizing his chance, jumped lightly into the hollow containing the pond. He crawled along the slippery muddy surrounds of the water. He was quiet and skilful. The intruders in front heard nothing. He risked a quick look. The nearest gunman was fifteen feet away. Between them was the thick trunk of the Blenheim apple tree. Some of its early windfalls already littered the ground. Two seconds and he was behind the tree. The gunman had stopped, he was staring at the house, his gun held at the trail. It took no more than a second for Dennis to cross the gap and swing the axe. The man turned, gawping in surprise. The axe would have split his head in two, had it connected; it never did. Dennis stiffened and slowly sank to the ground, blood gushing from his mouth. Experienced soldier that he was, he'd failed to check behind him, to see the third gunman standing at the pond's edge.

For ten minutes, two of the intruders ransacked the bungalows, ripping apart the meagre furniture and emptying drawers and boxes. The third man returned with a twenty five litre drum. Systematically

137

he doused both buildings with petrol, ending with a short trail to the outside. This he fired and without a backward glance the three walked to the road. Behind them, the fire roared and exploded as the ageing roof sheets cracked and crumbled.

The bodies lay in their blood, while flies began to gather speculatively. The little girl still clung to her pony. Silent now, she stared glazed eyed and trembling.

The short squat man jerked a round into the breech of his gun and aimed at the child from no more than a yard. She stared at him like a traumatised rabbit.

No! Not do, not do!' The second gunman shouted.

The man with the gun was unmoved. 'I give the orders.' His voice was coldly matter of fact.

The third man – the one with the long hair – lifted his own gun. 'You make one move, Larsen and I'll blow you away. If you wanna' kill kids, you do it in your own country, bastard psycho!'

The short man lowered the gun and walked away without a word. The others followed and a minute later the van drove off up the track.

CHAPTER 16

Sarah had hurried ashore and driven straight to work at the surgery. On arrival she had been surprised to see Francine Luterbacher's Golf GTI, in the car park. Sitting in the waiting room was Francine in person.

Hi, Fran,' said Sarah breezily. 'You're not one of our patients, what's up?'

'Sal, I need your help. Would the doctor give you the day off?'

'He might, but the reason had better be good.'

'I want you to come with me to Scotland.' Francine dropped her voice and glanced around. 'I think I can find something that will finish Ken for good...'

'Explain.'

'This thing that Ken's holding over Kaj Elgaad; it's all in some papers in a safe and I think I can find them.'

'Are you sure about this?'

'Yes, Ken as good as said so, but I never got to see them properly.'

'Where are these papers?'

'In Ken's house in Scotland.'

'Is anybody there? You can't just break in, and why do you want me?'

'Moral support and to be a witness, of course. And I won't be breaking in, I live there, my things are there.'

Sarah gave Francine a long searching look. 'OK, I'll come. Luckily Mrs Anderson's in today. I'll ask her to cover and I must leave a note for Dad.'

Francine's Golf, co-driven by Sarah, had annihilated the miles to the north. It was two o'clock in the afternoon when they finally stopped at Keele Services on the M6. Throughout the journey they had played tapes on the car stereo. They hadn't thought to turn on the radio and knew nothing of the other events that day. At Keele, they had a cafeteria meal and talked.

'Fran,' said Sarah. 'How well do you know Kirsten?'

'I don't really know her that well. The other day was the first time I've been to the Elgaad's farm. But I like her; she's straightforward, no messing about – different from Kaj.'

'I met him for the first time this morning, when he came back with us on *Glorfindel*. Kirsten really lost her cool, she punched him.'

'Kaj is a lovely sweet guy, but Ken's got him so tamed it's pathetic.' Francine pushed a forkful of chips into her mouth and chewed happily. 'Sal, I gather she and your dad are having a bit of a fling.'

'It's more than a fling, they're both serious. It'll be great if it lasts, but I worry about Dad being hurt again.'

'You know,' said Francine. 'I was there in the room when they first met. Your dad's all right – really dishy.'

Both girls were silent as they finished their meal. Then Sarah asked the question that'd been on her mind all day.

'What are we looking for in Scotland? Come on, I've played along with you so far. Tell me some facts.'

Francine nodded and leaned forward conspiratorially. 'I'll tell you as much as I know, but it's no big deal really. It may end in a let-down, but I've seen some papers, and I'm sure they're the ones he's using to blackmail the Elgaads.'

'What kind of papers?'

'Just three sheets: one of them's in Danish with a copy in English. The other's older and it's in German. I wish I'd read that first.'

'What did they say?'

'That's it, I never got the chance to find out. You see, it was last Christmas and Ken had drunk too much. He's got a safe in the drawing room. It's hidden and it's got an electronic combination. As I said, Ken was drunk. He opened the safe and took out an envelope. He started waving it about and boasting it was the key to his hold over the Elgaads. You see, Mummy had guessed he was blackmailing them, but Ken hates Kaj anyway.'

'That's what Kirsten told Dad, but do you know why?'

'I don't know except that they were kids together in this same house. Alfred Lindgrune was a friend of Kaj's father and he offered them a home when they were thrown out of Denmark. Alfred was quite a guy in the war. There's a medal of his in a glass case: the Military Cross.'

'What about these papers?'

'When Ken started shouting all this about the Elgaads, Mummy went wild. This doesn't happen often, she's a sucker for dominant males. The more Ken kicks her around the more she laps it up – she's made that way. My real Dad's a shit as well. Anyway this time she freaked. Said she was disgusted with the way he treated Kaj and Per.

140

Told him he was a bully and a sadist and he had no honour. Ken just laughed and then he stumped out to get another bottle of whisky. Mummy ran upstairs crying and there was me alone with the papers lying on the table.'

'So you had a look.'

'You bet I did. Trouble was I picked up the top one and it was in Danish. I couldn't make head nor tail of it. I wasted about two minutes before I tried the next one and would you believe it, it was the English translation. It was a long screed by Alfred – something about how he'd seen Nazis killing some children in Holland. Anyway, I could hear Ken clumping down the passage, so I snatched a look at the last bit of paper. It was a letter in German, typed in old-fashioned Gothic script. I only had time to see the date. It was July 21st 1939 and it was something about a government minister. By that time Ken had reached the door, so when he came in I was sitting there all innocent and the papers were just as he'd left them. He threw them back in the safe and that was that.'

'How are you going to open the safe?'

'No problem. I've watched Ken a dozen times and I know the combination inside out.'

'You're bloody crafty, sometimes, Fran. Are you sure he never saw you watching?'

'Ken never notices me. I hardly exist as far as he's concerned.'

'Why haven't you had a look before?'

'Simple, I had no idea of the significance of those papers until last week, and it wasn't worth the risk with Ken around.'

It was late afternoon when Francine turned onto the main A7 road heading towards Hawick. It had been a long tiring journey even with the two of them sharing the driving. They were now twenty miles from the Lindgrune family house. Sarah was struck by the scenery. She'd been born in the shadow of the South Downs and in some ways these hills were familiar. But the colours were harsher and already autumnal.

'Fran, this morning Kaj told us Lindgrune's ancestors ran a gangster mob in these parts. He reckons Ken's a throwback.'

'Wow, he means the "Black Armstrong". What a great idea! I never thought of that, but he could be right.' Francine was laughing.

'It's true then?'

'Too right, although I expect the story's been hyped up. But it's a fact, Ken's mother inherited the house from her grandfather, and that family were the Armstrongs. The first of them was the Black Armstrong; if you believe what they say round here he'd make Ken look like a charity worker.'

'I expect it's in his genes somewhere,' said Sarah.

'The only thing Ken's got in his jeans is a fat bum.' Both girls giggled.

Five miles on, Francine turned off the main road onto a side lane that shortly became a firm but unsurfaced forest track.

'Short cut, once over this ridge and we'll see it.'

The road led up a long sloping valley, before curving round and up a narrow shelf cut in the hillside. Sarah looked nervously down the three-hundred-foot drop, which seemed to start inches from the car's nearside wheels.

'There you are,' Francine lifted both hands from the wheel. 'Just like Switzerland.'

'Watch where you're bloody going!' Sarah snapped.

At the top of the hill, the track crossed a plateau before plunging towards another wooded valley, far below. On their left, a little stream tumbled in a series of mini waterfalls.

'That's the White Water Burn,' said Francine. 'It joins up with Teviot Water. But look, in that gap in the trees – The Lodge.'

Far below, the burn flowed into a little semicircular lake surrounded by green lawns. Beyond was the strangest house that Sarah had ever seen. It was tall and square and shone white in the evening sun, with little pepper-pot turrets at each corner, and a miniature green copper dome in the centre of the roof.

'It's like something from Disney World.'

'It's all kitsch though,' said Francine. 'The bit you can see is Victorian. The tower the old Armstrong lived in is round the back.'

She put the car in gear and began to drive down the hill. 'I'll have to see the Hendersons, to say we're here.'

At the end of the long sloping track, they joined a tarmac road that curled round towards the lake.

'This is the proper drive,' said Francine, 'We took a short cut.'

The car skirted the lake. Sarah could see wildfowl, and on the far side a folly in the form of a colonnaded Greek temple. Francine followed the drive round the house. Here were stables, a covered stockyard, and a sturdy Victorian-style manse house. A Land Rover stood outside and a column of wood smoke rose from a chimney.

'Good,' said Francine. 'Come and meet Bob and Janet. After driving the length of Britain, I could fancy tea and scones.'

An elderly man wearing corduroy trousers and a checked logger shirt appeared round the side of the house.

'Hello, young Francine. I thought you were down south.'

'Only a flying visit, Bob. I've come to fetch something I left behind.'

'Aye, come in then. I see you've got company and I dinna remember seeing this lassie afore, but come in and be welcome.' He had a warm smile for Sarah, who in her turn was relieved to find his soft Border speech easy to understand.

They were in a large room, apparently a kitchen and living room combined. At one end was a Rayburn with a simmering kettle, an oak table and a Welsh dresser. At the far end were a sofa, armchairs and a television showing a weather forecast.

'You've missed the news,' said Bob. 'There's been a terrible killing down south in Hampshire.'

'Whereabouts?' asked Francine sharply.

'Near a place called Alton.'

'Oh, that's miles from where we live.'

Sarah had noticed an oil painting. It showed a dour Victorian gentleman in a Norfolk jacket, with a springer spaniel seated on a rock beside him.

Bob followed her gaze. 'That's Sir Edward Armstrong last of his line – aye a tragedy. His good lady had eight daughters – would you believe that?'

'Why was it so tragic?' asked Sarah.

'Lassie, use your head. What good are daughters when a man needs an heir?'

'That's how the Lindgrunes came by the house,' said Francine.

'Aye, Sir Edward married his eldest daughter to her cousin Andrew Armstrong and it was their daughter who married Mr Alfred.'

'Bob,' said Francine. 'Are you saying that Ken Lindgrune's grandparents were first cousins?'

'Aye, but that's nothing for a grand family.'

'Yes, but the Armstrongs are no ordinary family. Kaj Elgaad reckons Ken's a throwback to the "Black" Armstrong.'

'Who did ye say said that?' Bob's voice cut in sharply. He was staring at Francine with a strange expression.

'Kaj Elgaad, you must remember him? He and his father lived here just after the war. He's staying at Chichester with Ken right now.'

Bob whistled softly. 'Kaj is staying with the Laird is he? I tell you

143

this, Francine – Kaj must be an awfa' forgiving fella to go staying with Mr Kenneth.'

'Why?'

'Because when Kaj was a wee lad, Kenneth tried to kill him.'

'Wow! You don't say.'

'Aye, Francine, I do say, and maybe I've said too much.' Bob looked pointedly at Sarah.

'You can say anything to Sarah. Ken's trying to ruin her dad, and they're both friends of the Elgaads.'

'Well having heard so much, perhaps ye'd better hear the rest. I'll fetch Janet. She was at Whitewater when the Elgaads first came. I was in the army overseas, ye understand.'

Bob left the kitchen and they heard him slowly tramp upstairs.

'Woman, ha' ye a minute? We've guests.'

'If my husband called me "woman" like that, I'd wrap a frying pan round his head,' said Francine. 'Take no notice though, it's just their way.'

Janet was a small, delicate lady, with a kindly smile and a painful arthritic limp. Sarah guessed she was in her late sixties. She was clearly pleased to see them, and to Francine's delight she set about making tea and filling the table with buttered scones and a chocolate cake.

'Woman, Francine here tells me Kaj Elgaad is staying with Mr Kenneth down south. Would you credit that?'

'Kaj, well I never, the wee Dane? I've often wondered about him.'

Janet set two chairs at the table and indicated the girls to sit down.

'Aye,' said Bob. 'As I've just said, Kaj must be mighty forgiving, and I let it slip to the lassies why.'

'Please, Janet,' said Francine. 'Sarah and I are friends of Kaj Elgaad's niece, and there's something else you should know. Ken is blackmailing Kaj about something that happened in the war, or here. We're not quite sure which.'

'Aye, I can see he might try that, though praise God, it was Kaj who was wronged. It's Kenneth who has to answer for anything that happened here. As for Kaj, ten years o' torment that poor wee fella suffered. You know, I used to worry as to whether I should do something. It was just that with Mr Alfred away so much, and us in a tied house. We didna' have the security.'

'But we have it now,' Bob intervened quietly. 'See, Francine, Mr Alfred left us the use of this house for life. There's a deed with his attorney in Dumfries. Mr Alfred, and the mistress too, they were verra determined to see that young Kenneth didn'a hurt us when they'd gone.' He turned back to Janet. 'I think ye'd best be telling them the whole story.'

'It was three weeks after the war ended,' Janet began. 'The two of them walked in here. Aye, it was raining and the man Eric was carrying the little lad on his shoulders; he could scarce move a step further himself.'

Janet explained that Eric and Kaj had arrived out of the blue. Eric had a letter from Alfred Lindgrune for Alfred's wife Kathleen. It asked her to give the pair shelter and to provide Eric with light work on the estate. Alfred would be home on leave in a few weeks and would explain.

'Well, the mistress didna' mind and their papers seemed in order. You see, at that time we all had to carry identity cards, and to feed, ye had to have a ration book, and these two had both. Trouble was the ID said they were Estonians, but the Polish lads on the farm said never – reckoned they were Norwegians under false colours. It was then that Eric admitted he was Danish.' Janet paused to refill the tea cups.

'After that, the pair of them settled in and we all waited for Mr Alfred to come home. Kaj was a fine little chap. He took quite a shine to our Maggie – she was only ten years old then. Kaj used to follow her everywhere, a lovely smile he had. He couldna' speak a word of English, but he soon learned. Oh he was a dear little soul. Everyone loved him, except Kenneth … Aye.' Janet's voice faded.

Kenneth, she explained, had resented Kaj from the start. Although Kaj was the older of the boys by a year, Kenneth was always the stronger, both mentally and physically.

'He was a mean-spirited child was Kenneth. He wanted to rule the roost and he couldna' abide this foreign lad getting all the attention.'

Kenneth had been crafty. He'd stolen small amounts of money and tried to make it look like Kaj's handiwork. 'Stitch him up is what they call it on the telly. But there was worse. He was the laird's son was Kenneth. The other wee lads around the estate – they didna' like him, but when he said jump they jumped. So Kenneth would be waiting for Kaj with a gang o' those boys and they would corner the wee lad and taunt him cruel. Many a time I rescued the little chap and Master Kenneth would stand there and he'd say. "Oh yes, Janet. Ye sides wi' this foreigner, but just ye remember I'll be the Laird one day".'

Janet laughed. 'When Mr Alfred came back from the army, he tried to take his son in hand, made him join a junior rugby team. They say Kenneth spent most of his time on the field kicking and biting and when the referee sent him off, he went through the other lads pockets in the changing rooms.'

The situation had continued for years, but it gained Kenneth nothing. The Lindgrunes, while doing all they could to bring their wayward son to heel, had taken a liking to Kaj and had drawn him closer into the family circle. There had been rumours, unfounded but widely circulated, that the Lindgrunes might disown their son and adopt the little Danish boy as their heir. It was in the summer of 1949 and Alfred, Kathleen and Eric were planning a children's party for Kaj's tenth birthday. Janet asked her husband to take up the tale.

'It was early July and the day before the kiddies' party. Mr Alfred asked me to set up tables and chairs on the lawn by the temple pool; that's the wee loch by the driveway. Well, I'd done that job in the afternoon, but later that evening it came over all dark and we could hear thunder in the hills. So I said to Janet here, I'd best put yon canvas chairs back indoors. See, it's ten o'clock, verra cloudy, but still light. The summer days are longer up here. It was beginning to spot with rain as I walked towards the temple. You must understand there's a sheer wall into the water there, and in those days we used to keep a rowboat by the steps.

'All at once there was a mighty flash o' lightning and I could see Kenneth on the wall pushing and jabbing at the water with one of the boat oars. Well, as far as I was concerned, everything that little devil did was trouble. So I run across and catches him red-handed. Aye, he'd pushed Kaj off the wall into the loch and he was holding his head under water with the oar. Well, I catches yon and I gives him a clip along the ear that sent him flat. Then I runs to the steps, and thank God, Kaj is crawling out, but the wee fella was gasping water and I guess he wouldna' have lasted much longer. Mr Alfred saw us from the windows and he comes out wanting to know what's what, so I tells him. I've never seen such a change in a man. He picks up his son and he lays into him for a whole five minutes, until the little cur was bawling for mercy. Then Mr Lindgrune says to me. "Bob, we'd best say nothing about what we've seen. Trust me – I'll see things are put right". Aye, and not long after that they sent Kenneth away to a boarding school and we all had a bit of peace.'

'Not for long though,' said Janet. 'He came back for holidays, and he wasna' in any way reformed. The older he got the worse it was. He raped that little girl Bella Hastie. Aye, I know it was all hushed up, but that was what it was. Then, when they were burning over by the

146

forest, he caught a sheep, wired its legs together, and threw it live on the bonfire, poor beast.'

'That's what he was like,' said Bob. 'Ye say he takes after the "Black" yin, well maybe, but the auld Armstrong had some logic about him. More than likely he'd cut your ears off, but if he did it was for a reason – never just for the hell of it.'

'Ken's not changed much, but he doesn't always have it his own way,' said Francine. 'Ask Sarah. A week back Ken forced his way into their house and Sarah's dad dumped him on the floor. Ken's still got a black eye and a plaster on his head.'

'Aye, good man! But he'd best be wary; Kenneth will repay him. He'll no forget a thing like that, and when he pays back it'll be in some mean and crafty way when you're no' looking.' Bob sighed. 'Ye'll be thinking I'm mighty disloyal to my employer, but that's the man he is.'

'When did the Elgaads go back to Denmark?' asked Sarah.

'In 1962; Mr Alfred took me a little into his confidence, but that was nearly thirty years ago, and I see no harm in telling you. It was May that year, and Mr Alfred told me he was off to Switzerland for a few days, to do some business for Mr Elgaad. It seems Eric was resolved to go home, but his life savings or whatever, were banked in Switzerland – in Zurich would it be?' He glanced at Francine.

'I expect so,' she said. 'That's the banking centre. It's where my proper dad works.'

'Now Mr Alfred was away four days and when he came back he sat up half the night talking to Eric, verra' private. I was checking the fires in the house that night, when Eric comes out of the study and he looked like one who'd seen an evil spirit. The man was white and shaking and he didna' seem to see me when we passed.'

Bob sighed; it seemed that even after thirty years the memories were vivid.

'Two weeks later they came to say goodbye and awa' they went, and I've never seen nor heard of them from that day, until now when ye two lassies come in here with your tale.'

'There's one more thing you should know,' it was Janet now. 'I dinna think I've told even Bob this. A few days after the Elgaads went home, I was for cleaning the big study, but there was the master working at his desk. He says, "Never mind me, Janet, ye carry on I've near finished", and he held up a bit of paper. He said Eric had asked him to guard it, but if it was his choice he'd burn it. Then he showed me some stuff he'd been writing in his own hand. "War's a terrible thing, Janet. Ye canna' always make the right choices".

'Suddenly the master was greetin', tears on his face, and him shaking all over. "Oh, Janet, I once witnessed an evil thing. I could ha' stopped it, but I didna' and it haunts my dreams to this day. Now I'm party to another tragedy. It hasna' happened yet, but I fear it will".'

'That was all, but my heart went out to the poor man. It seems he was burdened by some terrible secret, and just when he'd heard his good lady couldna' have more bairns and with his only son a villain and a scoundrel.'

Sarah and Francine left the Henderson's house an hour later.

'I've some things in the house,' Francine told Bob. 'Is it all right to go in?'

'Aye, the door's unlocked. You're welcome.'

The girls walked round to the front of the house, passing the original Armstrong tower. It was a plain, square building of ancient stone. To Sarah it seemed disappointingly small, though its entrance was grand enough. A grim archway, at least two metres high, its door owed nothing to its ancestry. It was a modern steel security shutter, which looked brand new.

'Ken fitted that last year,' said Francine. 'God knows what for. There's only old furniture and junk in there.'

Francine led the way into the great house. The entrance hall seemed vast and almost devoid of furniture. The focal point was a fine divided staircase, sweeping up to a circular gallery above. Francine ran ahead with Sarah following. On reaching the first-floor gallery, Francine headed for the third door on the left, opened it with a flourish and ushered Sarah within. The place was a lavishly furnished drawing room. A Victorian style veneer bookcase with glass doors stood against the far wall. Francine opened it, removed a book and fiddled with a catch. With a click the case swung back into the room to reveal a blank wall and the door of a safe.

Francine's expression puckered slightly as she carefully punched in a numbered combination. She gave a grin as the door swung open. The interior was empty.

Francine looked up in disappointment. 'Shit! It's gone. He must've taken it with him.'

The sole item in the safe was a rectangular cardboard box. Francine pulled it out, and eased its contents onto the table. It was a plastic radio transmitter with a short ferrite aerial.

'I think I know what this is,' she said. 'It's the gizmo that works that door in the old tower. I saw the men that installed it testing the thing with Ken.' She turned, grinning. 'Come on, let's play with it.'

'Should we?' Sarah was doubtful.

'Why not? If Ken's hiding something in there, our journey won't be wasted. Let's check that the tower's not locked inside first.'

Francine led the way downstairs, and then through a passage to the kitchens. From there they entered what was little more than a dusty tunnel, lit by a single light bulb. Sarah brushed aside a dangling spider with a grunt of disgust. At the end of the passage was a heavy studded oak door. It was locked. Francine stood on tiptoe to reach the lever of an ancient electrical circuit switch. She pushed it over with a satisfying clunk.

'That gear must be as old as the Armstrong. Let's try the main door; it should open now.'

Outside in the fading light, Francine fiddled with the transmitter. A bump was followed by the whine of an electric motor. The heavy door swung open, up and over.

'Open sesame! How about that?'

While some dim light filtered in from outside, the interior was mostly in shadow. Francine searched for a light switch, while Sarah strained her eyes and looked around.

'Fran, there's a car in here – a truck rather.'

The light came on. The room they stood in was large, perhaps twelve metres by ten, with a tiled floor and drab plaster walls. Opposite them was the same heavy door they had faced inside the house. In the left-hand corner Sarah could see the beginnings of a spiral staircase. The right hand wall was obscured to the ceiling by a stack of cardboard boxes, cellophane wrapped, and stacked on wooden loading pallets. To one side was a small battery-powered forklift truck. The whole centre of the chamber was occupied by a sparkling new white transit van.

'This one's a long way from home,' said Francine.

She pointed to a sticker in the rear window. It read, *T.C. Yapplington Commercial Motors Portsmouth.*

'Hey, Fran,' Sarah said. 'Frank Matheson told Dad that Terry Yapplington's a villain.' She giggled. 'He said Terry runs a call girl racket.'

'Tell you something as well,' said Francine. 'Yapplington's son is Ken's pilot, the one who flies the helicopter.'

'Let's look at these boxes,' said Sarah.

The stack appeared to be built of cardboard boxes. One had fallen from the top of the pile and part of its contents had spilt onto the floor.

Sarah examined the label on the box. "Elgaad Pharmaceutical. Aarhuus. Denmark. Contents – 200 – Decodon".

'Decodon's a painkiller, sort of aspirin,' said Francine in a voice of disbelief.

She picked up one of the bottles and unscrewed the safety cap.

'Sal, I've been an idiot. For Christ's sake it's been staring us in the face – it's Per. Him playing around in the lab with his remedy for peace...'

'What are you on about?'

'It's bloody obvious, if you think about it. It's history coming full circle. Imagine, if the Black Armstrong was around today, would he be rustling cattle? Not bloody likely! He'd be into drugs – and these are drifters.'

CHAPTER 17

'It was worth coming after all,' said Francine. 'Better than bits of paper – I guess we've cracked the mystery.'

Sarah was less certain. 'Wait a minute, I know Per played around with hallucinatory drugs, but he couldn't have made all this lot, assuming they're what you think.'

'No,' Francine was decisive. 'My theory is that Per invented the stuff, and that Ken is forcing Kaj Elgaad to mass-produce. It must be that, these pills are everywhere. I've tried them at discos and the college is swimming in them.'

'That's true – the doctors told me they're flooding every country in Europe.'

'OK,' said Francine. 'I'll take this bottle as a sample. Then we'll ring Mr Matheson and get him up here now. Come on out and I'll shut the door.'

Once outside, Francine pressed the close button on the transmitter. Nothing happened. She tried again, still nothing.

'This thing's got a rechargeable battery. Looks like it's flat; I wondered when I opened the door why it was so slow to respond.'

Francine began walking back towards the house. 'Come on, it doesn't matter, the charger's in the same box indoors.'

Sarah was listening, her expression puzzled. She could hear a distant humming noise, growing louder by the second, a sound both harsh and musical.

'Fran, there's a helicopter, coming straight at us and low!'

'I hope you're not thinking what I'm thinking,' said Francine. 'Oh shit! It's coming up the glen, along the line of the driveway and that's the way he always comes.'

It was eight o'clock and the last of the sun was sinking behind the hills to the west. Now they could hear the beat of the rotors and see the lights of the helicopter before it thundered close overhead, only to circle and move slowly towards them.

'It is!' Francine was showing traces of panic. 'That's Ken's – It'll land on the grass, right here by this bloody door, and there's naff all we can do. Come on Sal, we're getting out.'

Francine set off at a sprint remarkable for one of her bulk. They reached the Golf at exactly the moment the helicopter landed.

'Come on, we'll go!' yelled Francine as she scrambled behind the wheel. 'I'm not involving Bob and Janet, they've done nothing, it's all down to us.'

The Golf hurtled down the driveway before Francine braked in a desperate handbrake turn on the loose gravel that led to the forest track. Then she put her foot down. Sarah shut her eyes as a dust cloud erupted and stones and chippings rattled in the wheel arches.

'Where's that frigging chopper?' Francine grated the question through clenched teeth.

Sarah looked back. 'He's airborne again ... here it comes ... right over the top of us!'

The din of the aircraft drowned the rest of her words as it swept over them, heading for the ridge in front.

'Let's hope it's clearing out as well,' said Francine without conviction.

'If it's after us, it'll need more than just the pilot,' said Sarah. 'How many does it carry?'

'It's a Jet Ranger ... five seats. Can you see where he's gone?'

'No.'

'OK, keep watching.'

Francine steered the car up the steep zigzag road and over the brow of the hill.

'Oh shit!' Francine ground her teeth.

The helicopter was parked on its skids in the centre of the road not two hundred metres in front. Francine spun the wheel and drove the car off the track onto the open fellside. They bumped and banged for a short distance, before the steering became sluggish, and the drive wheels spun without effect. The car was in a bog.

'What do we do now?'

For the first time Francine looked wild-eyed and frightened. It was Sarah, in contrast, who found her inner strength growing.

'Split up and run in different directions. At least one of us should get to a phone. Good luck, Fran – see you.'

Without waiting for more, Sarah opened her door and jumped into the squelching mire. She waded to firm ground and then she ran. With her long blonde hair streaming in the wind, she ran in desperation, but also with the grace of a natural athlete. With the adrenaline pumping, she felt no sense of exertion. For a minute she seemed to be in a dream, floating on air. Then she heard the helicopter. It was coming for her and its noise froze her limbs. She was in a nightmare. Her feet were leaden. Her lungs were burning and her eyes staring. The noise was deafening, then the gale of the downdraught from the rotors seemed to suck the breath from her body. Sarah tripped, staggered, then fell full length on her face.

She knew the helicopter was stationary now and very near. The noise hurt her ears; she could neither move nor think. Then the engine roared and the helicopter sped skyward to hover like some malignant buzzard. Sarah lay still. She was trembling. Breathing in short painful gasps. Her limbs were locked and her eyes misty. Her hearing was as clear as ever. She could feel the wind through the grass and heather and with it the sound of footsteps crunching across the ground, nearer and nearer, until they stopped, and Sarah knew someone was standing, looking down at her.

'You, up! Come on. Up! Shift your ass.'

Sarah slowly raised her head. Beside her were two feet encased in soiled trainers. Very slowly she sat up and looked. Above her was a man, he carried a shot gun and the barrel was pointing at her head.

'OK, lady – stand up. You and me's goin' to have a talk.'

Sarah did as she was told. Her breathing was normal now and her heartbeat slowing. She felt calm but unreal. The man in front of her was a stocky figure no taller than herself. She forced herself to look him in the face. Two steely blue eyes above a grizzled moustache met hers. His face and wiry greying hair reminded her of pictures of the dictator Stalin. It was a stoneface. She shivered and then for a second she felt almost pity. It was a face that had never known the simple happy things of life. Behind those eyes lay only a cold, empty void.

'We're going to walk to the road,' said the man.

He was matter of fact, almost polite. The accent was American or Canadian she wasn't sure which.

Sarah did as she was told. She did not turn round but walked towards the track, avoiding the car in the swampy ground. All the time she could hear the man's footsteps a yard behind her. Another melancholy procession was moving from the other side. It was Francine, flushed and exhausted, with a second gunman. He was younger than the other and looked even more out of place on a Scottish hill. He was dressed in a stylish leather jacket, with shiny black trousers, and a fifties "rocker's" hairstyle.

'Hey, Dan!' he called. 'This one's a turkey. I'll swap the blonde with you – she's gorgeous.'

'Where's Kuo?' asked Sarah's guard.

'Tony's taking him down there. He's coming back with the van.'

'OK, we stop here. You two ladies will sit down together and we'll have some explanations.'

The grey-haired man indicated a spot by the roadside. Sarah caught Francine's eye. She wondered if the other might be at the end of her tether. If so, their survival would depend on Sarah's wits alone. She must stay calm and not provoke these men. Maybe the Hendersons would notice something and call the police; assuming they were still safe. She liked the old couple and felt sick at the thought of these men harming them. She must stay calm; anything might happen provided she kept calm.

'Just a minute, Dan,' said the younger one. 'Tony says this one's the boss's daughter.' He indicated Francine.

'You don't say,' said Dan.

'I was thinking. Play it safe for a bit. Lindgrune's my guvnor. He pays my wages.'

'Yeah, well I don't answer to him and maybe he ain't gonna be the boss much longer.' Dan looked at Francine. 'OK, young lady, say who you are and why you was meddling with that storeroom. And don't deny it, 'cos the radio key's in that car – I've seen it.'

'I'm Francine Luterbacher. I live in White Water Lodge. Mr Lindgrune's my stepfather and I've a right to do what the hell I like.'

Francine's breath had returned and with it much of her spirit.

'Where did you find that transmitter?'

'It was in my stepfather's safe.'

'Lindgrune says he's the only one who knows the combination.'

'Well, he's wrong then, isn't he?'

'Look, little girl, don't be funny with me, I ain't in the mood. Why did you open that store?'

'I wanted to show my friend the door working. I didn't know there was a van in there. Last time I saw inside there was only rubbish.'

Francine's air of injured innocence was just right and Sarah mentally applauded. She'd often laughed at Francine's ambitions to be an actress, but she had to admit, her friend was giving an Oscar-winning performance.

'OK then – who's this?' Dan pointed at Sarah.

'She's my friend. I brought her here as my guest to show her the lodge. I've never seen you before, but if you really work for my stepfather, I think we deserve a bit of courtesy.'

'Oh do you? Well, little lady, how come you lit out of here so fast when we arrived? You tell us that.'

Francine did not reply at first. Then slowly she began to sob.

'I saw the helicopter … I thought it was my stepfather, I'm frightened of him, he's horrible to me sometimes, I didn't mean any harm…' she broke off and sank her head in her hands.

'What d'ya think, Dan? Lindgrune can be a bastard, specially to women.' This time it was leather jacket speaking.

'OK, Reg, OK. You know this is a goddam nuisance.' Dan's voice was as cold as ever, but to Sarah's relief he'd stopped pointing the gun. 'All right, we'll pack'em in the van and take'em south. I'll decide what to do tomorrow.'

They sat for half an hour while the sun went down below the hills. The two men stood apart conferring quietly. Both looked at the girls from time to time and both still had their guns. Shortly afterwards headlights shone on the track and the heavy transit van came into view grinding up over the hill. It stopped beside them and Dan went over to talk to the driver. Then he walked back to Sarah and Francine.

'You two, on your feet. Walk to the back of the truck and stop, facing the doors.'

They did as they were told and again the man walked behind with the gun. The other one, Reg, opened the van doors, and Sarah could see the interior was three parts filled with cardboard boxes.

'Stand still and don't turn round,' sad Dan.

Sarah shivered as the man Reg walked behind them. He smelt of stale aftershave. Suddenly he seized her hand and she heard a click and felt something hard and cold. Francine gave a squeak. A quick glance was enough. The men were taking no chances; they had handcuffed the girls together.

'Get in the back,' said Dan.

'I want to have a pee,' said Francine.

'Use your knickers,' smirked Reg as he slammed shut the doors.

The girls huddled together, miserable and unwilling to talk. Shortly afterwards they heard the engine start and the van begin to move. The first few miles were agony as the vehicle sped along the forest road transmitting every bump through the hard floor. Then they felt the arrival of a normal road surface. The motion was better now and Sarah squeezed against the cardboard boxes, feeling dizzy and slightly sick.

She had felt no fear during their confrontation with the gang. Only exhilaration at Francine's successful bluff. It was different now. Cooped up in mounting discomfort in this swaying box her spirits sank into misery. She had no illusions about the man called Dan. She was certain their fate had been no more than postponed. If it suited the gang's plans, they would be killed – or at least she would be. The gang would probably spare Francine; they were, after all, Lindgrune's men. But Lindgrune would recognise her at once as the daughter of the man who was obstructing his plans. The very best she could hope for was to be used as a hostage.

Her eyes filled with tears. Oddly, in retrospect, she remembered less fear but rather a terrible sense of waste. She would never go sailing again, or ride on the Downs, or go partying and dancing with a date. All her dreams of rising in her profession, then marriage and children. She saw, dreamlike, her father in the bungalow at Fishbourne, knowing she would never come home again.

She was crying now and shivering all over. Inwardly she strove to get a grip of herself. She knew that in another minute she'd be hysterical. She bit her lip until it almost bled. She must stay calm. Perhaps in this situation one should try and pray. She tried to mutter the prayers she'd learnt in her childhood: the Lord's Prayer and a Hail Mary, but the words choked in her throat.

'Oh God, I'm in a bloody mess ... Oh God, I'm in a bloody mess.'

She repeated the words over and over again. Miraculously, the panic ebbed away. She could never, in retrospect, produce a rational explanation, apart from being mentally and physically exhausted; but not long after she fell asleep.

A while later she woke up; something was different. The engine had stopped, the vehicle was motionless. She looked at her watch; it was two-forty in the morning. The van doors opened. Outside were the bright lights of a filling station and roar of the traffic.

The man in the doorway was Reg. Sarah recoiled as a rush of fear swept through her. The man grinned as he handed them each a can of cola and a bag of crisps.

'Don't think about shouting, 'cos no one can hear you, and Larsen will turn really nasty.' He touched Sarah on the ankle. 'What's your name, darling?'

'Sarah.'

'You all right, Sarah?'

'No, of course I'm not.'

'OK, cool it. Think yourself lucky. If Larsen'd had his way, you'd have been topped by now.'

He leaned forward towards her. His breath stank of lager and Sarah shrank back.

'Look, Sarah. Larsen can't make up his mind about you. He's got more sense than to touch Kenny Lindgrune's little girl, but it don't mean he won't take it out on you. So take my advice. From now on, act dumb, and I'll do my best for you.'

With that he was gone and the doors slammed shut again.

CHAPTER 18

Steve and Kirsten stood watching the television in mute horror. The camera panned around the burnt-out bungalows and the pathetic remains of the trampled vegetable patch, then the turgid pond where the ducks still swam unconcerned. The human remains were gone, but the dead horse lay where he had fallen, though covered by a plastic sheet. The cameras had been kept at a distance but still close enough to pick out the bloodstained grass. Behind a taped-off area police were combing the road's edge and garden beyond. A policeman, named on the caption as Detective Inspector Hollins, made a statement. This, he said, was a brutal and senseless murder. These dangerous killers still at large. He pleaded with all members of the New Age community to co-operate with the police in apprehending the murderers. It was clear that both police and media were convinced the murders were part of some internecine hippie feud.

'Steve, what do we do?'

Kirsten was staring at the television, her lower lip trembling. Steve guessed she was on the edge of tears.

'Ring Fox,' he said tersely.

Alton Police Station was a modern building, part of a new courthouse complex. Steve and Kirsten were shown into the Crossfield incident room. Inside were nine persons with computers and three telephones in constant use. A PC took Steve's statement with polite scepticism.

'I'm sure you mean well, sir, but there's no doubt in our minds that this crime is internal to these travellers. Perhaps some feud with the motor bike lot. Let's face it, that's more likely than this theory of yours...'

'No!' Kirsten interrupted, her voice sharp and angry. 'Per was my cousin. He was part of this commune. These people knew his secret and he too was killed for it – so why not them?'

Her outburst silenced the room apart from the urgent ringing of a telephone. All eyes were on her.

'Ask the police at Chichester,' she continued, 'or Mr Matesen at Portsmouth.'

'Excuse me, miss.' Another man spoke from a nearby table. 'Are you talking about Frank Matheson: Portsmouth Division?'

'Yes, I think so.'

158

The man stood up, waved the PC aside, and sat down opposite.

'I'm Detective Inspector Hollins. How does Matheson fit into all this? I once worked for him before he was busted.'

'Chichester Police sent me to him,' said Steve. 'You see, we know this business has a link to Kenneth Lindgrune, the property developer.'

Hollins had a troubled frown. 'I hope you're wrong. I thought we were on for an early resolution of this case, but that would muddy the waters properly.'

'But why?' said Steve. 'You think Lindgrune's a crook. If you can find a link between him and these murders, that'd finish him, wouldn't it?'

Steve looked at the detective. Hollins was a round-faced, well-dressed, cheerful looking character, but young for his rank. A high-flyer, Steve speculated; surely he would seize an opportunity to succeed where the likes of Matheson had failed.

'Yes, Mr Simpson, but what you and this lady have told me is supposition. Frank Matheson was near to producing hard evidence, and it got him busted.' Hollins still seemed troubled. 'Now, I hear what you say. I will take it seriously, but these travellers are a strange lot, so I still say the truth will be some nasty bit of sub-culture rather than organised crime.'

Hollins walked with them to the reception area, and held out his hand. 'If you see Frank Matheson, remember me to him…'

'Save you the trouble,' boomed a familiar voice. 'You talk of the devil and in he walks.' Matheson had come out of the shadows by the desk.

'Welcome back, sir,' said Hollins, looking commendably startled. 'I expect you can vouch for these good people?'

'I certainly can, and what's more, if they've told you something you'd do well to believe it.'

'I'd love to believe them, but there's no evidence, and I don't like all this talk of Lindgrune.'

'Come on, Richard – positive thinking. Shop Lindgrune, and you'll be an Assistant Chief Constable within five years.'

'It's our real and actual Chief Constable that worries me. He thinks you've got a bee in your bonnet about Lindgrune.'

'But you know me better. Now, what about that poor little kid at Crossfield. How is she, and what's happened to her?'

'Charlotte Atrill,' said Hollins. 'She's at home under sedation. We had a WPC talk to her but she's still paralysed with fright. It may be a day or two before she talks, poor little mite.'

'I could see her,' said Matheson. 'I know the Atrills. They used to live in Stubbington before they moved to these parts. Dave Atrill worked in our vehicle service depot.'

'I can't stop you calling on her, Frank, but I would have thought you'd frighten her even more.'

'Oh, thank you very much.'

'I could do with a proper cup of tea,' said Matheson.

Outside the police station Steve had been bursting with questions but Matheson had not been forthcoming. They found a quiet coffee shop and a corner table. Matheson gulped his tea with relish.

'How did you know we were here?' asked Steve.

'Fox told me.' Suddenly he looked severe. 'How come you never mentioned these hippies to me?'

'When we went to their camp you were still in Italy,' said Steve defensively. 'When we saw you next, we'd just seen Julie Elgaad killed, I meant to tell you but it went out of my mind.'

Matheson sighed. 'We're a day too late, but tell me anyway.'

In turns they told him about Dennis and the commune and about their meeting at sea with Kaj Elgaad.

'You do realise that this Dennis and his girl were the only potential witnesses we had left?' Matheson grunted. 'We've nothing now except little Charlotte.'

'I know – I'm sorry.'

'Never mind. Lindgrune's got the Devil riding with him so it's no good crying over it.'

'What's all this about a little girl – Charlotte, you said her name was?' Steve was anxious to change the subject.

'Charlotte Atrill, poor little kid. She was there when it happened, saw the whole thing. The bastards shot her horse when they killed the others. Never touched Charlotte though, thank God!'

'But that is terrible,' said Kirsten. 'Poor little one. I expect she loved that horse.'

'Why shoot the horse and not the girl?' asked Steve.

'I don't know – I can't read the minds of psychopaths.'

'You said them,' said Steve. 'So did the TV report.'

'That's right. There were three men, all masked and carrying guns. That's all Richard Hollins knows because that's all Charlotte's said so far. She was shouting it out when the locals found her, since then she's clammed up – shock of course. The man at the pub saw the van they used, and it's turned up at another new age camp near Tichbourne. But I take that as a blind. I agree with you, I don't think hippies had anything to do with it. I think young Richard's got the message, but he's scared stiff Lindgrune'll ditch his career prospects, just like me.'

Crossfield was not a traditional village. It was a sprawling area with three churches and a number of small hamlets. Matheson took several wrong turns before he drew to a halt beside a flint-walled cottage behind a high hedge. Steve, who'd been following, pulled the Volvo tight against the muddy grass verge. The narrow driveway to the house was already blocked by a police panda car.

'This is it,' said Matheson.

'I don't like this,' said Steve dubiously. 'Should we be invading the privacy of these people?'

'Now look here,' said Matheson sternly. 'I've had to steel myself for something like this a hundred times. Believe me, it doesn't get any easier.'

Abruptly, he turned and strode up the drive to the front door. The cottage was clearly old, probably once it had been the abode of a woodsman or a shepherd. The garden was lovingly kept with colourful autumn flowers, a raised summerhouse, and a lawn as smooth as a golf green. By the garage was a wooden stable with an open door. Kirsten tugged Steve's arm and pointed inside. Visible was a feed of hay in the rack and a bowl of horse nuts.

Matheson rang the doorbell. Kirsten stood with him, while Steve hung back uncomfortably. The door opened a crack on its safety chain while Matheson had a quick exchange with an invisible person on the other side. Then the door opened wide. Standing there was a woman. She was short and dark, with hair and features almost Spanish. Steve guessed her to be in her early forties. Normally, he imagined, she was a jolly person, but today her eyes were red with weeping and loss of sleep.

'I'm sorry about the chain, Frank. I didn't realise it was you. I'm not opening to anyone at present. We've been pestered by newspaper people all day. There's a man from the *Banner* keeps pushing notes through the letterbox.'

'I know what I'd like to do with that lot,' Matheson growled. 'How are you, Angie, and how's Dave taking this?'

'He's brooding. I wouldn't trust him if he came face-to-face with those men. He'd kill them.'

'More likely they'd kill him. They're a very dangerous band of desperadoes I'd say.'

'Come on in, Frank,' said Angie Atrill. 'Who are your friends? Are they police as well?'

'Good heavens no! They're interested parties, who've suffered in different ways from these same criminals.' Matheson made the introductions.

It was a warm, friendly and rather untidy house, which surprised Steve after the beautifully ordered garden. The living room door was open. Steve could just see a settee with a tiny recumbent human form lying beneath a floral quilt. In a chair by the empty fireplace sat a young policeman.

'This is PC Ellams, or Bob as we call him, he's our local bobby,' said Angie. 'Bob, here's Superintendent Matheson from Pompey.'

The PC scrambled to his feet with an effort to straighten his tie.

'All right, lad,' said Matheson. 'I'm Superintendent retired now, so you needn't stand on ceremony. How's things here?' He lowered his voice as he indicated the motionless child on the sofa.

'She's still half asleep, poor kid,' said Bob. 'But I think the sedation's wearing off. I noticed she was awake and staring at me just now.'

'Thank you, Constable. You sit tight and I'll have a word with her mother.'

Matheson withdrew from the room and beckoned them into the kitchen.

'Do you want to talk to Charlotte?' said Angie. 'That woman policeman tried earlier but she got nothing. No reaction, nothing. It's not like Lottie – she's too chatty for her own good most times.'

'Not surprising after what she saw,' said Matheson. 'But she'll have to talk, she's our only witness and every hour that passes means the investigation runs a little bit colder. Have you tried to talk to her yourself? You're the obvious person.'

'Oh yes, I've tried, but it was awful. She wasn't my little girl any more. Her eyes were all glazed, like she was hypnotised. I couldn't hack it, I just ran out of the room. Then the woman copper tried, but she was all formal, like a school teacher – it was as if Lottie's done something wrong.'

'Please, please!' Kirsten was speaking. 'I will talk to Charlotte.'

'You!' Matheson looked startled.

'Yes, Mr Matesen, me. I think I know the trouble.'

A ghost of smile flickered across Matheson's face. 'What do you

162

say, Angie? I've developed a high respect for this young lady, she's full of surprises. I think we might let her try – if it's all right with you, that is?'

Angie said nothing for a few seconds. Steve had caught her eye and turned away quickly. For a split second the face expressed, fear, bafflement and despair.

'Please be gentle with her,' she pleaded with Kirsten. 'She's our only one – I just want her back again.'

She was sobbing now as Matheson put an arm around her, and sat her in a white wood chair by the kitchen range. Without a word, Kirsten slipped into the living room. She spoke to the PC who nodded, rose to his feet, and joined the others in the kitchen.

Angie occupied herself making a pot of tea. From time to time, one or other of them would glance at the closed door, but no one commented. Ten minutes passed, then distinctly, they heard the click of the patio windows opening. Charlotte was walking slowly, clinging to the arm of the larger girl. She was a slightly built fourteen-year-old, with long, jet-black hair like her mother's. Kirsten, with her similar colouring, could almost have been her elder sister.

The two of them walked up the flagstone steps to the summer-house and sat down on a rustic wooden bench. Kirsten sat with both arms around the child and they could see her lips moving, seemingly whispering in Charlotte's ear. Then Charlotte was talking, slowly at first, then animated, making little gestures with her hands. Then turning to Kirsten she said something, stood up, and amazingly smiled and laughed. It was for a split second only, then both girls ran across the lawn and back into the house. Another minute and Kirsten joined them in the kitchen, shutting the door behind her.

'Please,' she asked. 'Where can we find a digging machine? You know what I mean … a JCB?'

'A digger,' said Angie with a puzzled look. 'They've got one at the chicken farm and at Richards the contractor – but why?'

'It is as I thought. It is her pony – her Patch. He was the greatest thing in her life and she has seen him murdered. I know she saw those people killed, that is a terrible thing, and it will be with her for ever. But it is Patch who torments her now and it is he who she thinks of. You must bury him and she must see it is done. Will the police mind that?'

'The Scene of Crime is still closed but I believe they need the horse moved,' said PC Ellams, 'What had you got in mind, Mrs Atrill?'

163

'We were going to phone the kennels to take the poor beast away,' she said. 'But somehow we never got round to it.'

'You must bury him. That is what Charlotte wants. Then I think she will start to get well.' Kirsten was emphatic. 'She is a clever kid and brave. She has not told me everything, but now she goes to her room and she promises she will write down everything she remembers.'

'Well I never!' Matheson was staring wide-eyed. 'Miss Schmitt, you're a genius.'

'No, Mr Matesen, I am not. I had a horse once. His leg was broken on the road near our farm. The vet shot him in front of me, but my mother had him buried, and I still go there sometimes.'

Her voice trailed away before she shook her head and turned back to Angie.

'Mrs Atrill,' she said solemnly. 'When these troubles are over, you, your husband, and Charlotte, will visit our farm in Denmark. There we have horses, many horses, maybe sixty. Charlotte must choose one for herself to take home to England.'

Angie seemed doubtful. 'That's kind of you, miss, but me and Dave could never afford a trip like that or an expensive horse.'

'No!' Kirsten interrupted. 'These men Charlotte saw. They work for an evil man who has destroyed my family, and killed my aunt and my cousin. If Charlotte helps catch him I will owe her a debt for life, so you will come as my guests, and the horse will be my gift.'

'That's good of you to offer, Miss, and we're grateful for what you've done for Lottie. But if she knows so much, won't that gang come back for her again?' She spoke urgently, spilling out the worry that was at the back of her mind.

'No chance,' said PC Ellams firmly. 'Me and three others are watching this place around the clock, and we've got armed back-up on alert.'

'I do not think they will come back,' said Kirsten. 'You see, their leader was going to kill her, but the others stopped him.' She glanced sharply at Matheson. 'The leader was called Larton, Charlotte heard the name.'

'Larsen!' Matheson whistled, and then incredibly, his face broke into a happy grin. 'His name was Larsen, I'd bet a small fortune on it. As they say on the telly, we've got our breakthrough!'

'Who's Larsen?' Steve asked.

'A thoroughly bad lot,' Matheson was serious again. 'The Naples police told me about him. He's been working with the local Mafia out there. My police chief pal reckons Larsen's the man behind the Drifter drugs.'

'He can't be in Italy if he's here,' said Steve.

'No, he's not resident in Italy, he just makes a lot of visits. The Eyties will only deport him if they can't produce evidence to charge him, which they won't get – Larsen's too smart for that. I'll tell you some more. The Naples police gave me his mug-shot. They got the photograph from the FBI. I showed it to our friend Torrents. He confirms Larsen was the man who abducted Per Elgaad from that gay club in Southsea. He's quite adamant about it.'

Outside by the road, Steve felt the tension unwind. The emotion-charged hour inside the house might be all in a day's work for Matheson, but for Steve it had been an ordeal. He looked at Kirsten with admiration and pride. Goodness knows what she'd said to that poor child, but the result was dramatic.

Matheson grinned at them. 'One more call I think, to the licensee of The Fox and Goose.'

Ten minutes later they arrived outside the familiar shabby pub. The doors were shut, although half a dozen cars were parked outside. Matheson strode to the main entrance and plied the grotesque ornamental knocker.

'Sod off! We're not open,' came the voice within.

'Come on, Harold – let us in. It's me, Frank Matheson. I used to be with the law in Pompey.'

'I remember. I'm not open, and none o' my guests is driving. You'll not cost me another licence.'

'Get away, Harold, that was fifteen years ago, and I'm not in the force now. I don't give a bugger about your licence either way, but I must talk.'

'All right, hold on.'

The heavy door vibrated as the stiff bolts were undone. It opened a crack.

'Hello, Frank. Crikey, it's you two again – the boatman and the Danish crumpet. Come in quick. I'm trusting you not to grass me, Frank. You see, we've got company.'

The interior of the bar was laden with a pall of cigarette smoke, that made Steve's eyes water. Kirsten pulled a tissue from her pocket and with a grimace, held it over her nose. In the dim light of the room Steve could see ten people, all clutching beer or spirit glasses. None of them were the farm men of the previous visit. He counted seven men and three women. Their clothing varied from shabby suits to designer jeans and jackets. Something about them said, visitors and London.

'Hello, what's all this then?' said Matheson.

'And by the same token, what brings you here, Matheson?'

The voice came from a bright-eyed little man, dressed in cord jeans and an ill-fitting Barbour. Steve thought he had the face of an eager ferret.

Matheson stared at the man with distaste. 'Sid Everett, I've just heard how you've been tormenting the Atrills.'

'Oh come on, Matheson,' said the ferret. 'Two grand – two thousand nicker I offered that woman for her story. How's that for tormenting?'

'Mr Matesen,' said Kirsten. 'Who are these people?'

'This lot's the Rat Pack; scribes of the tabloid press. Sid here's from the *Banner*. Do you have them like this in your country?'

'Yes, we do.' She confirmed gloomily.

'Who's this bloke, Sid?' The questioner was one of the women, a thin-faced individual with enormous earrings.

'This is ex Chief Superintendent Matheson,' interjected another reporter. 'Two years ago. You remember, Tracy. I wrote the story – "Disgraced crime boss ... my men can never be above the law, says Chief Constable".'

'Don't give me those sort of quotes, Bill Allreed,' growled Matheson. 'What about those you didn't dare print because your boss is in hock to Ken Lindgrune?'

'Hey! What's all this about Bill?'

'Gee wizz – Lindgrune?'

'Go on, Matheson, tell us more.'

The whole rat pack had burst into an excited hubbub at the expense of the luckless Bill. Steve was reminded of an unruly schoolroom.

'Harold,' said Matheson. 'A word in your ear – in private?'

'Come upstairs, Frank, but not for too long.'

They followed the man to his living quarters on the first floor.

'I can't stop long, Frank, or that lot'll nick my whiskey.'

'How much have you told them?'

'Why do you want to know?'

'Because I'm tracking these murderers on my own account. There's more to this business than you realise, Harold.'

'OK, but as far as these press men go; I've told 'em nothing. None of 'em's offering enough dosh, but give 'em time and they will. They know I saw something.'

'What did you see?'

'I was standing as close to one of them killers as I am to you now,' Harold paused for effect. 'He was dressed like a traveller, but he was no more one than I am, and I'll tell for why. That long hair of his was a wig, a hairpiece. I know, I used to wear one when I played in a band.'

'That figures,' said Matheson. 'I don't think this is the work of travellers anyway.'

'That's not all. The bloke I spoke to was from these parts. By the way he spoke – could've been off the Island. I pride myself on a bit of an ear for accents.'

'Professor Higgins, eh?'

'Who's he?'

'Never mind. Answer me this. Do you think that man minded you having such a close look?'

'No, not a bit of it. He walked right up to me, asked for Dennis's place straight out – almost as if he was trying to call attention to himself.'

'Very cocky – would you know him again?'

'Without the hairpiece? I might if I heard him talking.'

Behind them they heard a light double knock on the door leading to the stairs. Harold walked across and opened it. A figure stepped quickly inside. It was Sid Everett of the *Banner*.

'I know, I know!' he said, waving aside the landlord's protests. 'I want a word with Matheson.'

'I'm not sure I want a word with you, Sid,' said Matheson. 'Speak anyway.'

From downstairs came the crash of breaking glass and a loud cheer. With an expletive, Harold scuttled from the room.

'That's better,' said Sid. 'Shifty little sod, that one. I didn't want to talk in front of him. What I've got for you, Matheson, is information, but it's off the record, and I'm not sure I should be talking anyway.'

'Don't speak in riddles, man.'

Sid nodded. 'Right, I'm in a different position to Bill Allreed. My boss isn't running scared of Ken Lindgrune. On the contrary, he's interested in the man. So interested that we've been give carte blanche to do a bit of investigative digging.'

Sid's voice had dropped to a conspiratorial whisper. Steve thought he looked more like a ferret than ever.

'Matheson,' Sid continued. 'I'll give you one tasty bit of info' for nothing, with one proviso. If anything comes of it, you talk to me first. Off the record to start with, but full co-operation if it gets to court.'

'That depends. No deals until I've heard what this information involves.'

Sid gave Matheson a hard look. 'Agreed, now, you've never had an inkling of what your girl Mandy discovered about Lindgrune? What got her killed?'

Matheson stared at Sid steely-eyed. A tense silence followed. Down below, Steve could hear the background chatter in the bar.

'Yes,' Sid continued. 'We liked Mandy; she was wasted on the provincial press. She'd have made her mark on the "Street" with any of the nationals.'

'Everett,' said Matheson. 'If you've something to say, then spit it out, and maybe I'll return the favour.'

'Here you are then, take this.' Sid handed over a folded scrap of paper. 'That's it. Keep in touch and we'll help each other.'

Matheson nodded curtly and put the paper in his wallet. Then he turned abruptly and walked down the stairs. Steve and Kirsten followed him out into the fresh air.

Matheson exhaled a deep breath. 'I didn't want to seem too keen in there, but Sid's no bullshitter, he knows something. Let's have a look.'

He took out the paper and read it. He grunted and passed it to Steve.

The words were printed in black ink with a fibre-tip pen.

> *Take a look at:*   *Unit 6.*
> *Goleigh Industrial Estate.*
> *Leigh Park.*
> *(trades under the name. Goleigh Electrical).*

CHAPTER 19

Sarah's note was still on the table, unopened. Steve hadn't noticed it before, so shocked had he been by the television report of the Crossfield murders.

The message was a rather terse memo. Sarah and Francine were off to Scotland and would ring home from there that evening. Steve glanced at the answerphone, but the tape was blank.

'What the hell are they up to?' he asked Kirsten irritably.

'I guess they go to Lindgrune's house in Scotland. Francine lives there for half the year. Maybe they do something while the house is shut and that man is safe down here.'

'It's no bad thing. I'm going to send you both away from here anyway.'

'Get lost!'

'No, it's for your own safety, both of you. Not for long, only until this thing's cleared up.'

'No, Steve, you will not send me away like I am some parcel. We face Lindgrune together. That way we win together or maybe we die together. I cannot say what will happen, only that my family have run away for too long. I stay with you. I can take anything if we are together.'

The words had the ring of another pre-rehearsed speech. She must, cleverly, have anticipated his thoughts and been prepared. Of course she was right. There would be no lasting relationship between them if she ran now.

Suddenly he had a vivid flash of that strange recurring nightmare that had afflicted him these last two years. The wind, the fury of breaking seas, and that other hidden companion. Now he knew that the unseen person was Kirsten, and that it was she who had been there, all the time, many months before he'd met her for real.

He looked at her pleading face and felt a chill of apprehension 'All right, love, I agree, we stick together. You're right, I think it's sort of meant.'

Outside, the sky was black with the approach of a weather front. Already it was beginning to spit with rain. Later, as they lay in bed, they could hear the rising south-west wind and the spatter of rain against the window. Tonight they did not make love, the tensions of the day had been too traumatic. Instead they lay together and talked.

'I wish Sarah would ring,' he said. 'I've no idea what she's up to.'

'Trust her, she will know what she's doing.'

'I suppose so. The trouble is that I guess this is one of Francine's capers, and they always mean trouble.'

'I know; Francine is one who likes to make things happen.'

'I know that from bitter experience,' he laughed. 'Francine's a one-off; the only Swiss with a sense of humour.'

'I know something else,' Kirsten said darkly. 'Francine has a big, big, crush on you.'

'Oh come on – she's younger than Sarah.'

'What difference does that make? Oh no, she has no chance – I have you,' she whispered gently in his ear.

The next morning the rain had intensified, with a swirling bank of low cloud and force seven gusts slamming across the Harbour. Steve had another exhilarating test sail in the Fieldman brothers' Fourteen. Kirsten sat in the car and waited. Steve returned in a cheerful mood. He waved goodbye to the twins, threw his sailing gear in the boot, and climbed in beside her.

'There has been a call on your telephone,' she said.

'Business?'

'No,' she sniffed with a whiff of disapproval. 'It was that Binbridge. He and Mr Matesen are waiting at your house.'

Two cars were parked in the driveway with Matheson and Chris Bainbridge sheltering in Chris's Jaguar.

'Come on in,' said Steve. 'I didn't know you two had met?'

'This is the first time face-to-face,' said Chris. 'But we've had a couple of chats on the phone.'

'This time it's a call to action,' said Matheson.

'Why?'

'Tell you in a minute.'

Despite her reservations about Chris, Kirsten gave the visitors a cheerful welcome and set about making coffee.

'I've been chasing a whole flock of wild geese,' grinned Chris. 'All my pet theories turned upside-down.'

'How so?'

'I researched Alfred Lindgrune, assuming him to have been a sleeping Nazi agent. He turned out to have been a superhero and as white as the driven snow. I rang up an old athletics friend, he's a sub-editor on the *Glasgow Herald*. Three hours later he faxes me some amazing stuff. A full-blown sex scandal – caused quite a flutter in high society circles at the time.'

'Sex,' said Matheson with a groan. 'Always is in a case like this. Well, tell us all.'

'Right, Alfred Lindgrune first came to Scotland in 1938, as an exchange student, at Edinburgh University. There he met a fellow student, one Kathleen Armstrong, and the two got engaged. Both were just eighteen, and this Kathleen was an heiress with a big fortune coming to her. You get the drift – a real Victorian hearts and flowers epic. Her family kick up, part the lovers, and Alfred goes back to Denmark. Two years later, in 1940, Alfred escapes from Denmark, comes to Britain and makes his way to Scotland again. First he joins the army, Kings Own Scottish Borderers. Then he looks up his old sweetheart and gets her pregnant. That way her family have to take the line of least resistance. The two marry and the baby is Kenneth, our number one pain in the rear.

Where my theory crashed was Alfred's war record. He was commissioned, then transferred to the Parachute Regiment, got wounded in the first hour of D-Day. He recovered and spent the rest of the war with the SAS. When it ended, he had the Military Cross and a Mention in Despatches.'

'Some guy,' said Matheson. 'I wonder why his son went to the bad?'

'I don't know but I suppose it happens. Anyway, Alfred became a naturalised Brit and settled down to run his wife's estate. Then he built up a timber importing business and made himself a millionaire in his own right.'

'But this is a lovely story,' said Kirsten. 'So romantic – I know nothing of this. My Uncle Kaj will say nothing about his time in Scotland, but he worshipped his Uncle Alfred and so did my grandfather.'

'I'm afraid I can't tell you much about your uncle either,' said Chris. 'The only thing my mate dug up, was that Kaj Elgaad went to George Watson's College in Edinburgh. He checked with a couple of ex-pupils of the period. It seems Kaj was a studious, low-profile, lad. He played a bit of rugby, went hill walking, and that's about the limit anyone remembers.'

'Nothing in all this to say why he's being blackmailed?' said Steve.

'On the contrary. Eric and Kaj seem to have been as harmless a pair as you could find. There's a secret somewhere, and it's probably staring us in the face.'

Matheson was looking grim. 'I'm afraid, Miss Schmitt, that we won't solve your family's problems without first exposing Lindgrune and this man Larsen. I really think you should talk to your uncle. Whatever this blackmail, the consequences for him will be ten times worse if he's criminally involved with Lindgrune.'

Kirsten shook her head. For a moment she looked as if she would say something, but she stayed silent.

'You mentioned the man Larsen,' said Steve changing the subject. 'Was he the one Charlotte saw?'

'Charlotte Atrill's statement says the leader of the gunmen at Crossfield was addressed as Larten. She says he was a short fat man and spoke American. Brave little kid, she was as near death as she'll ever be, but she remembers.'

'So, she's spoken to the police.'

'Richard Hollins says that once she started talking they couldn't stop her. All thanks to this young lady,' he nodded at Kirsten. 'There's a nationwide hunt for Larsen, but they're playing it quiet. No publicity on TV yet. They don't want the suspects to twig that we're on to them. There's nothing to connect with Lindgrune either but that may change tonight if we strike lucky.'

'Larsen's the man who runs Lindgrune's Mid Southern Security Company,' said Chris. 'I know that for a fact – they stole a contract from us; so Larsen's crossed me once already.'

Matheson looked at Chris searchingly. 'This is news to me. I didn't know that and I'm not sure the police do yet. You're sure it's the same Larsen?'

'Show me the picture?'

Matheson fumbled in his briefcase and handed a photograph to Chris.

'That's him.'

'Good work. By the way, Steve, we showed that picture to your lad Darren Stokes, this morning. He identifies Larsen as the man looking for Julie Elgaad.'

'You said something about tonight,' said Steve. 'Can I ask what's going on?'

'Yes,' said Matheson. 'I think the time has come for a briefing.'

He looked around his circle of listeners and continued. 'This address in Leigh Park, the one supplied by Sid Everett. I gave it the once-over this morning. It's an electric goods discount warehouse, seemingly completely legit. Next I checked who owned the building, and who runs the business. As I suspected, the site belongs to

Lindgrune, or rather, Winterbirch Holdings. Nothing unusual there, Winterbirch are big in that kind of property. Unit six, trades as Goleigh Electrical, and there is a Mrs Jennifer Mordemeade listed as Managing Director. The other two directors are Terry and Tony Yapplington. Terry, or Councillor Terence, is a hypocritical little toad and as smarmy a villain as you'll find anywhere. He's clever with it. I've spent half a lifetime trying to put him away and he's slipped me every time. Tony is his son, he flew helicopters in the navy before he was court-martialled and dismissed from the service.' Matheson chuckled. 'Very prim and proper, are the navy. Tony had two naked Wrens in his bed. He might've got away with that; trouble was all of them were stoned out of their minds on cannabis, and Tony was supposed to be on duty at the time. Anyway, he's still flying. He's the one who pilots Kenny Lindgrune's fancy helicopter.'

'What about Mordemeade?' asked Chris.

'Jennifer is Terry Yapplington's sister. No criminal form but she's got to know what goes on.'

Matheson was still grinning. He put his finger on his lips. 'There's more; it seems the shop's is a bit short staffed at the moment. I sent Torrents in to buy a Walkman. He said the fair Jennifer was chasing her tail. Told him both of her staff were off sick. So, I went to the Tax Office in Commercial Road and cashed in a favour. PAYE records say that Goleigh Electrical's two employees are, wait for it … Kuo and one, Reggie Thropping, who has a criminal record that'd fill a fair-sized book. He was also born on the Island. So bully for Sid Everett and I promise I'll never wipe my bottom on that stupid comic, the *Banner*, again.'

'What have you got planned, Frank?' asked Steve.

'Tonight, there's going to be a little unrehearsed pantomime.'

'Eh?'

'I'll explain. The police are reluctant to raise a search warrant on the say-so of Sid Everett. So tonight's charade is technically unofficial.'

'What are you up to, Frank?' Steve asked warily.

'Gather round and I'll show you.' Matheson unfolded a large-scale street map and laid it on the table. 'Right, Leigh Park, and here, Goleigh Industrial Estate.' He pointed with a finger. 'Unit six is this one. Basically it's a warehouse, with a shop in front, and an office upstairs. Two thirds of the building is storage and there's a wired-off compound surrounding the site with a locked gate. At ten-thirty tonight, Chris and me, will just happen to be passing. We'll observe

173

that the security gate has been forced open. So we'll immediately alert the two police officers in the police van, which by chance, will be parked here,' Matheson pointed at a cul-de-sac about a hundred yards away. 'We'll suggest to the officers that they investigate, and they will invite us to come with them. Incidentally, the security systems should have cut out by this time.'

'An awful lot of coincidences here, Frank?' said Steve.

'You could say that, but remember, we'll be doing no more than good citizens should. All open and above board. I'm not personally responsible for any of these things, but I know they'll happen – enough said.'

'If Lindgrune's men are inside the place won't they react if someone breaks in?'

'Even if they do, the last people they'll call to help will be the law.'

'It all seems bloody devious to me,' said Steve.

'You don't want to come then?'

'I never said that. You bet I'll come if I'm invited.'

'Me also,' said Kirsten.

'Oh no!' said Matheson decisively. 'This'll be no place for a nice young lady like you.'

'Bullshit! And I am not a nice young lady. Sometimes I am an evil bitch – like now.'

'If you don't take me with you,' lisped Chris, 'I shall scream and scream and scream until I am sick.' He laughed at her puzzled expression. 'Don't worry – literary quotation. Actually, I've seen this one under pressure. She's a cool customer and we could use a detached witness. Someone to stand back and remember every detail.'

'All right,' said Matheson wearily. 'But you are all civilians, unofficial and at your own risk.'

Steve huddled against the wall, although it offered no protection from the westerly, rain-filled wind that swept across the empty approach to the Goleigh Estate. He estimated they must be near the centre of the low-pressure system as it disgorged its rain on Southern England. The water running down his neck had already penetrated his shower-proof car coat, so that he wished he'd donned his sailing gear. The residue of salt spray in his hair was leaching painfully into his eyes. He dabbed at them with a sodden handkerchief. Kirsten was a few feet away, seemed rather better protected in a hooded jacket that shone luridly in the street lighting. Little Red Riding Hood, he smiled.

Matheson appeared round the corner, unmoved by the weather.

'Come on, time to do your bit for England.' He beckoned them to follow.

He led them down a path between two chain-link fences, and then through a wicket gate. They walked across an apron of concrete, towards the warehouse that towered above them. Steve could just make out some people standing in the shadows. As they drew closer these were revealed as Chris and two police officers.

'No sign of anybody in there,' Chris whispered. 'I don't think the CCTV is working either.'

One of the policemen spoke. 'This door's unlocked, Mr Matheson, and normally I'd expect the security lights to be on; and the shop lights. In the circumstances, I'd say we should take a look-see.'

'Go on then,' said Matheson. 'You make the official entry and we'll follow.'

The two policemen pushed open the door and entered. Glad to be out of the rain, the others crowded in behind. The leading PC switched on a hand lamp and searched for a light switch.

'Looks like the power's fused, sir,' he said.

'Not to worry, we'll proceed with torches.' Matheson turned on his own lamp, as did the other policeman.

The place was clearly an electrical shop. A crude chipboard counter ran the width of the room with cartons stacked on the shelves behind. On one wall was a display of burglar alarms and car security devices.

'Good selling line around here,' said the leading PC.

'Funny none of this gear's working for real,' said his partner. 'They've got a big security box on the gable.'

'Where does that go?' Matheson pointed at the stairway.

'Office above.'

'Let's take a look then. You lead the way, Rigby.'

The two policemen walked upstairs and the others followed. Expensive carpet Steve noticed, and newly decorated walls as well. At the top was a small landing, with doors to the left and right. Those to the right were evidently toilets with the usual gender signs. On the left was a glass door, and through it they could see the furnishings of an office. PC Rigby tried the door,

'Locked,' he said.

'You two had better have a look around for the intruders,' Matherson told the policemen. 'We'll stay here.'

The constables tactfully withdrew. Steve suspected a game was being played. All this was a bit too predictable.

Matheson nodded to Chris who examined the lock. He withdrew a leather pouch from his briefcase. Steve saw it was stuffed with bunches of keys. Chris tried two and the second one turned sweetly in the lock. The door swung open.

Matheson, without further ado, began to pull open the drawers of the nearest desk. Chris in his turn began a rapid check of the filing boxes.

'Nothing doing here,' he said. 'All legitimate business. Should we check the computers?'

Matherson shook his head. 'Waste of time – can't see we'd find anything there.'

He moved to a second desk at the far end of the room. By some chance whim Kirsten followed, and stood watching him, as he pulled open the drawers one by one. It was a heavy, old-fashioned roll-top affair with three deep drawers in each of its supporting pillars.

'Hello, what have we here?'

Matheson pulled out an object and dropped it on the desktop. It was a white shoulder bag with a long strap.

Steve heard Kirsten's gasp. 'That is Per's bag – I am sure of it.'

'Let's have a look inside,' Matheson undid the zip and began to unpack the contents. 'Well I never. What a lot of lolly.'

He was stacking the desk with piles of bank notes, all carefully sorted and tied with rubber bands. 'More than two grand in readies here. This could be the money Torrents saw Per with. Wait a minute, there's something else, yes: wallet, gold chain, watch and, I guessed it – clothing labels. That's why his body had no identity.'

'All those things were Per's,' Kirsten had a catch in her voice, and Steve put his arm round her. 'How ... how did he come to be in the sea?'

'My guess is they killed him and then pushed his body over Hayling Bridge. It's the obvious place from here.'

Steve agreed. 'The tide would be right for the harbour entrance, although it's a long way.'

'What happens now?' asked Kirsten.

'Strictly speaking we shouldn't be here. But I think that if you make a positive identification of all this stuff, we should have enough for the police to hold the three main suspects.'

PC Rigby had reappeared. 'Shop and main store are clear, sir, but we think there's someone in the loading bay.'

Matheson nodded and set off downstairs. At the bottom was the second policeman.

'This is PC Osbourne,' said Rigby. 'We work this area together.'

'Where's this loading bay?' said Matheson.

'Door's over there,' said Osbourne, pointing to the rear of the building. 'The main door leads on to the access road at the back. The internal door's locked. When we tried it just now, we thought we heard a voice ... it was only for a second and very muffled. Could've been a woman, or a kid.'

'You sure?'

'Yes, sir. We both heard it.'

Matheson looked at Chris. 'Can you get that open?' He pointed his torch at the heavy door of the loading bay.

'Let's have a look.'

They made their way through the store and looked at the door. It was a steel barrier secured by a single padlock.

'What's on the other side?' whispered Chris.

'Some sort of garage, there's another door onto the road. You could drive an average truck in there.'

'There's nobody covering the outer door,' said Rigby. 'Should we radio for backup?'

'Your decision, lad – but I'd say not yet. My being here is strictly unofficial and that would complicate things.'

'I'm ready,' said Chris. He was kneeling by the door with a key in the lock.

'Go ahead,' said Matheson.

It was a sturdy padlock in a heavy galvanised hasp. Chris turned the key and the hasp squeaked as he eased it free. Then he stood up and pushed the door open. Suddenly they were half blinded. Through the doorway came the cold white glare of two full- beam headlights. Steve heard Kirsten gasp and all of them froze. Somewhere behind the light a red flash winked, followed by an ear-bursting explosion. Something split the air as it passed his right ear with a sound like tearing paper. PC Osbourne staggered and fell to the ground. The air was filled with the smell of spent cordite.

Steve grabbed Kirsten by the hood of her jacket and threw her behind a stack of boxes. He heard the snap of the gun reloading and a second shot slammed into the nearby cases. In the silence that followed he heard the gun reload again.

The lettering on the box read, *Dishwasher.* He rolled protectively over the girl. He could smell the perfume in her hair.

Nearby Rigby was whispering. 'We'll need, the armed response team, sir. I'll have to go outside … radio won't get out from in here.'

'Too dangerous,' said Matheson. 'Only way out is down that alleyway. You'll be right in the line of fire. You wouldn't have a chance.'

'He mightn't shoot.'

'Yes he will. That gun's a pump-action, firing solid ball, same as they used at Crossfield. This lot will kill, they've nothing to lose.'

'I've got to try, sir. I'm worried about Mike. He's conscious but he's bleeding bad. He could croak if we don't get a doctor.'

'All right. How do you plan to do it?'

'If I can climb over this stack of goods, I can move up the room out of the line of fire.'

Steve listened with mounting disquiet. He tried to calculate the timing involved. Even a reasonably athletic man would take all of five seconds, but Rigby was full figured and well past thirty. Clinging to these boxes in the full glare of light, he would be a sitting duck. He had another quick glance. The nearest boxes nearest to him were all dishwashers, solid, square and immovable. The next stack was built of smaller items, transistors and irons. He could see Rigby about to move; it was crazy – suicide.

'Wait!' he yelled.

Steve rose to his feet, put his right shoulder down and hurled his body into the wall of cardboard. The move was instinctive, something recalled from boyhood, a goal keeper's dive. The impact almost knocked him senseless. His neck jarred with the pain of the old injury, but his momentum kept going. The whole stack, shook, swayed and a section collapsed into the room. He scrambled through the gap as the gun fired and the ball embedded itself inches from his head. Two seconds later and Rigby was there beside him.

'You all right, mate?'

'I think so,' Steve said, rubbing his bruised shoulder,

'Thanks, that was cool – mind over matter.'

Rigby shook his hand and was gone, running up the alleyway with a strange crouching gait.

The next sounds were the slamming of a car door and the whine of a starter motor as the van's heavy diesel engine came to life. Steve could just see Matheson crouching, peering into the lights through a gap in the boxes.

'Move it, Rigby,' he yelled. 'He's going to blast his way out.'

The van was moving in a series of violent tyre screeching shunts as its driver tried to turn in the narrow width of the garage. Forward, brake, reverse, then forward – it was like a manic dance. Steve heard a dull thud. The van had stopped, its engine in neutral, rear doors pointing at them. The engine raced at full throttle as choking acrid diesel fumes filled the space. Steve crawled back to Kirsten. He could see her face in the cold light, the reflection of her green eyes, and her expression; not frightened, but excited and interested. He forcibly pushed her to the ground again. She glared at him resentfully and then flashed a smile.

For two minutes the position was unchanged. Matheson crouched, watching the van. The wounded Osbourne groaned incoherently, and the engine drummed. Rigby appeared and spoke to Matheson. Then he crawled over to Steve.

'Firearms squad are on their way,' he shouted. 'It's all clear at the front door. Mr Matheson says you're to get the girl out of here.'

'No! I stay here,' Kirsten shouted. 'I'm supposed to be a witness. You men get lost!'

Rigby looked baffled, shrugged, and moved over to tend to PC Osbourne. Steve looked up to see that Matheson and Chris were now standing at the rear of the van. Steve, with more bravado than he really felt, crossed the gap and joined them.

'Looks like our man's shot himself,' said Matheson. 'I've just had a peep in the wing mirror. He's slumped over the wheel and not much left of his head.'

'Suicide?' asked Chris.

'More likely he left the gun loaded and propped up – probably on a hair trigger.'

'We've got to stop the motor,' shouted Chris urgently. 'This place is filling with carbon monoxide by the minute. Better we get out of here now.'

'No, Listen, there is somebody in the back.' It was Kirsten; she had an ear against the door. 'Steve, it's Sarah!'

'That's impossible,' he shouted.

For the first time she'd irritated him. It was a ridiculous suggestion.

'You come and listen!'

Steve moved to the back doors. 'Who's there?'

'Oh, Dad … Dad, it's me,' sobbed a small voice.

'Sarah – my God, it *is* Sarah! I'll stop the motor.'

Forgetting everything, he ran to the driver's cab and pulled at the door – locked. He could see the awful bloody ruin that had been the head of the lone occupant, the man at the wheel. He raced to the passenger door, barking his knee against the wing. It also was locked.

Now the others were with him. Rigby climbed on the sloping bonnet and tried, without success, to kick in the windscreen.

Chris appeared. 'Outer door's got an electronic lock – I can't open it.' Never before had Steve seen this man so alarmed.

Chris picked up a long nail bar and began to beat the windscreen in a fury. It must have been bullet proof, because the bar bounced off, leaving hardly a scratch.

The fumes were getting worse. Steve's eyes were streaming and his chest hurt. He was dizzy and feeling sick. He saw Kirsten tug the iron bar from the protesting Chris. She ran to the front of the van and began to lever up the bonnet lid. The catch broke with a crack that sounded above the noise of the engine. Kirsten threw down the bar and lifted the lid. They were all watching her now, fascinated. The girl leant inside the engine and with the strength of her hands and arms, snapped off the injector pipes one by one. The engine drummed, spluttered and died. The silence was broken only by the rain on the roof and the distant wail of police sirens.

CHAPTER 20

Steve still felt sick, although the diesel fumes had started to disperse now that the outer door was open. Gusts of wind and rain were beginning to swirl into the space and he shivered, partly from the cold, but more from shock. In those first seconds, as the tension unwound, Kirsten had clung to him, burying her head in the front of his jacket. She stank of diesel fuel but that mattered nothing; they all knew that she had saved the day.

Sarah was yelling and kicking the back of the van. The doors were heavy security pattern; nothing could be done to release her until the police came. They heard the sirens leave the motorway and race through the streets towards them.

'Those lads'll be psyched up,' said Rigby. 'I'll head them off, and we'll need an ambulance for Mike ... the sooner the better.'

Osbourne was no longer bleeding so badly, but he'd slipped into deep unconsciousness. Nobody said anything, but they were all worried. As Rigby vanished outside, they could hear the police convoy deploying to front and rear. Shortly afterwards, Rigby came back with a rather disappointed looking sergeant, dressed in a beret and flack jacket, and carrying a firearm. Further officers followed, and then a paramedic team who gently removed PC Osbourne.

'Shot's made a mess of him,' said Rigby. 'Lodged somewhere in his ribs, they think. Another inch either way...' He didn't finish but his expression said it all.

Two more policemen arrived dressed in overalls, carrying a disk cutter and an acetylene gas welder. Steve shouted to Sarah to move to the front of the van. Two minutes later the doors were open and she crawled out shaking and tear stained. She leaned against her father, though she couldn't throw her arms around him, as both were still handcuffed behind her back. The police tried their own keys without success until someone produced bolt cutters. Then she sat on the floor with Steve and Kirsten on either side. Slowly she began to stop shaking and spoke for the first time.

'They've taken Francine with them.'

'Who's they?' asked Steve gently.

'The Chinese man and the one called Dan,' she was shaking again. 'He wanted to kill me...' She could barely say the words.

After a long pause she continued, though Steve had to lean close to catch the words. 'Where's the third one … Reg?'

'He's dead.'

She shook with a sudden convulsion. 'I don't know what to think. He stopped the others killing me, but if you hadn't come … I know what he was going to do.'

She shook and began sobbing like a small child as they held her between them.

The sergeant in charge came over. 'We've got a car ready. Shall we take the young lady to hospital?'

Steve looked at Sarah, who shook her head violently.

'Thanks,' he said. 'But we'll take her home and I'll call her own doctor; he's a friend of the family.'

'It'll be OK,' said Matheson. 'Sussex force have their house under surveillance, they'll be safe enough.' He turned to the sergeant. 'None of my business, but I reckon there's not much doubt as to where that lot are hiding?'

'I know, Lindgrune's place. Well, that's up to the Sussex police, thank God. If they get egg on their faces we'll be well out…'

'Wait a minute,' said Sarah urgently. 'I'm a complete idiot. Tell them to look in the van. It's packed with soft drugs and Ken Lindgrune's house in Scotland … that's where they caught us. It's full of them, drugs that is…,' she ended incoherently.

'We thought that was their angle,' said Matheson. 'Larsen's background is drugs and we know he's been pushing drifters in Italy.' He shook his head and smiled. 'Very satisfactory, the jigsaw is falling into place.'

'Frank,' asked Steve. 'How come all the front doors to this place were wide open?'

'Don't look at me,' said Chris. 'I've a reputation to protect.'

'No, it wasn't Chris. Let's say, the Devil whispered in my ear, and I passed on the message.'

'You were cashing in another of your favours?'

'You could say that.'

'How did you know I was here?' asked Sarah.

'We didn't,' said Matheson. 'We were here on a tip-off. Finding you was the second big shock of the night.'

'I'm glad you did…' She was shaking again.

Spontaneously, Steve picked her up in his arms like a small child, and carried her to the car. When they reached it, she was asleep.

Back home, Kirsten put the exhausted Sarah in a hot bath. She smelt of sweat and the urine in which her clothes were soaked. They put her to bed, and shortly afterwards Dr Anderson arrived and injected a sedative. Steve took the doctor partially into his confidence and gave him a rough outline of what had happened.

'She'll get over it,' said Phil. 'Lots of resilience in that one.' He picked up his bag and walked to the door. 'I notice something else. There's been a marked improvement in you, my lad.'

That night, Steve had one final visitation from the dream. This time the scenario was different. He was high above the waves looking down, straight into the awful, mad, tumultuous sea. No orderly procession of waves, but a crazy, turbulent, boiling pot where the seas fought and clashed against each other and the spume blew like driving rain. Logic told him nothing human could live in such a sea. He was gripped by cold fear, because he knew he and Kirsten were somewhere in that churning water, without hope.

He awoke, wide-eyed and fearful. She was still lying in his arms; her naked body firm to his touch, her skin smooth and soft. He banished the horrible memory of the nightmare and drifted into deep and peaceful slumber.

At nine a.m. the phone rang; it was Matheson.

'Bad news,' he said. 'Not a trace of any of them. There've been three co-ordinated raids at four o'clock this morning. Sussex police have taken over Millbury House and the Scottish police are in Lindgrune's place up there. The other raid was on a factory in Denmark, and the Danes say they've found a production line for soft drugs. We've got everything we need for evidence but none of the principals – somehow they've slipped us. But they'll be caught; Lindgrune won't get any help in high places this time.'

'Either way, Frank, you're vindicated.'

'I suppose so, but it's a hollow victory. Also I've worse news as far as young Kirsten is concerned. There's an Interpol warrant out for Kaj Elgaad.'

'I'll tell her, but Frank, Kaj Elgaad is a decent fellow. He's only caught up in this because of the blackmail.'

'I know, and if he co-operates I doubt if too much will happen to him. I think you two should find him, and persuade him to go to the police of his own free will. You've got the whole of today because the force are full out searching for Larsen and Lindgrune.'

'Kaj is on his boat,' said Steve. 'He's over here to collect his boy's body for burial.'

Matheson rang off and Steve told Kirsten the news. She seemed calm and resigned. 'I always knew it would end this way. Lindgrune has destroyed himself, and we will be destroyed with him.'

Steve went to see Sarah. She was awake but bleary-eyed and still in the grip of the sedative. He left the bedroom quietly and shut the door.

'Kirsten, we'll see your uncle at once. The one thing he mustn't do is try and put to sea.'

'Why?'

'Because it'll look as if he's doing a runner.'

She frowned anxiously. 'I never thought of that. We must be quick – perhaps he has already started.'

'All right, calm down. High water's just after twelve. He can't move for at least two hours. All the same, let's get down there and get it over.'

Steve called the doctor's surgery and left a message for Phil. Then, to ease his mind about leaving Sarah, he walked outside and had a word with the police watchers. As he arrived indoors again, the phone rang. It was a relay ship to shore call; Steve recognised the voice of the operator at Niton. Then came the voice of Kaj Elgaad.

'Steve, how are you?'

'I'm fine, Mr Elgaad, but surely you're not at sea?'

'No the marine call is the only way I can reach you,' he paused and Steve sensed the man was uneasy. 'We are still at Itchenor, but we have Per's casket on board and we are planning to leave on the next tide in a couple of hours. I would be very pleased if you could both visit us before we sail?'

'Of course we'll come. I must talk to you anyway. Where are you moored?'

'We are in the channel at Itchenor. Please go to the landing stage and I'll have a boat fetch you.'

At Itchenor, Steve left the car on the Hard above the high water mark: an illegal place for parking, but that was too bad. Last night's rain had passed over. The cloud was breaking up, he could see patches of blue sky, and the sun was shining. Predictably, the wind had changed direction, and was now blowing fiercely from the north-west. It buffeted them as they walked down the pontoon and small dollops of water were breaking over the exposed landing area at the end. Steve estimated a force seven at least and probably gusting eight.

184

Kristabel's boat was moored alongside the pontoon in an exposed position. The boat was the same RIB that Kaj had used three days earlier. Now it was banging against its fenders under the eye of a single crewman.

Kirsten looked at the man in surprise. 'Uncle should have come himself, he usually does.' She spoke a few words to the man in Danish.

Looking at Steve she said. 'May I have the car keys? I have left something on the back seat. I will go for it and be back soon.'

'OK, love, here you are.' He handed her the keys and she trotted off up the pontoon.

Steve climbed into the boat and sat down. He tried to exchange a pleasantry with the crewman but had no response. He seemed a surly character, or more likely he couldn't speak English. Steve looked at his watch; Kirsten was certainly taking her time. She had already been gone ten minutes. The boatman looked uneasy. He scowled at Steve and then in the direction that Kirsten had last been seen. Then they saw her coming. She arrived breathless but cheerful and jumped into the boat. The boatman released the lines, and the twin outboards drove the boat away from the jetty.

Steve saw the huge bulk of the *Kristabel* at once. The great yacht was moored in the centre of the channel, against the floating pontoon usually reserved for the local fishing fleet. Even in the sheltered channel there was a nasty lop and the RIB was banging uncomfortably, throwing showers of spray. Coming towards them Steve could see the Harbour Master's launch with the HM himself at the helm.

Steve shouted to the boatman. 'You're way over the speed limit. Slow down or old man McKay'll book you.'

The man took not the slightest notice and Steve called to Kirsten. 'You tell him. This guy doesn't understand English.'

'Kirsten shouted a few words in Danish and the man throttled back. As the harbour launch passed them, Capt McKay RN Rtd, gave them a black look. Steve hunched down inside his waterproofs, hoping not to be recognised.

Kirsten moved her face close to Steve's left ear. 'We are in big trouble,' she said.

'Why?'

'This man is not from *Kristabel's* crew. He is not Danish either, and he speaks English OK.'

How do you know all this? He did what you told him.'

'No he didn't. You know what I say to him?'

'Tell me.'

'In Danish I say – go fuck yourself – and he comes off the gas just like you tell him in English.'

'Oh, Jesus, I see what you mean.'

'I tell you more. On *Kristabel* they have satellite communication. You know, talk to anywhere in the world. So why does Uncle give you that bullshit about only talking through Niton? Why he want the whole world to listen?'

'I must say, that point had crossed my mind.'

Something made them both look at the boatman. The noise was such that the man could have heard nothing of their words but he stared back at them and in his hand was a pistol.

'OK, folks, take it easy; the boss wants a word with you.' The accent was American.

'That is one bloody corny speech. You play in B movies or something?' Kirsten laughed derisively.

'Watch it, lady.'

'Piss off. Go ahead, shoot me out here and see what you get!'

The man could hardly avoid the logic of this. They were passing moored yachts with crews aboard.

Kristabel was close, towering over them, as the boatman brought them neatly alongside the yacht's landing platform.

'You go up there,' he said.

Steve shrugged and walked up the gangway steps to the deck. The *Kristabel* was vast. They were standing on the teak deck of a long quarter gallery. Above was the superstructure with its flying bridge, and a mast festooned with radio and radar equipment. Aft of the bridge the whole ship was covered by an elevated helicopter deck.

'You come with me please?' said a nearby voice.

Standing in a doorway was a man carrying a pump action shot-gun identical to that of the deceased Reg. Steve stared at him with interest. Here, without doubt, was Kuo.

'You go down there.' He jerked the gun towards a stairway leading down into the ship.

Kirsten led the way; here she was on home territory. Steve followed her down into a vestibule with pictures on the walls and cabin doors to port and starboard. The main saloon was straight ahead and its opulence made him catch his breath. Momentarily wonder-struck by the surroundings he almost overlooked the people in the room.

Opposite, sitting on a settee, were Trudi Lindgrune and her

daughter Francine. Trudi was white-faced and weeping, while Francine looked commendably defiant. Kaj Elgaad was standing by the ornate fireplace. Steve had been so startled to see this artefact in a yacht that at first he'd failed to notice him. The man was standing motionless, his eyes glazed and uncomprehending. To the left of the group sat Lindgrune slumped in an armchair. To Steve's immense satisfaction, the man looked more than just defeated, he had the air of a deflated balloon from which all the ego had run out. Steve's memory went back to the dinner party at the Elgaad's house a week ago. Here were all the players together again.

'Francine,' Kirsten called out. 'Sarah is OK, the police have freed her.'

'Wow, you don't say – that's great!' Francine let fly a whoop of delight, half rising to her feet.

'You sit – not talk!' Kuo yelled at her.

'You piss off,' said Kirsten. 'You people are finished and you also, Lindgrune. The police are coming for you. They have found all the drifters and they know how you killed Per, Dennis and Glenda and the newspaper girl. Now you go to prison for ever.' The scorching venom of her words startled Steve.

'You shut your mouth or...' Kuo thundered.

'Or what? Maybe you like to break my neck, Mr Kuo? Perhaps you think one more makes no difference to the time you spend in prison?'

'Now, now, Miss Schmitt, calm down, you are making bad feeling here.'

The voice was a new one and Steve turned sharply to see whose. Another man had come into the saloon from behind them. Recognition was instant; it was the man who'd bugged their rooms in Hellerup, and driven off in the Range Rover: Olle Morgensen's Eskimo.

At the sight of this man, Kirsten let fly a tirade in Danish. She was blazing with fury and whatever she was saying, she almost spat the words out.

'Steve, this man is Tostvig. Once he managed our Greenland office, but he, how you say, cooked the books. He sold vaccines on the black market. When Uncle fired him he smuggles drugs and liquor to the Innuit. Yes, he poisons his own people, and for that they put him in prison, but not for long enough. I tell you, he is one damned scoundrel.' The green eyes were blazing.

The Greenlander smiled and made a hand motion, as if brushing aside the words. 'Come now, Miss Schmitt, none of us are perfect. No doubt your new boyfriend knows of your sporting success. Yes, Mr Simpson, your little girl is a great person in Denmark. She brings them glory with her wind surfboard. Wrong sport – it should be cycling!'

The man stared at Steve, who, without thinking, took the bait. 'Why?'

'Why?' repeated Tostvig. 'So suitable. In Denmark, everyone rides bicycles, but I tell you this, there is not one bicycle in all Kobenhavn that has been ridden by so many different men as she has.'

Steve restrained his fury at the insult. His main concern at the moment was to stop Kirsten, now clearly in an apoplectic fury, from provoking these people to violence. What she'd just said about Kuo was probably true. The man was in enough trouble already and one or two more killings would be unlikely to make much difference. He reached out, took her hand, and gave it a supportive squeeze. Gradually the tension eased.

He stared at Lindgrune. 'Here we are then, what are you going to do?' Lindgrune seemed to barely hear him.

'You waste your time with him,' said Tostvig. 'Lindgrune no longer has a say in anything. I control things here while we wait for the chief.'

'You mean Larsen?'

'None of your business.' Tostvig seemed slightly put out that Steve should know the name.

'Look, said Steve wearily. 'If Larsen isn't here yet, he won't be coming. All the police in Europe are looking for him, and they're thickest on the ground right here.'

Tostvig seemed unconcerned. 'We wait and see.'

'Uncle,' snapped Kirsten. 'Look at me, you have not spoken to me!'

Kaj turned his head and slowly met their eyes. Steve was shocked; he'd been quite unprepared for the look of misery and despair on the man's face.

'I'm sorry,' Kaj's voice was barely audible. 'It's come to this at last; I'm sorry.' He turned away from them and resumed his original glassy stare.

'Uncle,' she shouted. 'Where is everyone? What has happened to the crew? Where is Jesper?'

'Captain Arnholt is dead,' intervened Tostvig. 'He was a very brave, but stubborn old man. As for the crew they are under guard in their quarters.'

'You murdered him in cold blood,' said Kaj. 'Yes, Tostvig shot

188

the captain on his own bridge, because he refused to take the ship to sea.'

'He was given every chance,' said Tostvig. 'Anyway, we have a new captain coming soon. That old fellow would've put us on the sand most likely.'

Steve gave Kirsten's hand another squeeze. She was crying now and unrestrained. He guessed correctly that this old sea captain had been more a member of the family than an employee. He began to quietly size up their position. It was clear that they were, as the saying went, on very thin ice. The fact that the gang were leaderless could make them even more dangerous. These men must know that time was running out, especially if they intended to make their getaway in the *Kristabel*. His watch said eleven-forty-five. High water was twelve fifteen. His understanding was that Kristabel could only safely negotiate the harbour entrance for one and a half hours either side of high tide. Today was a spring tide so perhaps one could extend the limit to two hours, but he wouldn't care to gamble. There was no big ship pilot in this harbour; yachts like *Kristabel* were rare visitors. Without a pilot they would need an experienced master.

He wondered who this new captain might be? Whoever he was, Steve would not fancy his chances of reaching the ship through the police dragnet. What if the gang decided to make a break for it without a professional? His one suppressed fear was that he might be forced to take the ship to sea. Steve was a fine sailor, but his power boat handling, though adequate, was not up to turning a ship like *Kristabel* in a narrow channel and certainly not with a gun in his back. Whatever happened, he would play for time. What about Matheson and the police? They really couldn't be so stupid as to forget about the *Kristabel*. Sarah would be expecting them back in the early afternoon. If they could only play for time.

His musings were ended by the sound of running footsteps. The door was thrown open and the RIB boatman appeared.

'Boys, the Chief's here!' He shouted.

Above the noises of the ship and the wind they all heard it; the droning rattle of the approaching helicopter.

CHAPTER 21

For a few minutes, the noise was deafening. Those in *Kristabel's* saloon could see nothing as the engine died away. Steve watched tensely to see what would happen next. He heard footsteps, then into the cabin came four men. Steve had never met any of them, but he recognised Larsen instantly. The hair was slightly longer and greyer than in the police photograph but there was no mistaking him.

Another was Tony Yapplington the pilot. Steve didn't know the man, but Yapplington senior was a customer of his and the resemblance of the son was striking. Larsen's two other companions were caricature heavies; nightclub bouncers Steve guessed. Both looked podgy and overweight. The nearest to Steve carried an unpleasant looking weapon that was probably a Kalashnikov. He made a quick calculation. These four brought the total number of the gang to seven, although there might be others guarding *Kristabel's* crew.

'What's the plan, Chief?' asked Tostvig.

'We get this boat moving and proceed as agreed.'

'That's a lie! He's going to kill us. They're taking the ship to sea and then they're going to sink her, all of us as well, while Larsen takes the helicopter.'

Lindgrune was shouting at the top of his voice. At last he'd come to life, although clearly half-mad with fear.

'You shut your mouth!' yelled Kuo.

He strode across and jabbed the barrel of the gun in Lindgrune's face. The man gave a yelp of pain, to which Trudi added a tearful wail.

'Hey,' said Francine. 'That chopper's only got five seats, who are you leaving behind, Larsen?'

'You for one, bitch. I've had about enough of you.' Larsen glared at her.

'The girl's got a point, Larsen,' said Tostvig. 'You said we were going to take the ship to Ireland, remember? What about that talk about trading guns for a safe hideaway?'

'Too late – your fault, Tostvig. We'd have gone last night if you'd got that goddam captain to play ball. Now, well, I guess it's too late. The Brits'll be scouring the seas for this old boat, and the Feds'll be hot after us too. So, we change the plan.'

The room was tense and the animosity open. Suddenly Steve felt completely relaxed. For the first time matters were no longer wholly out of control. It was like a tight-fought race. For the first time he could see an opening and he went for it.

To Kirsten he said conversationally, 'It's rather like Russian Sledges. We used to play that game as kids. You put eight characters on a sledge, then you decide which is the most superfluous and you throw him to the wolves. After that you carry on until the wolves have stopped being hungry.' He looked at Larsen. 'It seems you've already thrown Lindgrune to the wolves so who's the next victim? Tostvig I would guess.'

Larsen was unmoved. 'I wouldn't worry too much, Simpson, is it? Well I've got news for you. This could be your lucky day, because you, for one, are coming with us.'

Larsen grinned at him, or at least his mouth and teeth formed a smile.

'Why me?'

'Simple insurance. Nobody gives an asshole about Lindgrune, but they will for you. The Brits remember Steve Simpson with his medal and his little sailboat, so you're coming. I don't want any of your Navy jets messing with us this trip.'

Larsen laughed. The sound, like the smile was chilling. Kirsten dug her fingers into Steve's arm like a vice.

He felt strangely at ease. 'If I'm to be so honoured, then it's got to be Tostvig to the wolves…'

'You shut it, Simpson! You're talking shit – tell him, Larsen.' Tostvig had lost his confident veneer as he advanced on Larsen aggressively.

'That's far enough. Get back, Eskimo bastard,' said the man with the Kalashnikov. English north-country accent Steve noted.

'That wasn't a very nice thing to say, was it?' Dreamlike, Steve heard his own bantering voice.

Tostvig looked hunted. 'What are you playing at, Larsen? I've been straight with you. Now you play straight with me.'

His posh mid-Atlantic accent was breaking down. He was almost as terrified as Lindgrune. The gunman advanced a couple of paces and pushed Tostvig back until he was standing next to Kaj.

'Come on, boys,' Tostvig's voice trembled. 'Larsen's shitting out. He's not going to take any of you. What about you, Kuo? You worked for Lindgrune – Larsen won't want you.'

'He take me – I have gun,' said Kuo, tapping his shotgun fondly.

Steve saw he'd raised it from the floor to the ready position and it was pointing at Larsen.

'Yeah, sure, sure, you'll be coming – cool it!' For the first time Larsen looked less than confident.

'Only one seat left in the chopper,' said Steve. 'Would you like me to spin a coin for you?'

'I'll bust your guts for you, mate,' growled Kalashnikov man.

'I wouldn't do that, or he certainly won't take you.'

'OK, OK, cool it and listen,' shouted Larsen above the rising hubbub. 'Look; Tony will take the ship to sea, just as soon as it takes to get the engines warm. Now, no one, not Navy, not nobody will come near us on the seas, 'cos we've got hostages – OK?' Larsen had all their attention now. 'Sure, I'll take the chopper when we get near France. I can't say where we'll land, but arrangements have been made. Tony works for Lindgrune, and he's agreed to turn round and come back for the rest of you. OK, I can't speak fairer than that.'

'Is this on the level, Tony?' Tostvig asked doubtfully.

'You have my word as a naval officer.'

God, Steve thought, the clipped accent was just the part. It could have been John Mills in an old movie. The gang looked impressed; well, more fool them, because the little runt was lying through his teeth.

In the end, events were moving too fast for Larsen's plans. A rush of footsteps on the stairway announced the boatman – he looked flustered.

'Boss, trouble! The Harbour Master's alongside with a cop.'

'Just one cop?'

'Yeah.'

'OK,' Larsen pointed to the Kalashnikov man. 'Take Elgaad up on deck.'

The man raised his weapon and gave Kaj a light dig in the ribs. 'Come on, mate, let's be having you.'

'You as well, Simpson,' said Larsen. 'Watch him, Kuo.'

Kuo motioned Steve to walk in front.

'Elgaad,' said Larsen, 'you and Simpson will answer the questions. If you both want to go on living, you'll make them go away.'

Warily Steve led the party on deck. He still felt oddly detached and unafraid. The harbour launch was standing off a short distance from *Kristabel's* landing platform. The wind was still buffeting as strong as ever and the Harbour Master was being careful not to be carried down on *Kristabel* with an embarrassing bump. Kuo, standing in the doorway, motioned Steve towards the rail. He looked down; the launch carried a uniformed policeman. Steve recognised him as the local bobby from Birdham. Capt McKay was holding a loud hailer.

'I need to speak with the master of your vessel,' he boomed.

Steve turned round to see Larsen in the doorway. 'Tell him the Captain's sick. He can talk to Elgaad, but not face-to-face – on the radio.' Larsen handed Steve a loud hailer.

Steve took it and called. 'The Master is unavailable, but Mr Elgaad, the owner, will speak to you on the radio. Suggest channel six – repeat six.'

The Harbour Master acknowledged with a wave.

'OK so far,' said Larsen. 'Get up on the bridge and remember we're still watching you.'

He motioned to Kaj, who led them up a flight of steps to the bridge. They were entirely protected from wind and weather within a huge glass cocoon. The steering position was the centre of three luxurious pedestal seats. Visibility ahead and to each side was superb and a tribute to the yacht's designers. Aft of the bridge was the helicopter pad, accessed from two sliding doors. Steve could see the machine a few metres away, secured to the deck by webbing straps. Kaj was walking jerkily towards the VHF phone that Larsen was offering.

'Remember, one bad move and I'll shoot you, or maybe I won't.' Larsen held a large brown envelope and he waved it in Kaj's face.

Like a sleepwalker Elgaad took the telephone. The conversation with the Harbour Master became something of an anticlimax; just a series of mundane questions about the ship's registration. Was she a pleasure craft, or did she have a commercial purpose? Did Mr Elgaad intend to embark fee-paying passengers from Chichester? Steve was baffled. What had all this to do with the Harbour Master and the police? He'd have thought it was a matter for the Customs.

His attention began to wander. The bridge windows offered a magnificent view down channel. The wind was still gusting as hard as ever, so understandably, few craft were moving. The only vessel that Steve could see was a bulky fishing trawler powering upstream on the flood tide. She was *The Selsey Queen*, one of the larger local boats that moored on the same pontoon as *Kristabel*. The trawler was halfway through her turn now, with the whole of her starboard profile towards them. Clearly she intended to stem wind and tide and berth in the space in front of *Kristabel*. Kaj was still talking to Capt McKay, with Larsen and the other two listening. Steve returned to the scene outside. *The Selsey Queen* was passing by, her crew still huddled in

193

the wheelhouse. Lazy lot; in this wind they should be ready with the lines, however good the helmsman. Wait a minute – yes, he could see figures crouching behind the bulwarks in the centre of the boat. The trawler's helmsman cut his engines and glided the heavy boat expertly alongside the pontoon.

Two men jumped onto the dock and were busy looping the bow and stern lines on mooring bollards. Simultaneously, two more figures had left the boat and were moving stealthily along the pontoon close under *Kristabel*. Then one, with amazing agility, catapulted his companion up and over the rail of the quarter gallery. The first man leaned over and hauled his companion up beside him; the whole effort had taken five seconds. Steve was tense with expectation. These two super-fit mystery men were clad from head to toe in black and each carried a shoulder bag. Then from below decks came cries of alarm, followed by four thudding explosions. Now the pontoon was covered with running figures. The first two hooked ladders on *Kristabel's* side and swarmed over followed by the others. Here was another armed police unit, identical to the one they'd met the night before.

Larsen, Kuo, and the gunman were staring wildly around. Concentrating as they had on Kaj and the launch, they'd missed the activity on the pontoon. From below came a chorus of shouts and screams and an acrid smell of burning.

'Hell, what's going on down there?' Larsen, face expressive with fury, ran to the top of the stairs.

He began to shout again but as he did so the words died in his throat to become an awful rasping agonised gurgle. Elgaad held him from behind. Kaj had wrapped the cable of the radiophone round Larsen's neck and was winding it tight with a manic ferocity. As Larsen kicked and struggled, Elgaad turned the body to shield himself from the gunmen. Steve heard himself cry out in horror as he saw Larsen's face turn slowly to an ugly mix of purple and yellow. The eyes seemed to be popping from their sockets and the tip of Larsen's tongue protruded from his slobbering mouth. For one full minute Kaj mangled and shook the man like some demented bear. Then he flung the lifeless body to the deck.

Steve, watching in sickened disbelief, could not help noticing that neither of Larsen's henchmen had moved a muscle to save their chief. Both had stood watching intently, as if they were interested spectators at a wrestling bout. Steve waited for no more. The man with the Kalashnikov stood not two feet in front. Steve leapt on him, grabbing with his left arm around the man's neck. As he did so, he struck the gun-carrying forearm with a viscous karate chop. It was a skill that Steve had not practised since his late teens. He put every last effort and concentration into the one hit. It was a do or die effort and it worked. The bone cracked, the man screamed, and the gun clattered to the deck.

A single explosion, almost in his face, momentarily left Steve's ears singing as instinctively he ducked amidst a rain of glass splinters. He saw Kaj again, this time with Kuo in his grip. Unseen by Steve, Kuo had been aiming his gun. Kaj had caught him and jerked the gun skywards thereby saving Steve's life. A terrible change had come over Kaj. No one would ever know the extent of the mental torment the man had suffered these recent years. Perhaps some deep-laid ancestral force had awakened in this shy, peaceful man and gripped him with madness. Berserk was the old Viking word, and if ever it fitted a situation it was now. Kaj, despite his small stature, had lifted Kuo by his armpits. Kuo dropped his gun and kicked and struggled in angry desperation. Elgaad walked slowly to the head of the stairway and hurled his victim headfirst to the bottom. Steve winced as he heard the sound of a human skull cracking like an egg. Kaj bent down, picked up the Kalashnikov, and ran down the stair.

The falling body did nothing to deter a further group of people who were staggering upwards, all gasping, coughing, and wiping streaming eyes.

They were Tostvig, Tony Yapplington, and the boatman. Ignoring Steve they raced to the rear doors of the bridge. A blast of wind hammered into the room as the first man flung open the sliding panel. Tony hurled himself into the helicopter, followed by Tostvig. The third man began to unlatch the securing straps just as the engine fired into life. As the Jet Ranger's rotors began to turn faster and faster, even more disturbed air began to gust into the bridge deck. Steve saw the charts begin to peel off the navigation table and flutter around. Among them he saw the envelope that Larsen had seemed to use as a threat to Kaj. He reached out and caught it.

Another person brushed past, elbowing him aside; it was Lindgrune. The helicopter was stirring. Nobody could dispute the skill of the pilot. The machine had been parked head to the wind and it would need precise handling to stop it drifting back into *Kristabel's* superstructure. As it lifted off the platform, Lindgrune, running as if possessed, seized the nearest landing skid and hauled himself onto it, clutching the open doorway. At that moment the squall hit them. It came unnoticed, snaking and tearing across the mudflats from the direction of Bosham. The helicopter, with its extra burden, was clearly unbalanced. Above the sound of the rotors came an unpleasant grinding and snapping as the tail rotor scythed through the high masthead aerials. The aircraft was still climbing, but the sound had changed. From it came an ugly high-pitched metallic scream. Steve could only look on, helpless. Outlined in the doorway he could see a figure kicking and prodding at Lindgrune, still clinging to the cabin floor with his fingertips. Then he fell. Slowly the bulky form detached from the aircraft, and fell without convulsion or struggle, into the mud on Itchenor shore. Steve grabbed a pair of binoculars from the chart table and ran into the open. He trained them on the spot where Lindgrune had fallen, but there was nothing; only thick black mud.

He turned the glasses on the helicopter. It was inland now, above the treetops. Slowly it began to turn around on its own axis as it tumbled to the ground. Steve winced at the distant flash of exploding fuel. A thick cloud of black smoke, whipped across the horizon, and dispersed in the wind.

CHAPTER 22

Steve stood, the forgotten binoculars in his hands. He felt weak and physically sick. In the last two weeks he had witnessed death and violence beyond anything in his worst dreams. Now he felt an overwhelming craving for his old tranquil life.

The bridge deck was filling with people. The dead body of Larsen still lay doubled over in an undignified heap in the corner. The other gunman was lying face down on the deck with a policeman standing over him. As they searched his clothing, the man groaned with the pain of his shattered arm. Of Kaj Elgaad there was no sign.

Steve saw Kirsten at the same moment as she saw him and he ran to her. She clung to him and he knew she was still troubled.

'Steve, Uncle is going to kill himself – we must stop him!'

'Where is he?' said Steve. 'He was here just now. You know he freaked out. He killed Larsen and Kuo. Please, love, what happened down there – what were those bangs?'

'Stun grenades,' said a familiar voice; it was Matheson. 'Yes, you may thank your young lady. She gave the warning and saved the day. It gave the police time to set up the operation and borrow a couple of lads from the SBS. They were the ones who rolled the bangers down the stairways and ventilators. After that it was easy.'

Steve was baffled. 'Kirsten warned you?'

'Yes,' she said. 'Before we get in the boat, I went back to the car and phoned Sarah. You see I smell several big rats … but please!' She was urgent now, tugging at his sleeve. 'My uncle, I heard him shout in Danish. He is going to kill himself. He wants to die where Per was found.'

Her words were broken by the sound of high power engines, the twin outboards of the RIB, followed by shouts as the engines gunned. More shouts, then two gunshots. Kirsten sobbed and ran down the stairs to the open quarter gallery. Steve and Matheson followed, stepping over the still twitching body of Kuo. The RIB had cleared the pontoon and was heading down channel. They could see one man aboard and it was Kaj. The wind was gusting harder than ever and Steve could see the boat lifting and dropping in the unsettled lop.

An armed policeman spoke to Matheson. 'That man's got away. We tried to take out the motors with aimed shots. We think we've stopped one and it looks as if we've holed an air tank.'

Steve had a quick look through the glasses. Yes, the RIB was lopsided, and her port rear air compartment was deflated.

'Frank,' said Steve. 'I'm going after him. Kirsten says he's going to kill himself.'

'What are you going to chase him in?' said the policeman doubtfully. 'All we've got is this old fishing boat and you'll never catch him in that.'

'I don't know but I'll find something. Come on, Kirsten, let's go!'

He turned to Matheson. 'Frank, take this, I think it's important.'

He handed over Larsen's envelope and then ran headlong down the gangway steps. At the bottom he gesticulated to the Harbour Master who was still standing by.

'Hello, Stephen, I thought it was you up there. Is it all right for you to leave?' Captain McKay seemed totally unmoved by the mayhem he'd witnessed.

'Yes, it's all right. I'm going after the man in that RIB. We think he may be suicidal.'

'You won't catch him in this launch and none of my Dories are manned today.'

The local policeman was talking into his radio. 'They're going to let that fellow burn himself out. They were going to call inshore rescue, but it seems the man's got a gun so they're holding off.'

The Harbour Master dropped them at the Yacht Club pontoon. There on the slipway stood a "Fourteen" dinghy, her sails ready for hoisting. Beside her were the Fieldman brothers.

'Hi,' yelled Steve. 'Is there a fast power boat around?'

'Not today, mate,' said Dave. 'Racing's been cancelled. This place is almost deserted.'

Steve looked wildly around, then steadied himself. His mind was made up.

'Did you see that RIB that went down just now?'

'Yeah.'

'Look, we've got to catch him. He's Kirsten's uncle and we think he means to do himself a mischief. Can we use your boat?' Steve's voice was brittle with urgency.

Ross looked startled. 'This is a fast boat but I doubt you'd catch that thing.'

'I've got to try. Look he's lost a quarter of his buoyancy and he's only running on one motor. Down channel there'll be a sea running – he'll have to slow down. Your *Wendy* will be in her element.'

'Let us try?'

'Sorry, no. It's got to be Kirsten and me. I know you'll drive the boat faster, but only Kirsten can talk to the man. Trust us – it's life and death.'

'OK, Steve, yeah, go ahead ... but if it was anyone else but you...'

'Just help us get sailing.'

It took seconds to swap over harnesses and life jackets and they were away. The first mile of the channel was nearly a windward leg, with the sails sheeted in hard. Their combined weight was well under what was needed to balance a Fourteen in these conditions and Steve was forced to spill wind from the mainsail to stay upright. He shouted at Kirsten to keep watching the RIB. Visibility was awful. He could see nothing beneath the mainsail and they were half blinded by the backlash of spray. Then at last they were round the bend in the channel by Chaldock Point, and the whole of the lower harbour was in view. Kirsten was shouting and pointing. There, half a mile away, was a dot enveloped in foam: the RIB.

Steve shouted to Kirsten to half raise the centreboard. *Bendy Wendy* responded as her designer intended. She lifted out of the water and tore down the harbour on a scorching plane. Steve pulled in the mainsheet to adjust to the apparent wind. Suddenly everything had become smoother and quieter. It was the magic illusion, something he never tired of. It was as if one was flying several feet above the water. Steve had moved his position almost to the stern of the boat with Kirsten on her wire close beside him. They both had a quick look, the RIB was definitely closer. They could see small details. Only one motor was running and the deflated buoyancy tank was definitely affecting her. But Kaj was still pushing the RIB and they could see the craft buffeting and hear the howl of its engine over wind and sea.

Steve caught his breath; the waves down the harbour were even steeper than he'd expected. They were on the official time of high water, but clearly the tide was still flooding. Probably this northerly gale was slowing its entry into the harbour. They must reach Kaj before he came anywhere near the bar. Steve knew the grim truth all too well. There would be seas out there in which neither craft could live.

'I'm going to hoist the kite,' he shouted. 'Give me the lines – the green one and the blue. Now you take her.' Kirsten's face registered a shimmer of alarm as he pushed the steering extension into her hand. 'Steer off a bit, and spill wind until I'm back.'

The huge asymmetric foresail set with a crack. The dinghy

staggered like a boxer riding a punch. The mast strained, the carbon fibre bowsprit flexed, and they were away. Steve relieved Kirsten of the steering. He pulled in the main and brought the dinghy back on course. Faster than ever she lifted into an orgy of total sailing. This was to be the ultimate gamble. They were an underweight crew in wind gusting in excess of thirty knots. at the moment they were well balanced. In theory the extra speed should increase their stability. He concentrated on the chase ahead.

The RIB was no more than two hundred yards ahead, in trouble and slowing. He wondered if Kaj would connect this crazy racing dinghy with pursuit. Perhaps he did. The RIB was changing course. She was heading to cut the corner of the channel and head out over the fringes of the dangerous *Winner* Shoal. This would mean entering the troubled waters far earlier than was necessary. Steve steered to follow. The pressure on the rudder was phenomenal. He wondered what speed they were travelling. Behind them, their wake lifted in a great arc of glittering spray. A few hundred yards away was a lee shore, pounding white with breakers. They could almost feel the force, though they could hear nothing. The RIB drove on, and the dinghy followed, narrowing the gap by the minute. Ahead was the bar and the Pole Sands. Huge seas, green and white-topped, tumbled, fought and rended each other.

He felt a terrible sense of *déjà vu*. This had been his dream, perhaps it still was a dream. He was no longer certain if all this was real any more. He was gambling his life and Kirsten's. He couldn't turn back. They'd passed the point of no return. In no way could this lightweight racing boat with her exaggerated sail area work her way back against the wind. Even a full sized yacht might founder in such conditions. They had only one chance. He would charge this horrendous maelstrom head-on. The dinghy was fast, she weighed next to nothing. Let them see if they could ride the seas like a ping-pong ball.

They were entering the waters near the bar and the RIB was almost under their bows. Steve could see it twisting and bouncing. He could hear the tortured overheated engine scream as the propeller lifted from the water. Everywhere the spume blew horizontally from the waves like driving rain. Through it he could see gallons of water slopping around inside the RIB. Steve shaped to pass to windward. He would jettison the spinnaker and then spill wind from the sails, by luffing as far as he dared, and try to hold station long enough for Kirsten to call her uncle.

200

Already it was too late: they were nearly level. Steve glanced under the boom. As he did so he saw Kaj abandon the wheel and stand up. He was only a few yards away and he held the Kalashnikov in both hands. Then he lifted it and aimed at them. Steve was momentarily stunned and horrified, but there was no doubt, he saw the recoil of the gun. But, why – Why? He never heard or saw where the shot went, he was too intent on the RIB. It had turned broadside to wind and sea. For a second he saw Kaj clutch the wheel too late. Then the boat flipped. Turned over in the wind like a paper plate. Another vicious squall swept over them.

The wreckage was on their bows. He screamed a warning and tugged on the tiller with all his strength. The dinghy bore away. Her bows went down and the mainsail crashed over in a bone crunching gybe. The water closed over Steve's head. Instinctively he jettisoned the trapeze wire and surfaced to clutch the edge of the capsized boat. With relief he saw Kirsten's head beside him. He wanted to right the boat and start sailing. They would have to lower the centreboard and bring her head to wind. It was hopeless, he was hampered by both his harness and the buoyancy aid.

Another huge sea broke across them and slowly the dinghy rolled over. They both felt the shuddering crack as the mast fractured on the hard sand. Another wave crashed on top of them. Steve was deep under water. He could feel the pressure on his lungs and see the murky green light that filtered through from above. He surfaced and gulped for air. Kirsten had somehow climbed onto the upturned hull and was lying prone along the keel. She mouthed something but again the water crashed over, driving him down, deep, deep. His ears were drumming, his lungs bursting and when he surfaced his eyes hurt. He'd drifted yards from the boat. In desperation, he struck out towards her, but his limbs wouldn't respond. Again he was sucked down. This time the salt water began to slip silkily into his mouth. This was the end, just as the dream had warned. He felt detached, fatalistic, without fear. Oh why had he brought Kirsten into this? She too would die; such a waste.

The helicopter was back. Strange, he thought it had crashed. Perhaps he'd dreamed that as well, long ago, in another time. Again the sea swamped him, tugging him down with malice. This time he'd been ready and gulped a quick breath. He emerged in the sunlight coughing and spluttering. Somebody was shouting. Beside him was a man. He wore a crash helmet and drysuit. Steve wondered if he'd died. Was he being fetched to some awful surreal purgatory? Hadn't

Miriam warned him this might happen.

'Keep still, mate. Let's get this round you...' The stranger was shouting in his ear.

Steve clung to the man as another breaking wave swept over them. This time he remained just under the surface. The next few minutes became a jumble of half-conscious recollections. Little tableaux; like some crazy display of colour slides. They were clear of the sea, though the spray still blew around them. Above was the helicopter. It came nearer and noisier. Hands reached out from its bowels and dragged him in. He lay shivering and gasping on the hard metal floor.

'OK, mate, I'm going down again to fetch your little lad.'

'She's a woman,' he heard himself say as he vomited himself into unconsciousness.

Kirsten was there, her jet-black hair awry and plastered over her cheeks. She was kneeling, cradling his head in her lap, alarm and apprehension written all over her mobile face. He smiled at her and saw the expression change to joy and relief.

A voice was shouting above the roar of the aircraft. 'You yachties didn't ought to go out on a day like this. Not without proper experience.'

Kirsten flashed angrily. 'He has proper experience. He won Olympic gold medal.'

'Oh yeah, well, he never got it for synchronised swimming.' The man guffawed.

CHAPTER 23

Steve was awake. He no longer felt cold and sick, only extremely drowsy. With an effort, he opened his eyes. He was lying on his back in a small white room. Slowly he struggled into a half sitting position, but his strength had melted away and he had to grip himself as a spasm of vertigo took hold. From somewhere nearby came a voice; Sarah's voice.

'Relax, Dad. Just relax. It's all over and everything's OK.'

'Where's Kirsten?' He heard his voice tense and anxious.

'She's downstairs, waiting. The hospital discharged her this morning. She was with you earlier but you were asleep.'

'This morning?' He was puzzled. 'What time is it?'

'Two o'clock.'

'What day is it?'

'Sunday.'

'Sunday – I've been here twenty-four hours?'

'You were lucky. You had water in your lungs and stomach, and hypothermia.'

Steve smiled at her weakly. 'I remember now. I messed up; gybed on the bar – couldn't right the boat.'

'She ended up on the *Winner*. Ross and Dave collected her with a trailer. The boat's OK, but the mast and sails are a write-off.'

'Oh no,' he groaned. 'What can I tell them?'

'I shouldn't worry. Their serious competition is over for this season and Dave says the insurance will pay, seeing as you weren't racing.'

'But I was. Oh, my God – what happened to Kaj Elgaad?'

'He's dead. The lifeboat found his body almost exactly where we found his son.'

'I'm sorry about that. I did my best. I only hope Kirsten doesn't blame me. She was a brilliant crew, not even your mother would've done better in those conditions.'

'She won't. Not now we know Kaj's secret. It's a blessing really that things turned out like they did.'

'What was the secret?'

'We'll explain later. The doctor says you're to sleep another couple of hours and then we can talk all we like.'

He watched her leave the room and then sank dutifully back on the pillows. Next time he awoke, Kirsten was sitting on the edge of the bed, her hand closed over his. She smiled and a surge of relief swept through him.

'I'm sorry about your uncle,' he said.

'No need. It was what he wanted. He could never go home to Denmark. He did not want to face the world.'

'You know he shot at us before we capsized?' he said.

'I know, but I do not think he knew it was us. I saw his face at that moment, He was … I do not know how you say it in English, but the old Norsemen had a word for it. I think you would say, that in his mind he was already dead.'

Someone was peering through the glass door. Following a tentative knock it opened.

'Hello, Frank,' said Steve.

'Hello, young man. I see you're in capable hands.'

Matheson looked as lugubrious as ever. He sat down in a bedside chair and then shot them a rueful grin.

'What's happened Frank. Is it really all over?'

'Yes and no. All the principals are dead and our police and Interpol have netted nearly three hundred minor players. Yes, the drug operation's finished – from that source, anyway.'

'Why are you looking so gloomy? I mean, you've won, you're vindicated.'

'Not really, and definitely not publicly. You see it was blackmail. A bloody great spiders-web.' Matheson sighed. 'You know, at Millbury House, we found a strong-room in the cellar. Nobody could crack the code, and it was so rugged it would've needed dynamite to blow it – most likely bury it with the house. Now here's where you'll laugh. We found that it was your friend Chris's firm who installed it. So a quick phone call and we had the man himself and two technicians. They opened up just in time for us to vet some of the contents.' Matheson was laughing now. 'I still can't believe it. We found files, tapes, pictures, videos. Lindgrune had dirt on politicians, civil servants, council bosses, business chiefs, union men, even generals and admirals…' Matheson sighed. 'No wonder we were blocked every time we tried to get close to him. You see, he never took any money from any of these people. He was the puppet-master and how they danced. We only ever got to see a fraction of the stuff in there, but it was deadly, enough to bring governments down…'

'What's going to happen?'

'What's going to happen is bugger all. If you've got a strong

204

stomach you can read Lindgrune's obituary in the *Times*. Trudi even got a message of condolence from Number Ten, or so young Francine says.'

'Good God, you mean it's all being hushed up?'

'That's it. Two hours after we opened up the place, along come the Spooks,' Matheson's voice had a note of distaste. 'I mean Security Services – MI5, SIS, or some such. They came with two big vans and they shipped out the lot, or almost. There's one item saved, thanks to you, my boy.' Matheson took an envelope from inside his jacket.

'Is that the one Larsen had on *Kristabel*?'

'Correct; as I said, the spooks took away everything they could lay their greasy hands on, and that's the real reason why I'm not ringing the victory bells.' Matheson glared moodily. 'You know, after all this tribulation and God knows how many deaths, we break a group of unscrupulous blackmailing bastards. Then we're forced to hand over their dirt to another group of unscrupulous blackmailing bastards.'

He turned to Kirsten. 'I'd better explain. I once signed a piece of high-handed gibberish called The Official Secrets Act. That means that I can't tell you anything that I saw or read in that strong room, not what's relevant to the UK that is. But the spooks also took a file of stuff, written in English, but concerned with Lindgrune's dealings in Denmark. Now, the Elgaad blackmail papers are in this envelope, but there's also a nice line in detail in my photographic memory, as well as some jaw-cracking names. You can take them home with you to Copenhagen, and welcome. It won't be proof, of course, but it'll give the jokers a nasty fright.'

'Kirsten,' said Steve. 'We'll go and see Hansen. He'll advise us what to do.'

'Mr Matesen … Frank…'

Kirsten smiled at him, then suddenly became solemn. 'How did Larsen know about Dennis and his family? I feel more badly about that than I do about my uncle.'

'Me too – I'd been puzzling about it, I can tell you. Now one of Larsen's men has made a statement. It all happened through my goddaughter Mandy. I knew she was on to something but she had her own perverse pride. She wasn't going to let me in on the act until she'd completed her own investigation. It seems she identified Larsen and she twice followed him from Leigh Park to Lindgrune's house, Yes, followed him on that stupid great motor bike which was her trademark to half the population of two counties.'

Matheson paused, an uncharacteristic tremor in his voice, and they could see the emotion in his eyes.

'So,' he went on. 'The second time they were waiting for her. Kuo killed her, then Reggie Thropping went through her flat and the files at the newspaper. It seems she'd got a separate story about Per and his, drugs for peace, delusions. She found out about Per spending time with these hippies, and that he'd boasted about revealing a secret to them. You see, Larsen and co were becoming nervous of Per. He'd been useful to them as the inventor of the Drifter formula, but he was an unstable boy. He was always on the verge of blurting out the truth about his father and grandfather. It got to the point where they couldn't take any more chances. That was the night in the gay bar, when Torrents heard the boy ranting nonsense. Only it wasn't nonsense. God, I've been slow, Torrents as good as told us the secret and I never connected.'

'How did they know about poor Julie?' asked Kirsten.

'Just as I told you. Larsen's Mafia contacts were watching her. Lindgrune made a bad miscalculation there. When he told her the Elgaad secret I guess he never expected her to walk out on her husband.'

'What is this secret?' Steve could restrain his curiosity no longer.

'All in here, the so called *Nemesis File,*' said Matheson tapping the envelope. 'I'm going to give it to young Kirsten. It's hers to do what she likes with. But my choice would be to burn it today and scatter the ashes.' Matheson stood up. 'I'm going back home for an hour or two. I'll see you later and we'll talk some more then.'

He walked to the door and was gone.

'Well?' said Steve.

'OK, I will let you read these papers in a minute. Francine translated the German one last night. Only she and Sarah, you, Frank and I will ever know the truth.' She paused and stared at him half-smiling. 'There is something I will first tell you. Uncle anticipated his death. He has spent two years dispersing his personal funds abroad in my name. You see, I cannot inherit the Elgaad company. That would be against Danish law. So I have millions of Kroner and no job.'

'What'll you do, my love? What's going to happen to us?' Steve asked hesitantly.

'This morning I telephone Boston to talk to Mr Easterbrooke. I am to go to the States to meet him. If all is well, I shall be the new owner of Easterbroke Europe. So you will make sails and I shall be the boss. What do you think?'

EPILOGUE

Part One

EXCERPT FROM THE GLASGOW HERALD 25th May 1988

BUSINESSMAN FOUND DEAD ON MOUNTAIN

The body of Mr Alfred Lindgrune, Chairman of Anglo Scandinavian Timber Enterprises PLC, was discovered yesterday below the crags of Adnach Dubh, one of the Three Sisters of Glencoe. Mr Lindgrune, an experienced mountaineer, was staying at the Clachaig Inn, Glencoe, and it was thought he set out alone to ascend Mount Bidoain Nam Bian via the Dinnertime Buttress.

Mr Hector McIntyre, of the Glencoe Mountain Rescue, commented that Mr Lindgrune, although over seventy, was an experienced and competent climber. He was properly equipped for the route which was well within his capabilities. The recent frost had made some of the rocks a bit loose and it is possible that Mr Lindgrune misjudged a handhold, said Mr McIntyre. He added that Mr Lindgrune's body appeared to have been lying where it had fallen for some hours. It had been a particularly violent impact and death must have been instantaneous from an apparent clean break of the neck.

Part Two

THE NEMESIS FILE

Printed here is the English text of testimony by the late Alfred Lindgrune. MC. 1920–1988. This material remained hidden and unread for many years. Mr Lindgrune gave orders for the file to be destroyed on his death. However, his sudden and unexpected demise in a climbing accident was a great shock. In the confusion of that event no action was taken regarding the dossier until some weeks after the tragedy. It was then that the papers were found to be missing. Subsequent inquiries revealed, that agents of Kenneth Lindgrune, son of the deceased, removed the sealed packet from the office of the family attorney.

ITEM A. WRITTEN TESTIMONY OF ALFRED LINDGRUNE.

On February 6th 1945 I was in command of a group from the 1st Battalion Special Air Service Regiment, operating behind German lines in Holland. We had a dual mission. First to identify German armoured units. Secondly to destroy German rocket teams who might attempt to launch V2 missiles.

On the day in question we were concealed near an isolated farm on the edge of a forested area. We already knew that the greater part of a German armoured division was hidden in these woods a mile away. We also knew that the German pioneers had made a circular clearing in the trees five hundred metres from our position. I surmised that they would shortly attempt a rocket launch from this site.

A German military unit appeared in eight lorries and a staff car. We identified these men as Waffen SS from a Brigade we had seen the previous day. What happened next I will not record in detail. Suffice to say that not one week passes without a visitation of this event in my dreams.

The SS surrounded the farm and dragged out twelve civilians: three women, four men and five children. They forced the children into a wooden barn which they fired with petrol. As the adults tried desperately to break through the flames to the rescue, the SS shot them down one by one: target practice.

My own troops pleaded to intervene. I wish to God I could have, but they knew, as I did, that the discipline of our regiment forbade any deviation that would jeopardise our mission. The final allied offensive was due within hours and our failure would have cost the lives of our own forces. All I can say in mitigation is that I was able to positively identify the SS Unit and its commander. I gave evidence at the trial in Holland in 1947 and the man was executed.

Three months later on May 3rd I was dropped with my unit, close to Copenhagen Airport. Our mission was to stay concealed until the arrival of British Forces. We were to prevent the Germans from damaging the runway and installations.

The following night, May 4th, I ventured into the city on foot. I came upon a gang of youths tormenting and threatening to kill a small boy. They told me they were going to kill the child because his parents were collaborators. It was then, on the impulse of the moment, that I saw a chance to atone for my inaction during the atrocity in Holland. I rescued this child and took him back to my unit. The boy told me his name was Kaj Elgaad, and that he had become separated from his father only hours earlier. He told me where his father was hiding and offered to take me there.

I went and I found Eric Elgaad hiding in a cellar. I took him and his son back to my unit. On May 5th the Germans surrendered and the RAF took over the airfield.

As for Eric Elgaad: I discovered that his wife had been arrested as a collaborator and that their daughter and son in law were also detained. I was by now wholly satisfied that Eric had never had Nazi sympathies although he was much dominated by his wife. I resolved to smuggle Eric and Kaj out of Denmark as soon as possible. I needed to act speedily as my unit was due for withdrawal within the week. Through my own friends and relations I was put in touch with a man who was selling "liberated" German valuables to the British. He was suspicious of me but in the end introduced me to the crew of an RAF DC3 aircraft. These men had been smuggling goods on return flights to Britain. They agreed to take the Elgaads in return for one thousand US dollars. I just managed to raise this sum by selling some family heirlooms to an American Air Force General.

In due course the Elgaads were flown out, as luck would have it, to an airfield in Scotland just thirty miles from my wife's home near Hawick. The RAF men had undertaken to provide the Elgaads with papers. In the event the IDs were crude forgeries and the ration books turned out to have been stolen.

The Elgaads spent the next seventeen years in our household at Whitewater. Then one day we had a surprise visit from Eric's daughter, Anna Schmitt. Anna had brought her own baby daughter, Kirsten, with her, just six months old; Eric's first grandchild. Eric had been homesick for some while and had been worried about Kaj losing his Danish heritage. He now resolved to return home. I was due to travel to Switzerland on business and Eric had given me a coded number for an account with a Zurich bank. I was to withdraw the money in the numbered account. I was naturally glad to help but was astounded when the banker's draft revealed a sum of around three million pounds Sterling. The bank also gave me a letter from their records addressed to Eric as trustee for Kaj.

I think Eric suspected something of the contents of this letter, even so, when he read it, he broke down. He insisted that I read it and I can only say that I wish to God that I had not. Eric asked me to safeguard the letter for him, though I pleaded with him to destroy it. In carrying out his wishes I leave this my personal record with the original letter. I call them my Nemesis File, for I foretell that they will bring a tragedy that will one day engulf us all.

ITEM B. ENGLISH TRANSLATION.

Reich Ministry of Propaganda.
Berlin, 21st July 1939.
Personal testimony of the Reich Minister.

With these words I make solemn declaration of my love for Gerda. A year ago I first saw her, and from that moment she symbolised for me the perfection of Nordic womanhood.

For weeks I worshipped her from afar. Clearly she was in awe of my position and of my closeness to our beloved Fuehrer. I pledged my undying devotion to her and we became lovers. Now our child is born and I have held him in my arms. He is to be named Kaj and will take his stepfather's name: Elgaad.

I have to accept that my dear beautiful Gerda must now return to her homeland. Upon this the Fuehrer insists and Gerda and I know our duty, however painful.

To secure the boy's future I have placed a sum of money in a Swiss bank, one that is discreet and employs no Jews. The money is all my own, except for a generous contribution from the Fuehrer himself.

This declaration I will deposit with the money, in order that one day the boy will learn who his real father is and be proud of the part I have played in the preservation of our race.

Signed

Josef Goebbels.

***

Reviews of The Nemesis File

Olympic sailor **Cathy Foster:**

Rarely have I read such a racy book! It carries you along at pace, and holds you fast until the very end. Just then you think that maybe this is getting far-fetched, but the punch-line pulls you up short and makes you re-assess the characters and their relationship to events. Suddenly the plot hangs together again in a very satisfactory way, just as good detective stories should.

Instead of long descriptions to 'paint a picture' of all the venues and situations, the writing is succinct and carefully crafted to give the maximum impression for the minimum words. This gives the book its fast tempo, yet nothing is lost because the accurate detailing of locations and action bonds the reader into plot. As a past Olympic sailor myself, I know the sailing venues described in both Chichester Harbour and Copenhagen well, and I can reassure any future reader that the author has definitely done his research. In addition, he's right – you do build life-long bonds with other British athletes and other countries' sailors when you are part of the Olympic team representing your country. It is a pleasure and highly unusual to read a book which describes the joys of sailing and racing so well. Yet it's not a book about sailing, full of technicalities of the sport. Sailing provides the background framework for a story of murder and blackmail where the investigation chases over four countries and three generations of lives. A thoroughly enjoyable read.

Cathy Foster went to the Olympics in 1984 (finished 7th and made history as the first woman helm since the 2nd World War) and competed in two other Olympic campaigns, the last being 2002/3. She is a freelance Coach who specialises in top level racing, including Olympic and Paralympic sailors.

Journalist **Pamela Payne:**

The prologue of Jim Morley's book grabs you by the throat and the unfolding story holds you in its grip until the last page – do not, under any circumstances read the epilogue before finishing the book. With locations as diverse as the South Coast of England, Naples and Denmark, The Nemesis File's credible sailing scenes will either have you reaching for the seasickness-pills or signing on for a course; the sex scenes, however, are the most romantic I have read for a long time. A great adventure story, which will delight both sexes – sailors or landlubbers.